A Sleuth in Sausalito

a Mystery

Carol Sheldon

Published by Houghton 215 Main Street, #105 Sausalito, CA 94965

Most of the characters are entirely fictitious. Real names of the times have been changed, except for Jean Varda, Coroner Holmes and Sally Stanford.

Ordering Information: Best way: order directly from the author's email casheld@gmail.com or at Amazon.

Book Layout ©2014 WingSpan Press

ISBN - 13: 978-0-9905185-0-1

Other Books by Carol Sheldon

Mother Lode

Driven to Rage

Website/blog: www.carolsheldon.com

ΑcKNoWLedgeMeNtS

There are always a handful of eager readers willing to help by being proof readers, copy editors, etc. Pat Kampmeier, Wanda Henson and Marilyn Bentley proof-read the book. Wanda Henson overcame the difficulties of converting Mac to Word, and with perseverance and diligence returned a copy with professional comments. My friend Steve Olian gave invaluable help in matters of content, as did Vicki Weiland, a non-fiction editor and personal fan, who has guided me through all my books. She had an astounding amount of feedback for me.

Robin Sweeney, one of the local historians who keeps the stories of Sausalito alive was generous with her time, filling me in on life in the sixties.

D.P. Lyle, M.D. who loves mystery as much as medicine answered key questions for me, as did Lt. Boyd in the sheriff's office.

Crys Rourke helped make the opening come to life. Geoff Kidd helped with technical problems. Josephine Biasi created the cover. I am very grateful to all these dedicated people on my team.

A Sleuth in Sausalito is dedicated to Stuart Chappell posthumously, for all the support he gave for my previous books and plays, during the writing and the out of state book tours we took. In matters of furthering my career he was always there for me.

CHapter 1

Gwen Harris stood outside her rented car in downtown Sausalito. She took three deep breaths, straightened her skirt, and headed for the tiny hole-in-the-wall that was the police station.

With a dry mouth, and voice she was sure was shaking, she faced the detective. "If you've found my mother—I mean her bones, I want to know how she ended up where she died." She could feel the perspiration breaking out on her face.

"We don't have that information."

"Then I'm here to find out."

The officer shook his head. "We wouldn't have anything, if the remains weren't discovered here in Sausalito."

Gwen blinked. "Then who would?"

"Based on where you said the remains were found, it would be a matter for the Marin County sheriff."

"Oh."

Gwen could feel her face color, feeling stupid. She'd come on strong, tried to put on a tough face to get some answers. And then was deflated. Of course it was a sheriff matter; the letters had come from there. The police officer smiled patiently and gave her directions to the sheriff's office—a few miles north in San Rafael.

She left the tiny station, found her way to her rental car, and burst into tears.

She had held up pretty well on the plane, and finding her way to this town where she'd spent her first eleven years. She hadn't realized she was so emotionally vulnerable—one mistake and she was reduced to a puddle.

She remembered the first call. Her Aunt Marie had phoned her at the University of Michigan and given her the news.

"You're to call Sheriff Moss in Marin County, California."

"What about?"

"I don't want to shock you, Dear. Perhaps you'd better come home, and I'll tell you."

"No, tell me now."

She could hear her aunt breathing hard. She waited.

Finally, her aunt said, "They think they might have found your mother's bones."

"What?"

"It's just a possibility. Based on 'missing persons' from years ago, they narrowed it down to a few—"

"What are you talking about? Where were these bones found? Why do they think they could be Mom's?" The words came in a rushed swoosh.

"They want some X-rays if they can be located, to help identify or rule out the victim."

"What do you mean—victim?"

"Well, I guess the man didn't use that word. Anyway, the remains of the person who was found."

"Was she a victim of foul play?"

"Oh, Gwen, it's too early for that. We don't know. See if you can get the X-rays from that skiing accident she had back in 1953. I think it was a Doctor Ramsay in Sausalito. She had a broken tibia. I must warn you, though, they only found *parts* of the … skeleton. So the X-rays could be helpful … or not."

It was too much to take in. Gwen's head was swimming. Doctors, X-rays, bones. Most of all, for ten years she hadn't known what had become of her mother. And now, suddenly this information. *Possible answers were forthcoming.*

She hadn't heard the last thing her aunt said.

"Gwen, are you listening?"

"Yes, I'm trying to keep up with you."

"I know it's a lot to take in, Honey. Let's talk again tomorrow."

No sooner had they hung up than Gwen realized she didn't even know where the bones were found. In someone's attic? In the trunk of a stolen car?

She called her aunt back.

"*Someone's* bones were found in a steep ravine between Sausalito and Stinson Beach."

"Why weren't they found years ago?"

"I suppose the deep foliage covered them. I really don't know."

"Who found them?"

"A hiker."

Gwen dried her tears, took a few deep breaths and headed for the sheriff's.

When she finally got there, she was told that the person she wanted to see had gone for the day. It was Friday afternoon.

"Come back Monday."

She left totally frustrated. She hadn't come all the way to California from the University of Michigan where she was a senior in Journalism, to be turned away with no more information than she'd had before she came.

Two weeks ago she'd received a phone call asking her to get in touch with Detective Moss at the Marin County Sheriff's office. Parts of an old human skeleton had been found in a deep ravine off Panoramic Highway that led to Stinson Beach. An analysis of the remains had been made. There was the possibility that they were those of her mother, Patricia Harris.

Would she, the daughter of this missing woman, please send any X-rays that may have been taken of her mother? The detective gave her little hope that there would be a match. Only some of the skeletal remains had been found. They had contacted the families of two other missing persons.

Marie tried to contact the doctor in Marin who'd taken care of Patricia at the time, but he had retired.

"Do you remember the place where they took the X-rays, Marie?"

Marie didn't remember. But she called Megan Denison in Marin. Patricia and Megan had been friends for years. Gwen and her mother had lived with the Denisons until her mother's disappearance. Megan gave Marie the names of two emergency clinics. When Marie called the first one she was told yes, Dr. Ramsay had worked there, and they agreed to look in their archives for X-rays belonging to Patricia Harris.

The waiting period was agony. Gwen had difficulty focusing on her studies in Ann Arbor. She received a 'C' on a paper she'd written, the lowest grade she remembered ever getting.

Finally, she was able to get the film from the clinic where Dr. Ramsay had worked forwarded to the authorities in Marin County. Gwen held her breath. She reminded herself that she was not the only one who'd been contacted. The chances of these remains were not likely to be those of her mother.

But there was a match.

Gwen had spent her first eleven years with her mother in the artsy town of Sausalito. When her mother disappeared, her Aunt Marie came to take her to Michigan, where she'd lived for the last ten years.

Gwen was on the small side—five feet two inches, one hundred ten pounds. With curly brown hair, and green eyes, her aunt reminded her how much she looked like her mother.

~

Gwen couldn't let it rest at that. She was both elated to finally get some answers and horrified to think her mother's life had ended in such a traumatic way. Spring break was starting in two days at the university. Determined to get at the truth, she took the plane that Friday to San Francisco, rented a car, and drove toward the first town north of the Golden Gate Bridge—Sausalito.

She tried to stay focused on the road, but the surrounding beauty of the Bay, like a magnet, drew her eyes to it. Allowing herself glimpses off the bridge, she recognized Angel Island in the distance, the Coast Guard Marina below and the old prison Alcatraz out in the Bay. Old memories from her first years spent in Sausalito were coming alive.

As she crossed the famous bridge, knowing the first exit would take her to Sausalito, her stomach turned cartwheels. What would it be like returning to her home town after all these years, and under these circumstances?

Gwen took the Alexander exit, and followed the steep and curving road down to the south end of town, then along Bridgeway, the beautiful main street that overlooked the Bay on one side, and shops on the other. It looked quite different from when she'd been here as a child—more commercial, with new buildings she didn't remember. The arts community was still alive and thriving. Parts of the water side of Bridgeway had been cleaned up, and there was a park where there hadn't been one before.

Driving north, past the downtown area, where more tourists than she remembered enjoyed the sites, she could see the forest of sailboat masts in the Bay.

Taking her text books with her, and the journalism papers she was working on, she would only stay a week before returning to Ann Arbor to finish the term.

Gwen was on her way to meet Megan Denison, her mother's old friend, with whom they'd lived before.

Megan Denison cared for Gwen until the mother's sister came from Michigan to claim her. After several weeks all legal means of finding Patricia Harris came to a stop. Megan continued to question friends and strangers alike, but no leads were forthcoming.

What had happened in 1955 to make her mother disappear? Gwen had never known. Patricia's friend, Megan, had written to her off and on, and assured her whatever the cause, Patricia would never have left her.

"An accident of some kind. It's possible she drowned, although she was a good swimmer. Or had a sailing accident."

Megan Denison was the only contact Gwen had in Sausalito. She had phoned Megan in advance to let her know she was coming.

Now, as she approached their meeting place, Gwen felt the thumping of her heart—the dread of going over the past, the eagerness.

They met at the Roma restaurant on Bridgeway, a popular hangout on the main street of Sausalito. Their searching eyes found no difficulty in locating the other. They sat at one of the plastic tables outside.

"You haven't changed, Megan. I'd know you anywhere."

Not quite true: At forty-five Megan was heavier now—but still attractive. And her brown hair was already laced with white. The white hadn't been there the last time they'd been together.

"But *you've* changed, dear Gwen. Twenty-one years old, and the last time I saw you, you were only eleven." The older woman gave Gwen a hearty hug.

After some polite small talk Gwen got to the matter at hand.

"Do you think it could have been anything other than an accident?" she asked her old friend.

"Like what?"

"Like—something deliberate. Her remains were found at the bottom of a steep ravine!"

"You mean, was she pushed?"

Gwen looked out at the sailboat masts bobbing on the marina. "Yeah. I guess that's what I mean."

Megan put her hand on Gwen's. "We have no way of knowing for sure. You know she was riding her bicycle. It would have been easy for her to slip. I can't think of anyone who'd want to hurt your mother. She was well-liked."

"I want to meet some of the people she knew."

"Lots of folks left Sausalito. But I'll do what I can. Oh," she said suddenly, "you'll meet my son Alex when he gets back. Do you remember Alex? He was your playmate. He's with some friends up at Tahoe, spring skiing. He might be able to introduce you to some of the sailing community your mom knew. Patricia was a great sailor."

"Oh, yes. When will he be back?"

"A week from Sunday."

"I have to return to school then."

"Oh. Well, that is a shame."

They sat in silence for several minutes, Megan stirring her tea, Gwen wadding her napkin in her lap.

The wind came up and Megan's napkin flew off like a bird. "It's getting chilly," she said, retrieving the airborne miscreant. "Let's go."

Megan had walked to the café. They got in Gwen's rental car, and Megan guided Gwen back to her house up on Ebbtide Street. The structure was sixty or more years old, and of no particular architectural style. Several houses on the street were obviously built by the same builder, with small differences in portico and color. But Gwen remembered its charm, and Megan showed her to the same room she'd had as a child.

Her gaze travelled from wall to wall, corner to corner.

"It's my old room."

"Yes."

It felt very strange to Gwen to be suddenly back in the home she'd spent her first eleven years in, with her mother. Feelings she'd held back for a long time suddenly broke the dam and flooded through. Her breathing became jerky.

"Of course, we've seen many changes since then. Carpeting, new curtains."

Memories flooded in. She started to get dizzy.

"I need the lavatory," she said.

Gwen wanted to be alone. She allowed herself several minutes, finished by washing her travel-weary face, and returned to Megan, who was now leaving the bedroom.

"I'm sorry," Megan apologized. "I didn't –I should have realized."

"No, no, it's OK."

Megan prepared a cold chicken salad for dinner with white wine. They sat at the maple kitchen table with a plastic cloth very much like one Gwen remembered from her childhood. The table still wobbled a bit. Shored up with a series of match boxes, the short leg was still waiting to be fixed.

"Where's Chad?" Gwen asked.

"He has Lion's Club tonight. He left a bit early to run some errands. I think my husband wanted to give us some time for girl talk."

"That was thoughtful of him."

Megan asked her about school in Michigan.

After supper, Gwen asked Megan if she'd mind if she took a bath.

On the edge of the tub she saw a bottle of bubble bath. Indulging her desire, she poured an ample amount into the steaming water, and then immersed herself. How relaxing. She couldn't remember when she'd last had a bubble bath. Maybe in this house.

When she was dried and dressed she joined Megan in the living room. Still the same faux Tiffany lamp in the corner. Some things were so comfortingly familiar.

Gwen leapt to the question she'd wanted to ask all day.

"I want to know about my father, Megan. What can you tell me?"

She heard Megan's quick intake of breath.

"You must have known him. What was he like?"

"This is going to sound strange. But I don't know who he was, Gwen."

"You said as much in one of your letters. But is that really true? You and my mother were such close friends."

"That's one subject she avoided. She didn't want you to be involved with him. But she was always glad she'd kept *you*."

"She really was?"

"Yes, she was."

Just then, they heard Chad's car in the drive. Gwen sensed she wouldn't learn anything more about her father tonight.

Chad entered, gave his wife a kiss and held out a friendly hand to Gwen.

Chad Denison was considerably more roly-poly than she remembered him. He was balding in a Friar Tuck sort of way, had a smile which seemed to begin in his twinkling eyes, and a handshake stronger than his appearance suggested.

"My, it's been a long time. From child to grown woman, all in the blink of an eye."

"Not quite—a few more blinks than that," she laughed and gave him a hug.

"It's so good to see you. We've been looking forward to this."

"So have I. It's good to see you too."

"Can I get you ladies anything?" he rubbed his hands together. "A drink or something?"

"I think we're all set," Megan said.

They chatted for a few minutes and Gwen realized she was extremely tired. With a three hour time change, where it was already midnight in Michigan, she was ready to give her mind and body a rest.

"I think I'll turn in," she said.

"Of course," they chimed together.

Rummaging through her suitcase for her pajamas, she came across her childhood diary. The last minute, when she was packing, she'd decided to throw it in. If she going to open the pages of the past by revisiting her first home, she might as well take another look at these pages too.

The key had long ago been lost, but it took little effort to release the lock with a bobby pin. As she opened the old book, she heard its imitation leather crack. Leafing through the pages she noticed the handwriting changing from very childish to an older style, where dotted 'i's were replaced with hearts.

Then she read, "I'll always love you, Mama, even if you did run away."

She closed the book. Not tonight. She was already on overload.

CHapter 2

On Monday she was back at the sheriff's office.
Detective Bower was about thirty-five years old, had a military haircut, a ski-jump nose and a barely visible chin.

"Who found my mother's remains?" she asked him.

"A hiker. He reported it to the ranger's station, and a ranger went out there, and verified the finding."

The finding.

"Then someone from the sheriff's department—"

"What ranger?" she asked.

"I don't know, ma'am. I don't have that part of the report."

"Where can I get it?"

"You could call the Pantoll Ranger Station in the Mt. Tam State Park." He wrote a phone number on a piece of paper.

Gwen thanked him and turned to leave. "Sir," she called back, "where are her remains now?"

The detective looked embarrassed. "I'll have to look into that. Do you have a phone number where I could reach you?"

She left Megan's number with the detective, found a payphone, and slowly put her finger in each hole to dial the rangers' station.

Having prepared no opening speech, she was suddenly at a loss for words. Finally she said, "May I speak with the ranger who found some human bones two weeks ago?"

There was a pause. "Who's speaking?"

"I am the daughter of the person…" She stumbled, found it impossible to talk, made one more halting attempt and hung up.

What a fool she'd been. She should have thought it through ahead of time. Or maybe she just wasn't ready for this. What should she have said—*I'm the daughter of the woman whose bones you found,* or *Those bones you found belong to my mother.*

None of it sounded right.

She was agitated, and needed to do something.

She felt compelled to drive the road on which her mother had crashed below. Maybe she'd find a likely spot where the terrible accident had occurred.

She got directions at the gas station, took the first exit off the freeway to Mill Valley and followed signs on Panoramic Highway to Stinson Beach. She couldn't help notice the grandeur of the valleys and hills as she drove up the mountain west toward the Pacific Ocean. But it wasn't long before the twists and bends on the narrow road made her catch her breath. There were no shoulders, and no guard rails. Coming from Michigan where the land was generally flat, and even the slightest incline required a guard rail, Gwen was shocked and frightened by the steady climb, and steep drop-offs. She had never driven on mountain roads before. She gripped the wheel tightly as if that would make her safe. She knew her heart was pounding fast. No one had told her that this road was so treacherous.

At least she was on the inside of this two lane road. She couldn't even imagine what it would be like driving back. She had a dim awareness that the landscape was thick with all sorts of conifers and hardwood trees—even redwoods; but she dare not take her eyes off the road, for fear of crossing the center line, or driving into the mountain which rose on her right at ninety degrees.

The driver behind her was too close. Worse, he was honking. Well, what could she do about it? She knew she was going slower than the locals, but with all the switch-backs and blind curves, she didn't dare go faster. The driver honked several times, creating a near-panic state in Gwen. Finally, she noticed a pocket, or widened space in the road into which slower traffic could pull off, but she was too close to it, and the other driver too close to her to make a sudden turn. She watched for the next such turn-off. When she'd managed to get into it safely, the other driver honked and shouted obscenities. She sat there shaking for several moments, watching a whole line of cars go by, all faster than she'd felt safe driving. Her heart was beating so hard she could feel its throb.

Finally, she was calm enough to get out of the car. If she were going to see anything, look down those steep hills and ravines, she couldn't do it while driving. She walked across the road, nearly missed by a driver coming at break-neck speed around the curve from the other direction. On the far side she got as far off the road as she dared, but upon looking down, backed up. Below her lay a descent so steep she was certain anyone missing that turn, and cutting the edge would never survive. She began to feel a dizziness, a pull forward. She forced herself to look straight ahead to recover her balance. When she had regained her equilibrium, she crossed back to her car, sitting still in the enclosure, which gave her a feeling of safety.

Driving on, she got a breath-taking view of Stinson Beach, its crescent shoreline beckoning from below. Then for what seemed like several miles, as she traversed the switchbacks, the ocean was out of sight again. Finally, she approached sea-level and was warned or welcomed—she wasn't sure which—by a flock of screeching seagulls.

Driving along Highway 1, through the quaint little town of Stinson Beach, she reversed direction and went back to this village, parking by a little restaurant called *Seashells*. Entering, she wondered if her mother had ever been here. It looked old enough to have been there before the Ten Commandments. Living up to its name, shells hung in strings throughout the eating area. More shells were glued to edges of the booths. A couple of amateur paintings displayed shell-rimmed frames. The place held a strong odor of fried foods.

Being mid-afternoon, the establishment was deserted, except for two young men sitting near the back. Gwen sat in a booth, which looked like it had been painted many times over. Chipped in several places, she saw its former incarnations in shades of forest green, hot pink and yellow. Presently, it was white. A soiled menu was propped between the napkin holder and the salt and pepper shaker. She thought the prices awfully high for this one-star dive, but was tempted to order a lobster sandwich anyway.

The waitress approached her. "What'll you have?"

"I'm not sure," Gwen answered. "What do you recommend?"

"Hey, are you OK?"

"Why? What do you mean?"

"You're as white as these shells."

"Oh, I just had a scary trip driving over the mountain, or whatever it is, from Sausalito."

"First time?" asked the waitress.

"Yes."

"Where you from?"

"The mid-west."

"Figures. Pretty flat, huh?"

Gwen nodded. "Are there many accidents up there?"

The waitress nodded. "Some, yeah. Just a couple of months ago, two bicyclists were run off the road by a speeding BMW."

"Do you mean—were they?"

"Yeah, they went off the cliff. DOA."

Now, wishing to escape the subject, Gwen looked down at the menu and ordered the lobster roll. Tempted to get a beer to go with it, she refrained, knowing what lay between her and a safe bed in Sausalito. She settled for coffee.

The waitress came over and chatted with her. She had dishwater blond hair. Her hands bore the insignia of her work—they were red.

"Mind if I sit?" she asked. "I've been on my feet all day."

"Please."

She had a toothpick in her mouth and used it vigorously.

Gwen was grateful for the company, and used the opportunity to ask about the area.

"I was born here, so I guess I take it all for granted. But it's pretty special, huh?"

"Yes, very."

"Have you been to Pt. Reyes? Bolinas?"

"No, I just got here."

"Well, you'll want to see those places. Everybody does. You visiting?"

"Yes. Just for a week."

"Well, enjoy yourself."

When she had finished eating, Gwen braced herself for the drive back. The longer days would provide enough light; for that she was grateful. But nothing prepared her for the feeling of imminent doom, as her compact Honda climbed the torturous hills away from the water and up the mountain. She felt she was millimeters and moments from death, as the steep climb kept her nearly always on the edge of a precipice.

Again, vehicles jammed up behind her, and there were no pockets on this side of the road. Two cars passed her in the opposite lane in clearly marked no-passing zones.

Just as she rounded another blind curve, two bicyclists were right in front of her. Swerving to avoid them, she almost ran into a car coming from the other direction. She had never been so frightened.

Finally, she was in line with a group of cars held up by a truck. At least no one was blaming her for the slow pace. Bicyclists were taking their lives in their hands to climb these treacherous hills. At least that's what she thought.

So now, perhaps she could bring some closure to the mystery that had surrounded her mother's death for so many years. No wonder her mother had slipped off the road on her bicycle. Why had she taken such chances?

~

When she finally got back to Megan's, Gwen was so exhausted from her grueling drive, she lay on her bed and was soon fast asleep. She slept soundly until one in the morning, and then couldn't get back to sleep.

She picked up her old diary.

"Dear Mom, did you run away because you fell in love? Do you have another family now? Do I have a little brother or sister somewhere?"

"Mom, sometimes I get so angry with you. How could you have left me? Why didn't you take me with you?"

"Dear Mom, Didn't you love me? Was it because I still wet my bed? I'm so ashamed. I just don't know how to stop it."

"Dear Mom, I hope wherever you are, you are happy. Are you dead? Sometimes I wish you were, because then I'd know you didn't leave because you didn't love me anymore. But then I feel guilty."

"If you're in heaven, do you see God very often? Is he nice? Does he know I wet the bed? Please don't tell him."

"Dear Mom. Will I ever know if you had an accident or were murdered? Aunt Marie says I'm being melodramatic to think you were murdered, but that's the only reasonable thing that would make you leave me. Right?"

Gwen closed the diary, put it under her pillow. As she lay on her side a slow stream of tears flowed across her face and down the other side of her nose. Compassion for the child who'd written those notes filled her. How much of her childhood, teen-age years had been filled re-working, fantasizing different endings to the story of her mother's disappearance. She fell asleep with the familiar longing she'd never been able to quell.

~

The next day she called the sheriff's office only to discover that it was Officer Bower's day off. She had to do something. Action was the only thing that kept her sane.

She had studied karate at the university, first to satisfy a Phys. Ed. requirement. But she'd enjoyed it, and continued going to practice every week. Now she ran through many of the moves, and that used up some of her energy, but still she needed to get out and *do* something.

Call the ranger's station. Yes, that's what she would do. She didn't care how foolish she sounded. She'd just do it.

She was in luck. The ranger who'd discovered her mother's remains agreed to see her at Pantoll Station.

Oh, my God, she thought. I'll have to go up the mountain again. Well, what did she expect? If she was going to find the place where her mother had met her end, she'd just have to put fear aside. Perhaps her mother would be her guiding angel now, and keep her safe. The thought was comforting, anyway.

She pulled up in the rangers' drive and got out of the Honda. Hesitantly, she opened the door to the little wooden building, smelling of pine. A cool day, a fire had been lit in the wood burning stove.

She introduced herself, and the ranger told her his name was Carl.

"Would you be willing to show me exactly where my mother went off the road?"

Carl blinked a couple of times, but then, with the assent of his supervisor, agreed.

He asked her to follow him in her car. She must have looked pitiful, because he added, "Unless you'd rather ride with me."

"Oh, yes, please."

Being a passenger wasn't nearly as scary as being the driver, she discovered, as she was sure the ranger was well acquainted with roads and the safest way to navigate them.

Carl was friendly, about thirty and physically fit. He eased the situation by chatting with her about Michigan, where he'd thought about going to school—at Michigan State in Lansing. She told him she was studying at the University of Michigan in Ann Arbor. They laughed about what great rivals the two schools were.

"OK," he said suddenly, jerking the jeep to a halt. "This is as close as we can get. We'll have to get out and walk."

His statement had come so suddenly, her knees almost buckled as she got out of the vehicle.

As they walked a few yards toward the site he said, "There's not much to see from here—just this deep ravine."

It was similar to the one she'd seen the day before. Her imagination put her on the bicycle, flying off the edge, and almost straight down into the womb of the land. Covered with brush, all kinds of foliage, and exposed rock, her stomach was doing somersaults. She almost felt the blows, as in her mind she descended, down, down, down. Sensing her dizziness, Carl took her by the arm and turned her around.

"Have you seen enough?"

"Yes. For now, anyway."

He guided her back to the jeep, and they rode in silence back to the ranger station.

Finally, she spoke. "Who found her—I mean the bones?" She shivered as she said it.

"A hiker."

"And he called you?"

"Yes. I couldn't have located the spot without his help. Her remains were deeply hidden under years of undergrowth." He took a deep breath. "You have to understand," he went on, "that only part of her skeleton was found. It had been so long ago—"

"What part?" her morbid curiosity asked.

"Most of the rib cage, one fibula, tibia and foot. Animals probably carried off the rest."

"Animals?"

"Yes."

She was sorry she'd asked. She mulled it over, then tried to erase what the ranger had just told her.

"There's one other thing," he was saying. "Her bicycle was found about a hundred yards from her remains. Apparently, when she was thrown one of her shoes came off, and one stayed on the bicycle stirrup."

Gwen swallowed hard. "Was anything else found?"

"Like what?"

"I don't know."

"There was a button nearby. We don't know that it was relevant."

"What kind of button?"

"Looked like leather—from a man's sport jacket."

"Where is it now?"

"With the remains."

Gwen swallowed hard. "Do you think it was an accident?"

"Or what?"

She flushed. "Well, not suicide. I won't believe that for a moment."

"Then you're asking me if there was foul play."

"Yes, I guess I am."

She looked out the window and noticed a huge redwood clinging to its ground by what appeared to be a single root.

"We have no way of knowing that now. There was no investigation at the time, and there is no evidence to suggest foul play now. I can understand, Miss Harris that these questions torment you, but I think you'll have to put it to rest."

"That's not so easy,"

He patted her hand. "I suggest you go back to Michigan and watch the Wolverines beat the Spartans."

This statement came so suddenly, she gave him an astonished look.

"I'm sorry. Bad choice. I'm just saying I don't think you should waste any more time here."

When she returned to Megan's, she relayed what had happened that afternoon.

"Where was I when Mom was out biking?"

"At home with me."

"Who did she go with?"

"I don't know."

"How can that be?" Gwen could barely conceal her exasperation.

Megan picked up her tea, then paused, and set it down. "Why are you doing this, Gwen? What is it you hope to accomplish? It was all so long ago."

"I don't care how long ago it was. I want to find out everything I can about her death."

"Do you think that will make you feel better?"

"I have a right to know."

Why was everyone trying to steer her away from her search?

CHApter 3

The following day Gwen discovered that her mother's remains were at a forensic lab, where the X-rays of the broken tibia had been compared to the bone in question. She was to contact a Ms. Lewis and tell her what she wanted done with them. Gwen toyed with the idea of asking to see them, and then decided that would be macabre and gratuitous. She filled out a form indicating she wanted her mother's remains cremated. She would collect the ashes when they were ready.

Before she knew it, it was Sunday. She couldn't leave town now—not yet. She had just begun to find answers to her mother's death.

Alex returned from skiing. Although they had grown up together for the first years of their lives, neither found anything familiar in the appearance of the other. He was about five feet eleven, with stringy, long brown hair, generally well-built.

Alex was quiet and somewhat withdrawn, but he offered to show Gwen around. That evening they went to the *No Name Bar* downtown, where Joe Tate and The RedLegs were playing. Noisy and smoky, yet there was a real feeling of warmth among the comrades. It was small for such a popular hang-out. In predictable arrangement, the bar ran along one side of the establishment, tables in the middle, and on the other side a nook seemed carved out of the wall with a stage, just large enough to hold a small band.

"Maybe we'll run into some of your mom's old pals."

"I'd like that."

She didn't want to go to a bar alone. It was fun to have some company, and Alex introduced her to some of the other regulars in this popular establishment. But they didn't see anyone her mother would have known. Instead they talked about their childhood.

"We were married. Do you remember? When we were about seven."

He laughed. "Then the next day you said it didn't count because we didn't have a minister."

"I was probably mad at you," she smiled.

"Yeah, and that made me mad at you."

"Do you remember what you did?"

"No. What?"

She covered a smile.

"Tell me."

"You took out your wee-wee and peed on me."

"I didn't."

"Yes, you did."

"Wee-wee?" He looked totally stunned.

"That's what we called it then," she laughed.

"Was that the time you watched me get spanked?"

"Yup. To further humiliate you, your mom wanted me as a witness."

"Oh, God. I need another beer."

~

Two days later they went back to the *No Name Bar*, and two of her mother's old friends, Conan and Eric were there. They were part of the houseboat community. Although Conan was reserved, he had an inviting smile. Tall and handsome, with blue eyes and dark hair, he was on the slender side. He didn't talk as much as Eric, but quiet men often evoked a mystery, Gwen thought. She wanted to get to know him better.

Eric looked like what he was, a sailor—out of an old picture book. Shaggy beard, full head of wavy brown hair, and a pipe. He even had a pea coat and a captain's cap. His handshake gave Gwen an idea of how strong he was. Barrel chested and brawny he had sunken brown eyes which twinkled. He could play Santa Claus.

Both men were in their forties.

Alex told the others that Gwen was hoping to find out more about her mother's life and what led to her demise.

Eric shook his head. "That's still a mystery. Just disappeared. Nobody knew what happened."

"We know now," Alex said softly. "But not the how and why."

He told them what they knew so far.

"Jesus," Eric said.

Conan whistled. "Well, we knew she wouldn't just take off and leave you."

"I can remember seeing you as a kid," Eric said. "Playing by the water. Both of you, actually," he said looking at Alex. "Sometimes we did a little baby-sitting."

"Really?" Gwen asked.

"It takes a village," he smiled.

"Do you think it was an accident?" Eric asked.

"That's what I was hoping you could tell me."

Eric shook his head. "Haven't a clue."

"But who'd want to kill her?" Conan asked.

Gwen said, "I drove up on that mountain road a few days ago. It's really treacherous. I can see how easy it would be to have an accident up there—especially if you're on the outside edge."

"Yeah," Alex added.

There was a pause, and Eric ordered a round of drinks for everyone.

"What was it like living here in the fifties?" she asked.

"A lot like it is now," Eric said. "But not so quiet. It's a great town. So free compared to everywhere else. Lots of artists—still are. Waterfront people. And folks who anchor out and live on their boats. Beatniks, poets, even philosophers."

"The town's kind of wild," Conan added.

"Is that why you live here?" she asked the obvious.

"Yeah."

"Can you tell me how my mom fit into all this?"

Eric blew out a cloud of smoke. "She was a free spirit— one of us."

"But she didn't live on a houseboat."

"No."

Gwen waited for him to say more, while he played with his pipe, trying to get the embers going.

"She learned to sail. She'd often come out with us. And she could handle a boat in weather, too. Man, I remember once in a storm. I'd sprained my arm in the rigging, and she took us in." He re-lit his pipe. "She painted. I'm sure you knew that. Watercolors. She bicycled, swam, got into Yoga. All around gal."

"What did she live on?"

The older men looked at each other and shrugged. They didn't know.

"She sold a few paintings to tourists," Conan offered.

"For awhile she worked at a café—before you were born."

Gwen was dying to ask if anyone knew who her father was, but swallowed the question. Not yet.

Alex excused himself. "I'll be back."

Eric said, "He's at it again."

"What?" Gwen asked.

"Coke."

She figured he didn't mean Coca-Cola, but she didn't want to pry.

She changed the subject. "What do you guys do?"

"When I'm following my bliss, I'm out on the water sailing," Eric grinned.

"He doesn't just sail," Conan said about Eric. "He builds boats, repairs boats and cars. Anything you need fixing, Eric's your man. Wait 'til you see his houseboat."

"Tell me about it," she said.

Conan tried. "Built like a brick shithouse—well, not literally. It's kind of in the shape of—"he turned to his friend, "like what, would you say?" He gave up. "You'll just have to go and see it."

Those were the most words Gwen heard from Conan that night.

Gwen turned to Eric and raised her eyebrows.

"Sure, come, any time after four. I work until then."

"Thanks."

Eric said, "It's not the weirdest houseboat out there. You'll see. There's one they call the 'owl', another is like a beautiful contemporary chapel. And some are disasters waiting to happen. Most are jerry-rigged with whatever they could find to build them with. A real mix."

Gwen turned to Conan. "And what do you do?"

"I play at art."

"What medium?"

"I've tried several—oil, water color, mixed media."

"He does more than play with it—the guy's making money," Eric offered.

"Good for you. Maybe I'll get to see some of your work," Gwen said.

Alex came back and sat down with them.

Eric turned to Alex and Gwen. "I'm taking the *Wicked Winch* out tomorrow. You guys want to go out with me?"

Gwen looked at Alex. They both agreed. "That would be great," Alex said.

"It's not much bigger than a dinghy, but is she fast. Single sail, small cockpit, hull low to the water. I built her for racing."

"I hope you have life vests," Gwen smiled.

"Oh, yeah." He turned to Alex. "Be at Gate 5 Marina at two o'clock."

~

There was plenty of wind the next day when Alex and Gwen went to the marina to meet Eric. He threw them a pail with cleaning fluid and rags. "Swab the deck."

"Yes, sir," Alex said.

The boat was painted green—one of many coats over old wood, Gwen guessed. The mast looked too big for the boat; perhaps it had been sized down from a larger vessel. Painted on the side of the hull was *The Wicked Winch.*

Well, he had a sense of humor. Gwen liked that.

Eric started to identify parts of the boat for her.

"Oh, is this to be a lesson? I didn't know," Gwen said.

Alex lit up a joint.

"How else you gonna learn to sail?" Eric asked.

"Right, Captain."

He gave them each a life jacket and donned one himself. Then he said, "Do you know what a sheet is?"

"The sail?"

"Strike one. The sheets are the lines fastened to the sails. They control the sails. If the wind's behind you, you want to let the sail all the way out. But if you're trying to reach close to the wind, you have to use the sheet to pull in the sail. Tight. Whatever the tack, the sail has to be tight."

"If it's luffing—or flapping, you're not working it at maximum capacity," Alex added.

"And that will slow it down," Gwen said.

"Now you're talkin'."

They motored out into the open water, and Eric said, "This line is called the halyard. It raises the sail." He demonstrated.

He handed her the starboard sheet, and adjusted it for the wind. "Just hold it for now, but when I say, 'come about' grab the other sheet and pull it in, while releasing this one gradually. I'll be moving the tiller to the other side."

"What's 'come about'?"

"Crossing the wind. Can you feel which way the wind is coming now?"

"It's coming from the right side of the boat."

"Good. That's the starboard side. The left is called 'port'."

She looked up at the rising sail. She'd never seen one like it. He had painted a design on it of sea horses. Maybe it was to conceal the fact that the sail itself was old, dirty and patched. Or maybe it was just because he liked it that way.

Her first attempt at handling the sheets was a little slow and sloppy, but Eric was a patient teacher, and by the third try, he said she did it as smoothly as any old salt.

"I had no idea I'd be learning to sail."

She looked up at the cloudless sky, and down at the wiggly water, lapping and licking the sides of the boat.

Part of her felt guilty that she was sailing instead of learning more about her mother. But she was getting information, and from people who knew her. What more could she do?

They stayed in the harbor for the most part, while Gwen got familiar with the feel of the boat, and how far to move the tiller to achieve the desired tack. Then they moved farther south in Richardson Bay. She saw pocked pilings, each topped with a seagull, all facing away from the wind. They passed the entrance to Raccoon Straights, between Angel Island and Belvedere.

"It's gorgeous here. Why don't I remember this?"

"I don't think you got down to this end often, if at all."

The winds changed, and the tide was coming in.

"I'll take over now," Eric said.

An hour later they were back in the marina. When they came ashore, Eric asked if she'd enjoyed her lesson.

"I loved it."

"Let's go for a drink," he suggested.

"You two go," Alex said. "I have to get to work."

Gwen had almost forgotten about Alex. He hadn't said a word on the sail. Just laid back, and what? Meditated? Or was he stoned?

"Where do you work?" Gwen asked.

"At the post office, sorting mail."

As he walked away Gwen saw Alex light another joint.

"That was so exhilarating," she said. "I loved every minute of it."

"You're a fast learner. Ever been on a sailboat before?"

"Once or twice, on Lake St. Claire. But I never learned anything about sailing."

"Would you like to see my pad?"

"Sure."

They walked back to the array of jerry-rigged houseboats until they got to his.

She had never seen one of this size and shape anywhere.

He had fastened two enormous sheets of rusty metal salvaged from the war ship-building days into a curved arch, fastening them at the top, and at the two sides of a barge. On one end he had fitted plywood to fill in the space. On the other, more private end he'd cut glass to fit the opening.

"Wow, this is fantastic," she said.

He helped her onto the deck of this innovative home.

"Wait 'til you see the inside."

"This is terrific—you've divided the space into a living room, a bedroom and a bath."

"Or in sailors' vernacular—salon, berth and head. The galley's over there."

At one end he'd fashioned an indoor shop of sorts—at least a place to keep tools. Though, as he explained, he did most of his work outside. There was a deck on each end of the dock.

"You are really something, Eric. You did all this yourself?"

"With a little help from my friends."

When they were sitting with their drinks—Eric a whiskey, and Gwen a hot chocolate—she asked him, "How well did you know my mother?"

He lit his pipe. "We were good friends, but just friends. We had a lot of fun, a lot of laughs. We sometimes worked together, and sometimes partied together."

"Did she confide in you?"

"About what?"

Gwen shrugged. "I don't know. About anything."

"I don't know who your father was, if that's what you're getting at."

Gwen was embarrassed. "I guess I'm pretty transparent."

"I don't blame you for wanting to know."

"Do you think it could be any of your crowd?"

"Can't say for sure. In some ways everybody's an open book, but then everybody's got their secrets, too."

"What do you make of her falling off that cliff?"

"Gwen was a good bicyclist. I can't imagine her careening off the edge."

"I was on that drive. Those twists and turns are dangerous. If a car came speeding around the corner—"

"You said the ranger showed you the point at which she must have gone off."

"Yes."

"Will you show it to me?"

Gwen couldn't believe she'd heard right. "OK. Oh, yes."

It appeared she had an ally, someone who'd help her.

~

Eric didn't own a car, but he could drive, so Gwen talked him into taking the wheel of her rental car. She packed some sandwiches and fruit. She hoped he wouldn't think she was looking at this drive as a date, but it seemed the nice thing to do.

"Did you ever bike up the mountain?" she asked.

"Yeah, a few times. Usually with Patricia."

"But not that day."

"No, not that day."

"You don't know who she was with?"

"Nope."

"She could have been alone."

"I suppose. But she was usually sensible enough to have a buddy along."

Eric was driving faster than the ranger had. Gwen swung back and forth in the car, as Eric negotiated curves and switchbacks. She hoped she wouldn't be sick.

"Do you know who else she biked with?"

"Conan, Megan. Probably others."

They drove in silence for awhile. Then Gwen said, "I think we're coming close. I remember it was not far from this patch in the road." She sat up straighter.

"Here! Here!" She couldn't contain her excitement. "The ranger parked right over there."

Eric brought the Honda to a stop in the pocket and they got out of the car. "Show me," he said.

She crossed the road with him, and pointed down at the ravine. Then she looked the other way, as her stomach churned its disapproval.

After gazing down at the gorge for a minute or two, Eric looked at the road in both directions.

"Do you see any hidden curves around here?" he asked.

Gwen looked in both ways. "No. Not in the immediate vicinity."

"That's what I wanted to know," he said. "You see how unlikely it is that she was taken by surprise from a car coming around a bend."

Gwen nodded. A sinking feeling flooded through her. *Then what did that imply?*

In almost a whisper she said, "Are you saying you think she was pushed?"

"That would be my guess." He put his hand on her shoulder.

"Who would do such a thing?"

Chapter 4

A few days later Gwen got a notice from the University of Michigan. Her library books were overdue. She was suddenly jerked back into another reality. She had all but deleted the part of her life that involved school. She was stunned that she could have so easily turned her back on her studies. How long had she been in Sausalito? Almost two weeks, and she'd forgotten all about her plan to stay only over spring break.

At one point, after driving by herself up the mountain, she'd convinced herself that her mother's death was probably an accident, and would have gone back to Ann Arbor. But after what Eric pointed out on the last drive, she returned to the murder theory. How could she leave Sausalito now?

But she missed her old boyfriend, Brad. He was two years younger than she, and a sophomore, but there definitely had been an attraction. He was tall and blonde with an aquiline shaped profile, and a strong jaw line. He was already on the Varsity basketball team, and she loved watching him play. He had a good sense of humor, and their sex life was more than satisfactory.

Sex. When she'd first thought about losing her virginity, she assumed most girls were virgins, and she certainly intended to be one until she married. Then a report came out—Kinsey, she thought— saying over fifty percent of college students were not virgins. So when her hormones soared with Brad, it wasn't too long before she succumbed. One night they made a rational decision to go ahead. Brad said he'd buy some protection, and they knew where they'd go.

A stable of university buses was corralled behind the Dental School on campus. One night they discovered that these vehicles weren't locked. So that had become their home away from home, a place to play. Not a perfect solution, having to assume acrobatic positions on the cold seats; and unless all the windows steamed up, which never happened, they were in risk of forfeiting privacy. But at least they were the only ones on the bus, and no one ever came by. Hey, they were young.

Of course, with all that preparation and anticipation, it wasn't too surprising that when the moment came on their first attempt, Brad couldn't perform. They both fussed with the condom, but he shrunk more with each attempt. Finally, they gave up.

Future evenings proved to be more successful.

But he was a med student, and it would be forever, she thought, before he'd look at any relationship seriously. He was just a lot of fun, and she'd try to tell herself all along that that's all it was meant to be. Maybe it was just as well that they were separated by so many miles. She knew it wouldn't last. She might just as well start getting used to being apart now.

Well, she had to make a decision. Go back now and try to make up her classes, or kiss this semester good-bye and stay on where she was. Except for the tuition that would be wasted, and missing a futile love affair, it wasn't a hard decision. She liked it here in California, and besides, she told herself, she was doing important work—trying to solve a ten year old mystery of her mother's disappearance.

~

Conan called her at Megan's and asked her if she'd like to see more of Marin.

"Sure," she said.

"We'll have to use your car, unless you want to ride in my old truck."

"We can use my car. Will you drive it?"

"OK."

He took her south, and turned off the freeway just before the bridge. They drove up a hill to a vista where many cars were parked in the headlands.

"Let's get out here," he said.

They joined the others hovering near the edge of the cliff watching the incredible view. Below lay the Golden Gate Bridge, separating the Bay from the ocean, and on the other side, the city of San Francisco. A myriad of boats skated across the bay. Though most were sailboats, there were also large shipping vessels, kayaks, and canoes.

"What a view! I should have brought my camera," Gwen said.

"There'll be other times."

They continued driving up the hill and stopped again, where they walked around and saw old bunkers and barracks built a hundred years ago.

"It's really good of you to take me on this tour," she said. "I think this area is the most beautiful place in the world."

"I haven't been here for awhile, so it's a treat for me too."

"What do you call these hills?"

"It's all part of the Headlands, belonging to the military, but they're going to turn it over to the national park system. There was a big fight over transforming all these hills into a huge development. Fortunately, some wise souls are protecting it from that fate. So it will retain its natural beauty."

They drove on, and came to a point where they could go farther up, or go down.

"Which way?" Conan asked.

"She pointed to the left, where the road first went up, and then took a sharp dip down toward the sea.

"Wow," she cried out. "And I thought Michigan was beautiful!"

"I'm sure it is, just in a different way."

"True. Lots of lakes, and in the fall the autumn colors rival New England."

"Well, there you have it."

"Have you ever been there?"

"No. Sorry to say I haven't been any farther east than Nevada."

"Were you born here?"

"In San Francisco."

They followed the road down, which became one-way, and was carved out of the hill very close to the sea. The sun was dancing on the waves, and wispy clouds floated across the sky.

"Now hang on," Conan warned.

"Oh, my! Like a roller coaster!"

They sped down the steep hill on the water's edge.

"You like it."

"Oh, yes." She looked around. "Marin is gorgeous." She rocked back in her seat, waving her arms in the air.

On the way back to Denisons, Conan said, "I'll come in with you. Have to see Alex about something."

When they arrived, she didn't see anyone in the house.

She looked out her back bedroom window and saw Alex and Conan together. Conan was handing over a small package of something to Alex. Then Conan turned and walked out to the street without going through the house.

It surprised Gwen, but then why should it? It could have been a loan from Conan to his nephew. She decided it was none of her business.

When he came in the house, Alex said, "Where were you all day?"

"Conan and I took a ride out to the Headlands. They are so incredibly beautiful, Alex."

"You don't know Conan very well."

"Oh, he was fine."

"Still, you should be cautious with everybody. Can't be too careful."

"Everybody? Suspicious of all Mom's friends? And you, too?"

"Well, I'm the one person you can rule out. I'm not as old as you are."

"Six weeks younger. So I should be paranoid about all the older guys."

"I'd just be careful; that's all I'm saying."

They fixed supper together. Spaghetti and meatballs.

"Dad thinks it's not spaghetti if there aren't any meatballs," Alex said.

They finished their meal with strawberry ice-cream.

Since they were alone, and there was something on her mind that Gwen couldn't let go of, she burst out with, "Alex, can I ask you a serious question?"

"What?"

"Do you suppose there's any chance my father is the villain?"

"Why would he want to kill your mom? He loved her, didn't he?"

"I don't know, but he probably didn't want her to keep me, and when she did—"

"The accident was ten years later."

"That's true. But they could have had a lovers' fight. Afterward, he felt guilty, and sent all that child support money to Aunt Marie."

"I don't think so." Alex said.

~

The next evening, like many others, she could hear music coming from the waterfront. Restless, she decided to venture down a few blocks, and follow the sounds until she came to the arena of color and music. Seeing it for the first time at night, and pulsing with electricity, Gwen was enthralled by what she encountered. Several musicians were performing, while many others, including children, danced. Some seemed to just enjoy the rhythm. Others, dancing alone, were allowing the music to transport them to ecstatic states. Colored lights were strung above from the masts of several boats. Surrounded by boats and boats-in-the-making, she thought the whole scene was a work of art.

Smoke from nearby drifted to her face and invaded her nostrils. The smell of food made her realize she was hungry. She walked over to a concave table laden with food of all kinds. Chicken thighs were browning on a nearby grill.

"Want some?" a voice asked.

She looked up, startled.

"Help yourself."

"I'm crashing your party." She smiled at the stranger.

"It's alright. Happens all the time."

"Maybe later."

The man put a piece of chicken on a paper plate and handed it to her. "For starters."

"Thank you." She accepted the plate.

"I'm Louis."

"Gwen."

"Where you from?"

"Michigan. I'm just visiting."

"A lot of 'visitors' never leave."

"I can understand. The whole area is breath-taking. And you—where are you from?"

"Chicago. Seems like another lifetime. I've been here about twelve years."

Gwen's heart jumped. *Did he know her mother?* Instead she said, "What do you do here?"

"Don't tell anyone, but I sell insurance," he half-whispered. "Not to this lot, but in the city."

"Insurance, that's a new one on me."

"I know. And I intend to change that. But I had some college debts to pay off." He changed the subject. "Lots of artists in the houseboat community. Also boat builders, poets, renegades. It's a lively place."

"I can see that."

Louis suggested they walk around, and he introduced her to a couple of his friends.

"It's free-living. I don't know how long it can go on. But it's good while it lasts."

"What do you mean by *free*?"

"Well, we're not paying anybody any rent. We're like one big family. We all help each other—unless we don't."

"Unless we don't?" Gwen asked.

He laughed. "Oh, I was remembering a couple of creepy guys we wanted to get rid of. Told them there was a party up the way, did they want to go? So we took them up there, and left them."

"And the party?"

"There wasn't one."

"Oh."

"Most people are welcome, though. If they aren't free-loaders."

They wandered over to where the musicians were playing, and found a log to sit on.

"Rock and roll."

"That much I know."

"Of course you do. Sorry. This group is called the *RedLegs*."

"There's not much about this lifestyle I'm familiar with. Ann Arbor is about as liberal as it gets in the mid-west, but it's nothing like this. However," she said proudly, "we do have the five dollar pot law. Did you know that?"

"No, I didn't."

"That's the fine—five dollars, that's all it is. Pretty amazing, considering what it is in other parts of the country—or in the state, for that matter."

"Well, I'm impressed."

When she bid him good-night, he made her promise to come back.

"How often do you party like this?"

"Sometimes once a week. Sometimes every night."

"Every night?"

"Not always the same people."

She didn't make any specific promise, but as she walked home, she knew she'd be back.

Chapter 5

A few nights later, when she heard the music coming up from the waterfront, she decided to go back and look for Louis. She'd find him and ask him if he knew her mother. How was she going to solve this case if she was afraid to ask questions?

She wandered around the grounds, but didn't see Louis anywhere. She sat and listened to music, thinking he might show up. She looked at the motley assortment of houseboats, and wondered which one was his. Some had been deserted boats or barges, and the ingenuity of these non-conformists had built houses or cabins on top of them, with the abandoned materials left by the military, she'd learned. Many were lashed to each other, as there seemed to be only one actual pier, so docking space was tight. They presented a haphazard overall look and were laid out in no particular pattern.

Part of her wished she could live in this carefree lifestyle, instead of the prescribed, restrained life of academia. But then, what of her degree in journalism? Was there too much of the mid-west imprinted on her to let go of that and live this life of hedonism, where friendships and freedom meant more than degrees and decorum?

She came out of her reverie and realized someone was watching her. She'd seen him two or three times as she'd walked around in the crowded setting. Now he was leaning against a pile of used lumber that seemed to be free for all who needed it to work on their boats.

The music ended, and she walked home, frustrated that she hadn't seen Louis.

She made sure she wasn't being followed.

~

Gwen sent for her clothes in Ann Arbor, and decided it was time to turn in the rental car. She could get along with a bike. Eric took her to a popular shop on Bridgeway. Lots of bikes—many for rent to tourists. She decided on a Schwinn. It had three gears, which she knew would be good for hills, although she vowed she'd never go on the mountain trails with any bike.

On Saturday Alex asked her to go the movie that night. They saw "Psycho" on Caledonia Street.

Gwen said, "I didn't know murder could be so cold-blooded. It was awful."

"Don't take it so hard."

"I can't help it. I wonder if whoever pushed my mother over the cliff did it as callously as the Anthony Perkins character killed the girl in the shower."

They walked home— Gwen licking an ice-cream cone, Alex smoking grass.

"Alex, do you think it was a crime of passion, or done with calm malice aforethought?"

"You mean your mother?"

"Yes."

"I don't know. Maybe it was a mistake to go to that movie. It's got you all upset again."

"Sorry."

"No, I'm sorry. Getting you more distressed is the last thing I wanted to do."

They had gone to the early show. It was only nine o'clock.

"Want to go down to the waterfront? I hear the music," Alex asked.

"Sure," she said.

She felt safer in his company. They wandered down to Bridgeway, then toward the north end of town where the waterfront community thrived.

Gwen tried to buy some fish from the guy tending the grill, but he insisted on giving it to them.

"We're not vendors," he insisted with a smile. "But you can make a donation." He indicated a coffee can.

So they accepted the fish with thanks, and put some money in the can.

Wandering through the *natives*, as she thought of them, and the voyeurs, she was hoping to see Louis. They mingled through the crowd, but he was not in sight. Finally, they settled on a log near the musicians.

"I guess if you have resident musicians," she said, "you can have a party every night."

"That's true. They do a lot of community cooking outside, anyway. So throw in a few musicians, and you've got a party."

"Do you come here often?" she asked.

"Every week or so."

Suddenly, she felt a body sitting on the other side of her. She looked up to see that it was Louis.

"Hi, there," he said.

She introduced him to Alex. She didn't want to talk to Louis about her mother in front of Alex, although there were no secrets from him. She wasn't sure when she'd see Louis again. After several minutes of raving over the freshly caught, grilled fish, she opened up to him.

"I lived here when I was a little girl. Alex and I lived in the same house. We're almost brother and sister."

"Why'd you move away?" Louis asked.

"My mother died."

"Ah."

"Maybe you knew her. Her name was Patricia." Gwen held her breath.

He thought for a minute. "Yeah, I think I did. She was an artist, wasn't she?"

"Yes. What do you remember about her?"

Louis looked blank. "She was good-looking, had a little girl. Well, sure—that was you, right?"

"Right."

"She hung out with Megan Denison, Eric and those guys."

"Yes. Did you ever go bike riding with her?" Gwen could feel she was entering dangerous ground.

"Nope. I'm about ten years younger than those guys. We did sail together with Eric once or twice."

"Do you know anyone she did ride with?"

"I doubt it."

Gwen could feel prickly hair on the back of her neck. She had to ad lib. "She died when she went off the mountain road coming back from Stinson Beach. She was on her bike. She probably wouldn't have gone alone. I just thought if you biked with her you might know who else did."

"Sorry. Can't help you there."

Another dead end.

Two days later, frustrated, and not wanting to ask Alex to accompany her again, Gwen went to the waterfront alone. She didn't see Louis, and left early.

On the way home she felt she was being followed, but when she turned she saw nothing. *I'm just nervous,* she concluded. But two blocks later, when she'd turned up the quiet Ebbtide Street, she knew she was being followed. Suddenly someone stepped up quickly from behind and snatched her purse. He ran off with it quickly. Gwen ran after him, yelling to him to give back her purse. But he was too fast for her, and disappeared around the corner. She hadn't even gotten a look at his face.

Megan wasn't home. Chad sat watching a game on television.

"I've just been robbed!" she shouted.

Chad turned off the TV and looked at her. "What did you say?"

"I'm still shaking. I lost twenty bucks!"

Chad got off his favorite chair and guided Gwen to the sofa.

"Tell me what happened."

"I was walking home, minding my own business, and somebody came up behind me and grabbed my purse."

"Did you see his face?"

"No. He ran off too fast. At least nobody is trying to kill me."

Chad was thoughtful.

"What is it?" she asked.

"Nothing. I was just thinking."

"Tell me."

"How can you be sure it was your *money* he wanted?"

"What else?" Her eyes opened wide. "Are you saying he wanted my ID?"

"Could be. If you're his prey, he wants to make sure he has the right girl."

"I'm nobody's prey!"

"You might be. You've been telling people why you're here, what you hope to find out. If your mother's killer is still around, and he thinks you're getting too snoopy, you could be a target."

"Oh, Chad, that makes it awful."

"You have to be more careful. You shouldn't be out alone—especially at night."

She nodded. "What am I going to do?"

"Well, if you want my advice, go home. We'd hate to see you go, but you're not safe here, Gwen."

"I can't go back now."

"You're not going to change the fact that your mother is dead. Right now, your primary concern should be your own safety."

They were silent.

"I don't mean to sound harsh; my concern is keeping you safe."

She nodded.

She looked so dismal he suggested they have some ice-cream.

~

Eric called and offered to take her sailing. This time it was just the two of them. He taught her more about the parts of the boat and how to control it. He let her take the tiller, which gave her a great feeling of power and control until she accidentally jibed and they would have capsized if it were not for Eric's quick response in righting the boat.

"What happened? What did I do?" she asked.

"It's called a jibe. It happens when the stern crosses the wind instead of the bow. It's dangerous, as you just saw, unless you're an experienced sailor and know what you're doing."

Eric opened a can of beer. "Want one?"

"No thanks. It might make me sick out here."

She was shaken enough to hand the tiller back to Eric. They sailed smoothly for awhile on a broad reach.

Finally, she said, "I know you said you didn't know who my father is. But do you have any idea?"

He shook his head. "My guess is he was a married man. Otherwise, I can't think why your mother was so secretive about it."

"I thought of that too."

"Coming about."

She released the sheet and grabbed the other one. She was proud of how smoothly she could make this transition now.

"She worked in a café when she first came, then after you were born she didn't seem to need the money. I suspected she was provided for by your daddy."

Daddy. She hadn't dared think that word since she was a little girl.

"I have a secret," Gwen said. "My aunt, with whom I lived after Mom died, received allowances for my care when I went to live with her."

"Did she say who was sending them?"

As Eric prepared to come about again, Gwen moved her knees so the tiller wouldn't hit them.

"She didn't know. They went through some bank, and were sent anonymously to her. She still gets them—until I finish college or turn twenty-two."

"Has to be from your father."

"I would think so."

"So at least you are taken care of, financially."

"Yes. Please don't tell anyone else, Eric."

"I won't. That's another angle. Tracing your father by finding out where the money's coming from."

"Can we do that?"

"Long shot. I'll think about it." He opened another can of beer.

Chapter 6

I haven't seen any of your work, Conan. Will you show it to me?"
"Sure."
They arranged that she'd come to his 'studio' the next day. He used the term loosely. Like many others he had fixed up an old abandoned boat for use both as place to live and as a studio. It was tied up to two other boats, which had to be negotiated to get to his.

"Don't they mind—your neighbors?"

"I try to compensate."

"How?"

"I gave them some art work. And sometimes they come over for a meal."

The next day, following Conan's directions, Gwen found the part of the marina she was looking for.

This part of the houseboat community looked different from what she'd seen on the other end; each houseboat was painted a bright primary color—red, purple, orange and yellow. It gave the marina a cheery feel, which perhaps helped to conceal the poor repair many of them were in.

She walked out on the pier until she found the red, green and white boat he'd told her to look for. This was the one she was supposed to trespass to get to Conan's.

"Hello," she called. "Anybody home?"

A friendly voice answered, "Come aboard."

The water was choppy; boats and houseboats were bobbing. Gwen was smiling at the woman, and almost lost her footing in the long stride required to get onto the Italian boat, as she called it.

"Thank you. I'm going to see Conan."

"Go right ahead," the woman said.

She would have to make an even bigger leap to get to the next boat, where no one appeared to be home. Then she called out to Conan. He came out on the deck to meet her.

She looked at the gap between the houseboat she was on, and Conan's.

"I can't make this leap!" she called to him.

"Yes, you can. I'll catch you."

She thought she might fall in, but she didn't want to appear to be a scaredy-cat, so she took a deep breath and visualized herself on Conan's deck. Then she jumped.

"See, you made it," he said, swinging her away from the edge.

Conan's boat was called an 'ark'. It was almost flat-roofed, built on a barge with an overhanging roof on each end, and a deck. He had recently painted it aqua.

Conan ushered her inside. Gwen remarked on how well-maintained it was, compared to some she'd noticed. He had divided the space, as had Eric, into a cooking and eating area at one end, a salon in the center, and his studio at the other end.

The studio, Gwen noticed, appeared to be locked.

"I'll get us some beer."

He went out on the deck and pulled up on a rope. Gwen watched as he removed two beers from an old lobster trap, brought them in and uncapped them.

"That's a handy way to keep them cool," she said.

"Yeah, not much ice around here. The water's cold."

He offered her one of the beers, and they talked about the houseboats, how many of them seemed jerry-rigged, and barely hanging together.

"Yup. That's the way it is here. I spent the morning helping a guy re-fasten his cabin to the deck after last week's wind storm tore it half way off."

"Do you like it—living on the edge?"

"Sure, or we wouldn't do it. We've exchanged comforts and security for freedom."

"It's tempting."

"You think you'd like to live this way?"

"I don't know. It's scary, but exciting, too." She paused to sip the cool Coors he'd given her. "I see a lot of kids around."

"Families. We have lots of them."

"Aren't the parents afraid they'll fall off and drown?"

"Some of them wear life-jackets until they're older."

Some of them.

Gwen looked around the space. The walls were adorned with pictures.

Gwen studied one, and said, "It's lovely. I can really see the movement in the water and the boat."

"It's not mine though. An exchange I did with another guy."

Oops. Of all the art around, she'd chosen to comment on the one thing he hadn't created.

"Sorry." She rose to her feet, and looked at the others more closely. "They're all fascinating. Is this recent work?"

"Yeah, most of it."

She saw something on the floor, leaning against the wall. It had its backside facing her. She picked it up and looked at it. "Oh, what's this? It's a totally different style."

"From another lifetime."

"It's a collage."

"Yes."

"It's full of vibrant color, and—Why did you stop doing this kind of work?"

"I wanted to turn to something different, I guess. You've heard of artists' periods—his blue period, his grey period." Conan smiled and tossed the rest of his beer down.

They laughed.

"Anyway, I moved on."

His current work was watercolor, but Gwen wasn't as nearly taken by it as she was with the collage. Then she saw a watercolor that was better than the others, but it didn't look like it was the work of the same artist. She looked in the corner. In very small lettering she read "P. Harris."

She involuntarily sucked in her breath. "My mother."

"Yes. She gave it to me a long time ago."

"She must have liked you a lot."

"At one time, yes."

She couldn't get over having stumbled across her mother's painting. It was so visceral, so present. She started shaking. To cover her feelings she turned away, toward the studio.

"Do you have more in there?" she said, pointing to the studio.

The smell of food cooking wafted into the room.

"Yeah, but I'll have to get something ready to take out there," he said, motioning to the gathering crowd outdoors.

"Let me help you."

He had the ingredients of a salad near his makeshift cutting board— something rescued from an old dresser, he explained. She was glad for this activity to avoid talking. There wasn't room for both of them to work there, so he assembled some plates, found a bottle of wine, and watched her wield his sharpest knife against tomatoes, cucumber, lettuce, beets and radishes. He gave her a large bowl to hold it all.

She could hear the chatter of people outside. It was a relief to get in the open air. Someone was cooking barbecued ribs that smelled scrumptious. Conan placed the salad bowl on the concave table, and helped himself to it and the ribs. There was potato salad and corn on the cob, a delicious relish, and an assortment of other dishes.

Gwen was surprised how hungry she was. While trying nearly every tasty dish on the rickety table, Eric came up to them.

"You ought to try my fish," he said, nodding to another grill. "I caught some nice halibut today. Alex and I took the *Wicked Winch* out by the island."

"What did Alex catch?" Conan asked him.

"He couldn't catch a cold."

"Why?"

"Stoned, as usual."

The men laughed, as they strolled over to Eric's grill. Eric gave Conan a nicely browned slice of the fish. Although it smelled wonderful, Gwen was too full to try this delicacy.

"It looks great—another time."

"You going to the party tomorrow night?" Eric asked.

"What party?" Gwen inquired.

"Varda's. On his boat."

"I'd love to." Gwen said. "Can you get me on?"

"Sure."

"How about you, Conan?" Gwen asked.

"No."

"Why not?"

"No," he repeated.

The threesome chatted for awhile and listened to Joe Tate and The RedLegs band. Then Conan excused himself, smiled at Gwen and said, "You're in good hands."

"Why doesn't Conan want to go to Varda's party?" Gwen asked Eric.

"He had a falling out with him a long time ago."

Gwen decided not to pry further.

When they parted, Eric said, "Wear something funky tomorrow night. We'll have a good time."

She wasn't sure what she had that qualified as funky, but she'd discuss it with Megan. In any case, she was looking forward to the unusual experience.

~

Megan was more than happy to let Gwen choose one of her costumes.

"This is terrific," she said, looking at a tie-died one-piece outfit with Scheherazade pant legs and a sequined belt.

The next night she met Eric, and they walked down to the Vallejo, an enormous old hulk, which had started life as a ferry and was now the home of Jean Varda and Alan Watts, who had split it down the middle.

She could only see Varda's side, but even that was huge.

Eastern music permeated their ears before they'd even climbed the gangplank. But it was the aroma of foreign food that invaded Gwen's nostrils that most caught her attention. Varda was known to be an excellent cook. The place was alive with stimulation for all the senses.

She recognized him from a distance from the way he'd been described to her. He was a big man, bigger than she expected. Somewhat rotund, he was wearing a full-length glittering gown with a train. Crowned with a huge shock of white hair, he stood out among all his guests. Gwen could hear his robust laughter from across the room.

The artist had used his talent to redo the flooring, carving little niches here and there of clowns and gargoyles.

The wall covering was imaginative and different in every room, mostly hand-painted, or fabric of contrasting colors placed at different angles.

Then she noticed the art work. When she looked closely she saw a remarkable resemblance to the collage she'd discovered at Conan's. She looked at them all closely. Yes, they were collages, with bits of fabric, yarn, sequins. Conan must have been very influenced by this man.

She mentioned this to Eric.

"You can hardly tell the difference. Conan took classes from him a long time ago."

"I wonder why he gave that style up."

Eric shook his head. "Moved on to something more personal, I think."

"I saw his watercolors."

"What did you think?"

Gwen glanced at Eric. "Oh, I don't know. They seemed kind of depressing, I thought. But don't tell him."

"I won't."

When it came time to eat, they sampled Varda's Turkish Turkey. This was a concoction of pine nuts, Eastern spices, turkey and raisins. Though she'd never tasted anything like it, Gwen enjoyed it. The ouzo, or whatever it was, did not go down as well.

As dinner came to a close, Varda and his friends put on a show—a combination circus and Greek theatre affair. Totally charming, his appreciative audience gave a standing ovation.

Later, when Eric introduced her to him, she thought he looked at her like he'd like to see her with less clothing.

He held her hand a long time. "You're welcome here, anytime, my dear."

She blurted it out, "Did you know my mother, Patricia Harris?"

"Yes," he said. "I did. We'll have to talk about her sometime."

Just then someone else took his attention, and reluctantly, she thought, he dropped her hand and turned his gaze away.

"Be careful," Eric said. "He's a womanizer."

"But he's way older than I am."

"That never stops him."

She turned to Eric. "Did you know he knew Mom?"

"I hadn't thought of it in a long time. But yeah, he did. This isn't the first time you've met him, come to think of it. I took care of you once in awhile. I had some repair work to do here for Varda one day and brought you and Alex with me."

"What? I can't hear you."

The volume of noise from the music and people trying to talk over it was deafening.

"Let's go out on the deck." He led the way.

Compared to inside it was quiet here. The moon cast a strong ray of sparkling light across the bay. Neighboring sailboats made their presence known by the occasional chorus of halyards banging against their masts, while the willow trees on shore undulated in the breeze, creating a dance between nature and boats.

Eric repeated what he'd said.

"I don't remember being here. When was this?"

He said softly, "It was the day your mother didn't come back."

Gwen was stunned. "The day she died?"

"Must have been. Megan said she had other plans when Patricia asked her to take care of you, so she recruited me."

"Oh, no!" Gwen covered her mouth.

"It's OK. I enjoyed your company. You were a funny kid. Always asking questions."

"But Megan said *she* took care of me that afternoon!"

"She must have gotten confused with the days."

Gwen said no more about it, but her thoughts were whirling. How could Megan have gotten confused on such a day as that? What was she doing? Gwen remembered that Megan didn't know who her mother had gone biking with.

Gwen went home that night with a mixture of feelings—kind of a euphoria from the party, and a chill from what Eric had told her.

Something was wrong. Something Megan wasn't telling her.

She was glad Megan was asleep when she returned. She went straight to bed, then lay awake a long time, thinking what Eric's information might imply. She didn't want to believe it, but there it was.

Could Megan have pushed her mother over the mountain cliff? Why would she do that? They were friends, weren't they? But why had she lied about baby-sitting? Was she jealous of her mother for some reason? What could that be?

Could her father possibly have been Megan's husband? The thought brought on chills.

No, she was letting her imagination run away with her. She scolded herself for thinking such a thing. Why would Megan have invited her to stay with her, and have been so gracious if she had that on her conscience?

For now, the question would have to lie dormant.

Chapter 7

O f course! Why hadn't she thought of it before? She'd write a feature article for the newspaper and see if they'd publish it. Human bones, a decade old, had been found. That's newsworthy isn't it? And they'd been matched with a woman who'd disappeared ten years ago. Circumstances pointed to it being a murder.

It would be a human interest story, and she'd ask if anyone knew anything about the woman who'd disappeared. If so, would they please come forward to help the daughter find the perpetrator of this crime? She gave a contact number—Megan's.

The article was published in Marin Scope, and Gwen waited for the phone to ring. During the next week she did get a few calls, from people who remembered her mother, and or recalled that a local citizen had disappeared in the fifties. Gwen met with a few of them, and some offered interesting details about her mother's life.

A lady in her sixties asked if they could get together for lunch. When they met at Dayton's, Gwen thought the woman looked undernourished. She called herself Pip, and ordered a huge plate of roast beef, potatoes and gravy. Sort of a mid-western meal, Gwen couldn't help thinking. When Gwen tried to question her regarding her knowledge of her mother, Pip gestured that she wanted to finish her meal first. Gwen tried to be patient, studied the woman's features.

She had an enormous amount of grey hair piled carelessly on top of her head. Strangely, it was held by expensive looking clasps. She wore a frayed, but at one time probably, very expensive wool coat.

When, finally, Pip had scraped every bit of her food up with the last piece of bread, Gwen asked again, in what way she had known her mom.

"I'd like some cherry pie now."

"Oh."

"A la mode. And coffee on the side."

Again Gwen waited for the woman to consume the large dessert and finish two cups of coffee. By this time, she'd concluded that Pip just wanted a free meal and had nothing to say.

Finally, Pip wiped her mouth, let out a sound of deep satisfaction, and smiled with a twinkle in her eye.

"Now, about your mother," she began. "I liked her watercolors. I purchased two of them."

Gwen was stunned. Where would this woman get the money to buy art? But she must have known her mother; how else could she know Patricia Harris was an artist?

"I know what you're thinking," Pip continued. "How could the likes of me ever afford to buy paintings? Well, it wasn't always like this. I had an art gallery, right downtown, and it did real well. A friend of mine, another artist, brought some of her work in for me to see. I bought two, and put them up on the wall in the shop. Customers noticed them, admired them. Once I got your mother to come in and look at them. She looked real pleased—had two little kids with her. Guess you were one of them."

Pip paused, and Gwen tried to absorb what she'd said.

"Another time she came in with a man—I took it to be her boyfriend."

"What did he look like?"

"I don't remember, but I took him to be a lawyer. He told her he had a court case in an hour."

"Did you ever see her again?"

"No. Life changed for me not long after that."

Gwen waited for her to continue. When she didn't Gwen felt it would be too intrusive to ask this stranger for details.

They were silent.

"I guess I didn't give you much. But that's about all I have to say."

"Thank you, Pip. I appreciate the information."

Gwen paid the bill, and they parted on the street.

She wondered about this lawyer-boyfriend. Could that be her father?

She didn't think the story had contributed anything useful toward the solution of the crime, but she was overjoyed to even get this vignette of her mother's life. How happy her mother must have been to see her work displayed in a real art gallery.

~

When she next saw Eric, he was upset with her. They were sitting in the *No Name Bar*, and a tenor was singing a soulful song about lost love.

"You did a very foolish thing," he said.

"What?"

"That article in the paper."

"Why?"

"Are you trying to bring the murderer to your door? Why do you want to draw attention to yourself like that?" Eric threw his sailor's cap on the table.

"I didn't think of it like that."

"Don't you realize you're a target now, too?"

"You really think so?"

"Look at it from the murderer's point of view. He thought all danger of being caught was long over. Now the daughter shows up and starts digging, looking for clues. Don't you think he'd either be on the run, or after the daughter?"

Gwen covered her face. "I don't know."

"It was stupid. And dangerous. Don't you see that?"

There were tears in her eyes. "Yes."

"Now you'll have to watch your back all the time. Don't go anywhere alone—especially at night."

"But—"

"No buts. You've even given the murderer your telephone number. Jesus."

Defensively she said, "We don't know that he's still around here."

"Small comfort."

He saw how distressed she was. Gently he said, "Detectives act undercover. They don't put up billboards stating they're on the case, and where to find them."

She tried not to look at Eric. "It was stupid. I see that now. Oh, God, how could I have been so dumb?"

He bought her a drink, and said, "Let's listen to the music."

~

Eric walked her home.

When they got to the house, Megan was still up and said she wanted a word with Gwen.

It was obvious from her tone that something was wrong. Eric wasn't the only one upset with her about the article in the paper. Megan paced with her arms crossed.

"A man phoned here tonight. Said he had some important information, but didn't want to give it over the phone. He asked for this address."

"Oh, God."

"Yes, oh God."

"You didn't give it to him, did you?"

"Of course not. But it may not be too hard for him to find."

"I'm so sorry, Megan. Really I am. I certainly never wanted to put you at risk."

"Well, it's you I'm worried about."

"I think it's time I moved out. You've been gracious with your hospitality. But I know I've worn out my welcome."

"Don't put it like that. But you're in danger. I think you're right—to find a safer place."

The next morning Gwen told Megan that she would move to the hostel in the headlands.

"Are you sure that's what you want to do?" Megan asked.

"I'm going to check it out. It's cheap."

"You plan to stay on, then."

"Yes."

Megan nodded thoughtfully. "You'd be safer back in Michigan."

"Megan, I'm not giving up now. Eric convinced me it was murder, and I'm going to do everything I can to find out who did it and why."

~

Exhausted, Gwen lay in bed that night, half aware of talking in the living room. Chad and Alex. She started to drift off to sleep, but was jerked back awake by the escalation of their voices.

Chad was barking at his son. "We've had enough. I know when you're stoned. You either get clean and sober or you're out of here."

"Yeah, Dad."

"You should be on your own by now anyway. I don't know why your mother puts up with you and your drugs."

"Sorry, Dad."

"Sorry? How many times have we heard that? It means nothing." Gwen could hear Chad pacing the floor. "And how the hell do you pay for your habit?"

"I have friends."

Chad raised his voice higher. "Dopeheads aren't going to give it to you free! You take me for an idiot, boy?"

"No."

"This is your last warning. You get clean, or you're out. I don't care what your mother says."

CHapter 8

The next morning Gwen set out for the headlands. These undeveloped hills posted themselves as guardian between the Pacific Ocean and the little town of Sausalito below. Highway 101 was in the hills above the town.

"Thank God," Megan had said. "There were serious plans to build the highway and all that traffic down the hill and right across the waterfront in town."

"Sausalito?" Gwen was astonished.

Megan had nodded. "Fortunately, the townspeople made a big enough fuss—it didn't happen."

"Good."

She set out on her bike, and just before the Golden Gate Bridge, turned off the highway and headed west through the tunnel. The headlands were vast, with high cliffs, views of the sea, and wild life, from a myriad of birds—even to mountain lions, she'd heard. She'd failed to ask where exactly the hostel was, so she rode around in the hills. Much more open to the wind and sun than the mountain, it was covered with different kinds of grasses and shrubs, not so many large trees.

She was getting very tired. She realized she was out of shape, hadn't ridden a bike since she left Michigan. She was also very thirsty; she'd have to remember to bring water next time.

After peddling a few miles, she could see the ocean in the distance. Sparkling in the sun, it seemed to beckon her. She followed the road through the marshes, spotting blue heron and egret. When she reached the beach, she parked her bike and stretched her legs in the sand.

What a sight. Windswept and exhilarating, it was sheltered to some extent by cliffs to the north. Waves crashed against colorful pebbles adorning the beach. Farther out, whitecaps sculpted the blue green sea, and surfers danced across the most promising waves. Gwen had never seen surfing before. She'd heard of it, knew it had become popular in California, but never imagined what she was seeing— the way the surfers would catch a wave, spin lightly across its crest, and follow it sideways as long as they could.

Although it was sunny, it was also cold and windy. She'd gone from hot and sweaty to cold. Although mesmerized by the surfers, she returned to her bike. Another time, more appropriately dressed, she would return to this lovely spot. She went back the way she'd come, up to a point.

Then seeing a few buildings up on a hill, she headed in that direction. She pumped hard, even in low gear, glad she'd bought a three-speed. She finally crested the hill and stopped in front of one of the buildings. A gardener was planting something near one of them. He gave her directions to the hostel. She rode on, found the right building, and went inside. She spoke with the house manager and discovered that although the hostel held both private rooms and dorms, the private rooms were all occupied. There was space in the dorm. They would put her name on a waiting list for a private room.

She decided that for awhile, anyway, this would be a safe haven. Anyone looking for her in Sausalito wouldn't find her. She'd have no phone, but calls could be made in town. The hills were beautiful, but also very isolating. Well, there was a tradeoff for everything. The hostel itself looked comfortable, if not luxurious. There was a kitchen where residents did their cooking, and two large refrigerators for storing food. Everyone had chores, and she was assigned kitchen sweep and mop-up after breakfast.

"And what do you think about my new living quarters?" she asked Conan.

He rolled his eyes and smiled. "One extreme to the other. Don't leave your toothbrush in the bathroom," he joked.

There was no way she could take all her clothes to the hostel.

"Would you mind, Megan, if I left some of them here?"

"Not at all."

Gwen packed up what she thought were the most necessary items for a 'camping' trip, as she thought of it, and headed for the grocery store. Again, she was careful to select only essentials, as her allotted space in one of the refrigerators was small.

The next day Conan helped her move the things she'd decided to take with her to the hostel dorm. She'd packed a duffel bag of sport clothes, walking shoes, and toiletries. She took nothing of value.

"You're planning to get a job, right?"

"Right."

"Are you sure you're up for a bike-ride to work every day?"

"I'm tough."

"Still—you'll arrive all hot and sweaty."

She hadn't thought of that. She smiled at him. "Thanks, Conan. You've been a marvelous help."

~

Gwen had been wondering if there were any way she could trace the checks that had been set up from her anonymous benefactor. She wasn't at all sure that her idea would pay off, but she decided to give it a try.

At least she had the name of the bank, and it was in Marin. Now, the next step was to get a job there.

She dressed as professionally as she could, put the high heels she hadn't worn since she left Michigan in a bag, and set out to find the bank. Expecting an impressive stone structure, such as all the banks she'd known in the mid-west, she was surprised to find this one a low wooden edifice near a park graced with two huge stone elephants. She locked up her bike, slipped on her high heels, ran her fingers through her hair, took a deep breath and went inside.

She asked to speak to the manager.

"I was an 'A' student in math, and I'm a major in accounting. I'm afraid I can't give you any work references, as I'm still in school. I can give you personal references."

"Why are you looking for a full-time job if you're in school?"

She realized she'd put her foot in it. "I'm taking time off to earn money to go back."

"Then," the manager continued, "you would only be with us for a short time."

She gave him her most dazzling smile. "Well, that would depend on how well I liked banking."

The manager gave her a non-committal smile in return, and an application to fill out.

When she handed it back to him, he thanked her, and told her she'd be hearing from him if they had an opening.

She left feeling discouraged. He'd said *if he had an opening.*

But in two days he called her. "We can take you on as an intern. If you work out, you'll have the job in four weeks."

Gwen was elated.

At first intimidated by the tall, striking black woman who was to be her mentor, Gwen soon learned to appreciate her patience and skill.

Most of what she was expected to do the first week was to follow Denise's every move, and when they weren't too busy to ask questions of this head teller about anything she didn't understand during the previous transactions. She caught on quickly, and after the second week, the roles switched, with Gwen making the transactions and her mentor, Denise, looking over her shoulder.

Gwen didn't mind the work, and couldn't wait for the day when she'd be on her own. Her drawer checked out every evening. She hadn't made any mistakes.

She made a point of arriving early enough to freshen up and change into her job clothes in the restroom, but Conan had been right. It was a long bike ride. She guessed she'd have to buy a car if she stayed at the hostel.

She became friends with this woman twice her age. Sometimes they went out after work for a drink. She had to be careful not to reveal her real reason for working at the bank, or for living in Marin, for that matter.

Once Gwen was left on her own it was not too difficult to find out the procedure for sending an anonymous check. She went to another bank, and said she was thinking of making an anonymous donation to a charity, and asked how she could set that up.

She was told the process. She nodded, and then said, "But how can I make sure the payee doesn't find out who the money is from?"

"Only the sending bank would have that information."

"I see." She thanked the manager and left.

But now she was at a roadblock. The files were kept by the name of the payer, not the payee. Of course, it was the payer who held the account. And that was the whole point, to find the name of the payer. It appeared that she'd have to go through hundreds of outgoing checks and records to find her name attached to that of a payer. And she couldn't spend a lot of time on this without the risk of being caught. For now she was stumped.

~

Gwen decided to open a bank account in Sausalito, now that it appeared she'd be staying for awhile. It would be easier to cash checks if she had a local account.

Two weeks after she'd done this, she checked the balance in her account and realized it was three hundred dollars more than she'd deposited. This could only mean one thing. The money her father had been sending her in Michigan was now coming to her Sausalito account. But how could he have known where to send it?

She called Marie. "I know nothing about this," her aunt said.

She decided to confide in Denise, on a theoretical level, at least.

"If a person is sending money monthly to an account in a certain state for someone else, and the one receiving the money moves to another state, how would the payer know where the new account is, if she doesn't tell him?"

"Probably the bank of the payer would advise him, and suggest the new account."

"But how would the payer's bank know where the new account is, if no one had advised them?"

Denise looked puzzled. "I'm not sure." She was thoughtful for a moment. Then she said, "Why?"

"Just wondered."

When that didn't satisfy the curious Denise, Gwen added, "OK, my aunt's been getting money from her ex, but she's changed banks. She doesn't want to contact her ex directly to tell him."

"She could tell her new bank to get in touch with him."

"Hmm."

Gwen continued to muddle over this. She hadn't told either bank to contact the payer.

She'd had the money in her Michigan account sent to Megan's address in a cashier's check. She'd then taken it to a local bank and opened a new account. How could anyone have known? She hadn't even told her aunt.

Chapter 9

Gwen held the small package of her mother's ashes. It didn't weigh much. With nervous fingers she opened the box, then the plastic bag in which the ashes were contained. She pulled the bag out and looked at the contents through the plastic. She opened the plastic bag reticently and touched the ashes. Just ashes, she told herself. No, the human remains of my mother. She plunged her hand deep into the grey stuff, discovered it was not all fine ash. There were little pieces of bone, and then, good God, a dog tag. She pulled it out and read: *Tuffy*. My God, how did that get there? Wouldn't it have melted?

They must cremate animals in the same place, she thought with distaste. Then she read the disclaimer that came in the box. "In the interest of full disclosure, we cannot assure you that the contents of your loved one's ashes are theirs alone. Residue from others may be included."

This was hard to stomach. But there it was. She wasn't at all sure that she wanted so much disclosure.

We must have a memorial service for her now, she thought. There must be some finality to her death, if not why she died.

Megan liked the idea. They set the next Saturday at three in the afternoon, and invited everyone who knew her mother. Megan helped her plan it. They would have a circle on the ground in the backyard with her mother's ashes in the middle. There would be incense burning next to the ashes, flowers and petals spread around. Megan had some sage which they would burn, and waft around those willing to be cleansed by it.

It wouldn't have been done that way in Michigan if Gwen planned it by herself, but she was entranced with Megan's plans, hippy-like as they seemed to her.

"I could play my flute, if you'd like," Megan offered.

"That would be lovely."

"I want to give you one of my pots with a lid, to use as an urn for her ashes."

"Thank you, Megan. That's very kind of you."

"You pick out the pot—any one you like."

Tears brimmed her eyes, and she gave Megan a big hug. She chose a grey one with a lid. A subtle design of field flowers was stamped into the clay around the base.

There would only be a few people, and Gwen was glad for that. It would be more intimate. Everyone would get a chance to say something they remembered about Patricia.

Then another piece appeared in the local paper.

"I didn't write it," Gwen protested. "Who did this?"

On the obituary page an announcement stated that a memorial service for Patricia Harris, whose remains had been recently identified, would be held at the home of Megan Denison, 399 Ebbtide Street. It gave the date and time. The implication was that anyone could come.

"Who would have done this? Who did you tell?" Megan asked.

"Besides the guys coming? At least I don't remember telling anyone else."

"Well, somebody let the cat out of the bag."

"Oh, my God, what are we going to do?" she implored of Megan. She didn't want curiosity seekers, who only knew about this woman disappearing.

"Do you remember the story of *The Three Little Pigs*?" Megan asked.

"Yes. Why?"

"Do you recall how the pigs outwitted the wolf?"

"Yes! We'll change the time."

So it was decided that the service would be at two o'clock. If anyone showed up at three o'clock it would be too late.

Gwen and Megan prepared refreshments, including champagne to serve afterwards. They would celebrate her mother's life. And Megan talked about having some kind of communion, which Gwen didn't understand, but agreed to.

"I'll start us off, shall I?" Megan asked.

Saturday came, and the women made the yard ready, then created a circle in the middle with stones from the garden's edge. Inside the little circle, they placed the urn of ashes, incense, a bronze statue of the goddess Quan Yin, a small iron pot for burning their prayers, and a bowl of grapes.

There were only to be six of them—Gwen, Megan, her husband Chad and Alex. And their friends Eric and Conan. Oh, yes, and she had invited Louis, but she wasn't sure he'd come. She let them know the change in time.

When everyone had arrived they were directed to the backyard, where Chad offered the smoke of sage to any who desired it. It was meant to be purifying. For her part, Megan began playing her flute. Gwen didn't recognize the melody, but felt a sad resonance with it. Megan, in a long white dress swayed with the evocative notes of the wooden instrument. She then offered up a prayer to the goddess Quan Yin. Gwen wasn't at all sure that her mother knew anything about this goddess or any other, but it all felt healing to her anyway.

Megan picked up the bowl of grapes. She passed it around, asking each to take one, as a unifying bond and communion with the friends of Patricia Harris.

Finally, Megan invited anyone who wished, to speak.

Gwen said, "I'd like to say something about my mother. I only knew her for my first eleven years, but I have many memories. She was kind, she told me—actually Alex and me—bedtime stories, often acting them out, and taking different parts. She took us to see interesting things. Sometimes it was just to feel the difference between the bark of a sycamore and the bark of an oak tree, but it was always fun, and we learned a lot." She paused and smiled to herself. "I don't remember ever being spanked, but I probably was, because Alex and I got into a lot of mischief. Once we painted the bathroom walls with our new watercolors."

"I remember being spanked," Alex spoke up loudly.

The laughter that followed loosened everyone's tongue, and soon they were all sharing memories of Patricia Harris, and what a delight it was to be with her.

"So cheerful," Chad said.

"Until near the end," Eric commented.

"What do you mean?" Gwen asked.

"A couple of weeks before she disappeared, she was worried, or agitated. I didn't pay too much attention. Women have their moods."

"Oh, and men don't?" Megan countered.

Gwen was flattened by Eric's remark. No one had said that before. No one had even hinted that her mother had been disturbed at that time. She would have to ask Eric more about that in private.

The service ended with everyone writing a prayer or good wishes for Patricia on a little piece of paper and submitting it to the little pot of fire. The smoke wafted up in the air, and Gwen liked to think the messages were being carried to her mother's soul.

Indoors, they popped the cork of the champagne, the mood became lighter, and two or three conversations were going on at once.

Gwen took her champagne to the back room, preferring to be alone. She looked out the window. There was a man stooping beside the little iron pot and placing a note beside the remains of the other notes. Then he lit a match and burned it. He just stood there for some time, before walking away. He looked vaguely familiar, but try as she might she couldn't place him.

Gwen had been too mesmerized to go out and ask him who he was, and what he was doing there. Obviously, someone who'd read the notice in the paper. It was three o'clock.

By the time she thought to go to the front room to summon the others to see if any of them knew him, he was gone.

Her father? Another sleepless night.

~

Conan came to take her for a ride the next day. This time they rode in his 1955 Chevy truck. Gwen was cautious; she had suspected Megan. Who would be next? Conan? Eric? Maybe Louis.

They drove out to the shoreline road on Highway 1, and then north, through patches of redwoods, through more winding roads, a bit away from sight of the ocean.

"Smell it?" Conan said. "We're coming to eucalyptus."

The scent was unmistakable. Shedding bark lay strewn on fields and road alike.

"A messy tree. Not a native. Worst part, it's taken over native plants," he said.

But Gwen inhaled its tangy perfume with pleasure.

Farther on, the blue of the water showed itself again. Sea lions lounged on tiny islands barely more than sandbars.

"Let's stop," Gwen cried. "I've never seen them up close."

They parked on the side of the road, and ran across it to watch them.

For the most part, the sea lions lay in repose, as if in a still life. Occasionally, one would raise its head and bark. Its neighbors ignored him, except for one who dove into the water to cool off, before returning to sun himself some more.

"Lazy beasts," Conan said.

"Maybe you envy them," Gwen said.

He gave her a wry smile. "I'll take you to Bolinas. Picturesque little town." They drove on, missing the turnoff. When Conan was quite sure they'd passed it, he stopped and asked someone on horseback if she knew where the road to Bolinas was.

The woman laughed, and told him the residents did not encourage visitors, as the town was small and they wanted to keep it that way, so every time the authorities erected a sign, the locals took it down. She gave him directions, and they backtracked a mile. They found the road, and about half a mile down the road they found the town.

Like a movie set, it jutted out into the sea, its narrow streets difficult to negotiate as the truck slalomed past double parked cars, and reclining dogs in the street. And nowhere to park. No wonder the natives didn't abide visitors. Nevertheless they drove through the few lanes, quaint with artsy shops and inviting eateries.

Finding nowhere to land, they rode out to the edge of town on the beach road. No parking there, either, until a Ford pickup managed a four-step maneuver to get turned around on the narrow road, and relinquish a spot.

At low tide the beach on the little inlet was covered with a kind of rock Gwen had not seen on any other California beach. Many of these large and small stones were pocked with holes. She examined some carefully.

"What made the holes?" she asked.

"Probably some critters before the minerals took final form. One of the things kind of unique about this place."

"Fascinating." She collected several and got Conan to gather some too.

On the way back, they stopped at the Pelican Inn by Muir Beach. They found a table on the pub side, and Conan went to the bar to order the drinks. Gwen took in the setting: low ceilings, dark paneling, brass fittings and a cozy fire. The six inch wide floor boards were polished black. A very English pub. She heard a rhythmic thudding, and turned to see a man throwing darts at the board on the far wall.

Conan returned with two pints of Guinness. Dark and heavy, Gwen had never tasted it before. It struck her as thick and syrupy.

"I hope you like it," he said. "Goes with the atmosphere, don't you think?"

"Oh, yes, it's just … different."

"Let's order some food. Are you hungry?" he asked her.

"Something smells awfully good."

They decided on oyster stew. Gwen wasn't sure she'd like it, but Conan assured her that if she didn't, he could handle both bowls.

The stew was certainly different than anything she was used to, but she decided, what was life without adventure? *As if she hadn't had enough of that.*

They sat and talked by the fire for a long time. Gwen found herself telling Conan a lot about her life in Michigan, and the differences between Ann Arbor and Sausalito.

"I thought Ann Arbor was liberal," she laughed, "but nothing like the Bohemia of Sausalito."

She told him about the diary she'd kept as a child that was mostly about her mother.

"I still keep a diary," she added. "I guess I should call it a journal, now. Diary sounds so juvenile."

"Do you think your time here has been well-spent?" he asked.

"I don't know. I have two quests, you know—one to find out who my father is, and the other to find out who killed my mother."

"What makes you so sure she was killed?"

She thought she saw a tic on Conan's face.

"It didn't happen at a place where she was likely to have slid off. There wasn't a twist or bend near there."

Conan nodded. "Any clues yet?"

Gwen sighed. "No. It's discouraging."

"Have the police or sheriff's office been helpful?"

She shook her head. "They don't know anything. As they say, it's a cold case."

"That's true." Conan lit a cigarette. So you've turned up nothing."

"Oh, it's too depressing to think about."

He smiled sympathetically. "Let me buy you an after-dinner drink."

"As long as I don't have to drive."

He went to the bar, and waited for the drinks. He brought back two glasses of brandy.

He held up his glass. "To the answers of your quests."

They clicked glasses.

"I've never had brandy."

"Another adventure."

She made a face at the first sip, but forged ahead.

When they'd finished their drinks, he said, "Let's go. It's getting late."

Outside, they could see that the fog had descended in the lowlands. Conan drove slowly and carefully. In the near distance they could hear the call of a fog horn from the lighthouse, and the response from a ship entering the gate. They went through spots where they were absolutely blinded by the murkiness. Then there'd be a brief clearing, before the miasma, like an enormous ghost would halt their progress again.

Finally, by some miracle, or with the guidance of an angel, they reached the hostel.

"Thank you, Conan. I had a wonderful time, even if the trip back was scary. You are a wonderful driver. I don't know how you got us through it."

He walked her to the door. "Which room is yours?"

"I'm in the dorm—upstairs."

They said 'good-night', and Gwen went inside.

She was so tired, she couldn't wait to get to bed. She woke up once in the night, thinking she'd felt movement. But she had all she could do to turn over and go back to sleep.

Despite the usual noise around her, she didn't wake up until after ten o'clock. And she still felt groggy. She went downstairs to fix some breakfast and noticed someone else had done her chores. She felt guilty, but fixed herself a bowl of oatmeal and some coffee.

With the most awful headache, a walk outdoors seemed the best solution. It did help to clear the webs entangling her brain, and she felt better when she returned. Going back upstairs to retrieve her diary, she decided it was time to catch up with her life. She hadn't recorded anything for at least two weeks. She fumbled in her duffle bag for it. It wasn't there. To make sure, she dumped all the contents out on the bed. Still no diary. What could have happened to it? She felt under her pillow, even inside her pillow case.

Then she had the most sickening thought. She'd told Conan last night that she was still keeping a journal. If he were the guilty party, he'd want to know how much she knew—if she'd recorded anything important in this book. Damn, she thought. And what was that movement she'd felt in the night? A rustling? Someone going through her belongings? Why had she slept so soundly, and why did she have such an awful headache?

He'd drugged her. He could have done that at the bar while he got the brandy. That had to be it. So that he could come in after she was asleep and riffle through her stuff without her waking up.

There was still no private room available. She lay awake thinking how foolish it was to believe that she was safe here, where anyone could walk in and do anything.

Maybe she should call it quits and go back to Michigan.

Chapter 10

At the bank the next day Denise picked up on her mood.

"C'mon," she said, after work, "Let's go for a drink."

"No alcohol." Gwen thought of her hangover, which she was barely getting over.

"OK, but let's go out. We can talk."

Gwen felt she shouldn't talk to anyone. But of all the people she knew, she least suspected Denise of anything. She wasn't part of her mother's crowd.

The smell of hamburgers and onions permeated *The Hamburg Joint*.

When they were seated, Gwen said, "I don't know what to do, Denise. I was so sure I could solve these problems. I think I'm losing faith in myself. And everybody else—I don't trust anyone—none of that crowd, anyway."

"What happened?"

"Somebody stole my journal. I don't feel safe where I'm living, after last night. "

"That's awful."

The tables were close together, and someone kicked her chair as he tried to pass by. Gwen was so on edge, she broke into a sweat, as if she'd been attacked.

"I'm getting paranoid," she said.

"Come live with me, Gwen. I'd like to have a roommate."

"You mean it? You're not just being nice?"

"No, I'm not being nice. And I could use the money." She drank some of her coffee. "And don't give up, Gwen. You're a fighter."

Gwen could read the sincerity in her friend's face.

She liked Denise, and it would be a lot closer to work. She wouldn't mind giving up the long bike rides through the headlands. And she wouldn't have to buy a car. In town she could get along with her bike.

"Actually, I would like that. Thank you."

They went back to the hostel, gathered up her things and checked out. Gwen paid her bill, and was asked to fill out a form giving her forwarding address. They tied her bicycle to the back of the car.

On the way she saw signs for people running for political office—Alan Shoemaker, Richard Thurman and Sally Stanford. Politics. She wasn't involved with politics here. Too much else to think about.

They pulled in a drive on the south end of town, on Third Street, off Main Street.

"This end of town is called 'Hurricane Gulch'. Where you were living with the Denisons down by the boats on the north end is called the 'Banana Belt'."

"Oh, thanks," Gwen laughed.

The house was unremarkable, probably having been built at the turn of the century. The shingle siding, painted white some time ago was looking weary. There were seven steps up to the porch, and one of them was broken.

"Be careful of that step," Denise said too late.

But Gwen managed to avoid the broken part.

"I have the downstairs unit," Denise told her, "with two bedrooms. Just let me get my stuff out of yours."

"No hurry," said Gwen.

The house had an odor, not too unpleasant, but definitely present. She tried to think what it could be. Not a cooking odor, nothing spoiled. She concluded it was just old house smell.

~

When she left for work the next morning, she was stopped short by the view up the headlands. Fog was coming down through the hills. Its edges very defined, like a dragon it undulated its descent through the slopes as if choreographed by a master. The wonders of Marin would never cease to amaze her.

The next week went without incident. For the first time in ages Gwen felt safe. And she enjoyed Denise's company.

"How are you coming with those records?" Denise asked over a bowl of cereal.

"I'm only about half way through. I don't dare do more than a few at a time."

"Why don't I help you?"

Gwen considered this.

Denise said, "It would go faster."

"That's true. But I wouldn't want to put you at risk."

"It'll be OK. Really."

They finished eating and put the dishes in the sink.

At work, Gwen showed Denise how she was going through the files.

"It's no wonder it's taking so long," Gwen said. "Records of the anonymous payer checks are mixed in with all the others."

"That's right. And hundreds are sent out each month."

"Jesus."

At four o'clock, Gwen said, "I have to run. Have to get my driver's license. I've been here, how long? Almost five months? And I don't have a California license yet. Shouldn't have waited 'til the last minute."

"But you're not driving now."

"No, but I might need to some day. My purse was stolen—remember. I don't have any ID. I should have a license."

"You're right. When's your birthday?"

"Friday."

"Then we're going to celebrate, Friday."

Gwen smiled.

"I'm taking you to dinner at the Valhalla."

"Oh, Denise, you don't need to do that."

"I know I don't need to. I want to. And you can meet Sally Stanford."

"The madam?"

"She ain't no madam no more. She's a respectable restaurateur." Denise laughed. "However, she still has a red light in the upstairs window.

"What's she like?"

"She's full of vinegar and piss. Doesn't take flack from nobody. But she's kind and generous, too. Supports the Little League. Haven't you seen the posters? She's running for city council."

"Yes, I did see the posters."

Getting her California license was no easy task. With no out of state license or birth certificate in hand, she had to wait a few days while DMV requested information from Michigan.

On Friday night, they entered the famous Valhalla at eight o'clock.

"Reservation for Carter," Denise told the host. "By the window."

Gwen couldn't believe her eyes. The unmistakable Sally Stanford was sitting on a pumped up barber chair. On her shoulder sat a parrot. And in her mouth a large cigar.

Gwen giggled.

"You better hush, girl. Or we'll be thrown out. Act dignified," Denise finished with her own giggle.

The whole décor was in reds—velvet drapes, deep crimson carpeting, chairs upholstered in red satin. And of course, the red light in the upstairs window.

"Is she trying to re-create the famous house she had in the city?"

"Oh, shush," Denise whispered. Then she added, "Perhaps for some old customers it is nostalgic."

When they were seated with menus, Denise said, "Order whatever you like, Honey. This one's on me."

Gwen couldn't get over the view. "It's just beautiful. Look at the moon shining on the water."

"Not bad, huh?"

When she pulled her eyes away, Gwen studied the menu. "Everything's so expensive."

"Don't even look at the prices."

Gwen ordered steak béarnaise, and Denise had lobster. A lovely salad of fresh greens, beets and cheese was presented to them first.

Looking around, Gwen could see that the customers looked well-heeled. Not the rag-tag group she'd gotten to know in the waterfront community. These were no doubt the *hill people*. Dressed to impress, each table was flanked by born-on-the-right-side of the tracks people.

When they'd finished eating, the waiter came by and asked if this was their first time at the Valhalla.

When they replied he said, "In that case, ladies, the dessert is on the house."

He brought over chocolate soufflé topped with whipped cream. While they were consuming this decadent delicacy Sally waddled over to their table. She removed the strong cigar hanging from her mouth, introduced herself, and stated that she was running for city council.

"I've run before and lost, but I'm not giving up," she said. "I love this city, but it needs a kick in the you-know-what."

The young women listened attentively as Sally laid out her platform.

"This town needs toilets. Public restrooms in the downtown area. The merchants are all for it—it will bring them more business. That's one thing."

She could see she had a captive audience and continued.

"There's another matter that's whipped this community into a cloud of dust, and that's the houseboat folks." She stooped to whisper. "Now the hill people would like to see the lot of them washed out to sea. Most of the people in this room are hill folks. But you two look like you might listen to reason." She turned to survey the cash register, which drew her eye like a magnet at frequent intervals.

"Would you like to sit down, Miss Sally?" Denise asked her.

"No, thanks. I got to keep moving. But I want to say this. I was born poor, grew up poor, and though I may be well situated now, it wasn't always this way. I still know what it's like to not have enough. And if those poor people down at the waterfront are ingenious enough to make something out of nothing, like the abandoned and rotting boats the military left, then I say, more's the power to them."

She blew her nose. "Now I got to move on."

She placed two pamphlets on the table, and left with the cigar dangling from her lips.

On the front was written in large print "Sally Stanford for City Council." Inside, was a picture of her and statements of what she stood for. One was, *You shouldn't have to hold it!*

They saw her move to the next table, and then the next, handing out her leaflets.

When they rose to leave, Sally followed them to the door, with a wake of strong smoke trailing her. "If either of you feel strongly about these matters, I'd invite you to attend the council meetings. They're on the third Wednesday of the month at city hall. You know where that is?"

"No," Gwen answered.

"It's right downtown, kind of kitty-corner from the park with the elephants—a store front. There's a sign on the door."

"That might be something worth doing," Gwen said to Denise. "I don't want to see the houseboat people thrown out. They're my friends." And then she thought about how she didn't even dare see Conan any more.

They walked the short way home. Gwen said, "It's weird. Sally seems to be represent the hard-working boat people, but her customers are all hill people."

"Or people from San Francisco. Folks get a kick out of coming here, as if they're doing something scandalous. Everybody knows she was a madam in the city."

"And not here?"

Denise moved her hand this way and that. "Not openly, anyway. I think she has other fish to fry."

"You mean the council seat."

"Yup."

They reached the door. Gwen thanked and hugged Denise for treating her to such a wonderful time.

"It was delicious—all of it."

~

Gwen decided that going to the town council meeting was worthwhile. For one thing she was impatient waiting for a break in the mysteries she was trying to uncover, and needed to keep herself busy. She really did like Sally Stanford's platform. It would be awful to destroy that industrious community on the north end of town.

"Do you want to go with me?" she asked her roommate.

"Can't. I have a class."

Denise was taking night classes in the recently developed personal computers field. She hoped to get ahead of the game, be able to show her stuff at work, and eventually rise to a management position.

Gwen found City Hall downtown by following Sally's directions.

An unpretentious space, it was crowded in with the police station on one side, and a grocery shop on the other. Although the meeting hadn't started, the room was already noisy, with opinionated citizens of every feather talking with friends or neighbors. And already hot. The single fan did little to dissipate the stifling August heat.

Gwen found a seat near the back, and spent the next ten minutes taking in the ambience, overhearing various conversations, getting the feel of what it was like to be at a Sausalito council meeting. Mostly her sense was that the room was too small for the number attending.

She noticed that the some of the houseboat people were sitting in the back, segregating themselves from the hill folks.

Gwen saw Sally Stanford take a seat in the front of the room.

Mayor Lindsay brought the meeting to order. Gesturing lavishly, his hands seemed too large for the rest of him. His appearance struck Gwen as probably being from the working class.

The council members were introduced. One of the names she'd seen on posters, Richard Thurman, was an incumbent and part of the current council. They went through a rather boring agenda, Gwen thought, until the issue of the waterfront community came up.

After the council had its say, the public was allowed to speak.

It was about this time that competition came from across the street. Bongo players and singers had gathered, as they usually did, in Elephant Park, so called because of the two huge pachyderms guarding it. Many people in the park were from the waterfront community, joined by local hippies and spiritual types. Others, high on some ingested substance, came to heighten their experience in the 'zone' with the rhythmic drumming of the bongos.

Council members groaned, as the vibration of African drums buzzed their ears.

"It's impossible to carry on business with that racket going on!" a vocal member of the council spoke up.

"Please identify yourself before speaking," the mayor said.

Someone from the hill insisted the water community was a blight, and had to be disposed of. Three others spoke to the same issue, saying much the same thing.

To the last, the mayor said, "Please speak up; we can't hear you."

Then Sally Stanford rose and presented the opposing view. It was much applauded by the crowd in the back, who whistled and gave her a standing ovation. Two of them followed her in a lively encore of their own.

As tempers rose, so did the temperature in the room, contributing to body odors.

She had not planned to speak, on this, her first meeting. But she was so roused by others, she found herself standing.

"I'm Gwen Harris. I agree with those who have spoken in defense of the waterfront community. I see no reason to condemn this hard-working group of people, who, among other things, have cleaned up the mess the military left to rust and rot, by recycling this material into actual homes."

She sat down to rousing applause and loud boos. What a lively place this was. Finally the mayor closed the discussion.

On the way out, Conan approached her with a smile. He took her arm, and said, "Glad to see you here."

She was surprised and shocked. She hadn't seen him earlier.

"Let go of me," she said with real anger, jerked away, and as she ran from him, called over her shoulder, "I want it back."

She couldn't hear his reply as she was racing out of the building.

Still breathing hard, she tore down Bridgeway. How dare he act as though nothing had happened? Did he think she was so stupid as to not have noticed that her journal disappeared on the same night he left her at the hostel?

She stopped by the waterfront, gazing out at a hazy moon. The fog hung motionless, muting the streetlamps, softening everything in her vista.

A motorboat churned past, its wake sloshing high among the pilings.

Somehow the scene calmed her. These sites were familiar and had the effect of dampening her anger.

~

"There's a package for you," Denise called, when Gwen came home the next night.

Gwen saw it on the table by the door. It was from the hostel. She wondered what it could be.

Tearing off the wrapping she could see right away that it was her journal. She could understand how Conan might have returned it, but the hostel? Well, maybe he'd dropped it off there.

Then she noticed the note tucked inside the book.

"We found this on a shelf in the common room after you left. We know you'll be glad to get it back. Hostel staff."

Gwen had to sit down. *In the common room?*

She ransacked her brain, and then she remembered. Yes, the last time she'd written in it *was* in the common room. She'd totally forgotten. It seemed so long ago.

She felt terrible for blaming Conan for something he hadn't done.

Chapter 11

The annual art fair, held on Labor Day weekend was coming up, and Megan was unusually busy forming, firing and glazing the pots in her kiln. Gwen, who by now had been assured that there had been no more scary phone calls, offered her services, and soon was loading the kiln, removing pots from it when they were cool, and putting price stickers on finished work.

"You must join us at the fair," Megan said.

"Tell me what's so special."

"Besides all kinds of art laid out in booths, there are jugglers, people on stilts, magicians and musicians. The best part is when Varda—do you know who Varda is?"

"Yes."

"Oh, my Dear, He puts on an elaborate event every year at the art fair. He calls it the *Masque*. It's full of magical costumes, seemingly death-defying acts of balance and arterial efforts. He holds it all together with a compelling story that keeps people enthralled. Sound effects, moveable props—he has it all. Sometimes an Egyptian slave mart, or a Turkish bath. It's great fun!"

"Sounds exciting."

"It's mind-blowing. And the best part, it's free."

Gwen helped to carefully wrap Megan's treasures. Gwen got caught up in the excitement she could feel all around her.

"He has these parties on his boat too."

"I know."

The Fair was not always at the same site; this time it was on Caledonia, near Central School. Part of the street was closed off, and the school lawn was drafted as well to accommodate the vendors and attendees.

Gwen accompanied Megan to help set up the booth, and assist with customers. Megan's pots were unusual and she sold several the first day.

Toward evening, Gwen saw a troupe of costumed characters enter the fair grounds. The veiling that had covered a stage area at the south end was pulled aside, and a wild and imaginative set revealed. Lights came on, and a mid-eastern type of music began.

Megan encouraged Gwen to go join the merry-makers by the stage. Gwen was only too happy to do so. Within minutes she was so captivated by the sight of Persian clowns, majestic potentates and acrobats that she forgot where she was.

On stage a sort of trial was going on, and it appeared that the accused was about to be decapitated. But the chorus, or was it the jury, was singing, clapping, applauding the sentence of the judge. Some of the actors were winding their way through the crowds, dancing and playing small wooden flutes. Many patrons were in costume, too, reveling in the drama and flagrant display of themselves. Bawdy and maudlin, the night was in full swing.

She hadn't come in costume, but Gwen got caught up in the flush and fury of the music and movement. She cavorted with some stranger in gold metallic costume of an era she couldn't identify. She had never moved in such a wild and carefree manner. She was totally lost in the moment. If she had any worries she was not aware of them now.

The first partner left her, as a clown cut in and introduced her to his style of frenetic movement.

While she turned to watch someone on her left, a raspy voice on her right whispered in her ear, "You will die!"

Gwen turned quickly to see who it was, but the person had already disappeared in the crowd. She wasn't sure if it were one of the masked actors, or someone else in the crowd.

Her lungs were heaving.

"Did you see who that was?" she asked the clown. But he only kept moving in that crazed jerky manner of his with the same glassy smile on his face.

Her heart thumping wildly in her chest, Gwen pushed herself away from the dancers.

"I'm not even safe in a crowd!" she cried to herself, running across the grounds.

Suddenly someone grabbed her. She nearly fainted.

"Hey, what's the hurry?" It was Conan.

She was so frightened she fell into his arms.

"What's the matter?"

He guided her to a bench, and sat with his arm over her shoulder. Gwen told him what had just happened.

"Probably just a prank."

"I don't know—maybe, but I'm not even sure it was one of the actors. What if ..."

"Stay by me," he said.

She could see his gaze surfing the crowd. Was he looking for someone he knew who might have provoked this incident? They sat in silence, while Gwen tried to regain her composure.

"Are you hungry?"

"No. Yes. I think so. At least I was."

"You wait here. I'll go get us——-"

"No! Please don't leave me."

"OK." He took her hand. "Come with me."

They walked across the grounds, past tents and tables, other musical groups, and over to the food vendors.

Conan bought them both a hotdog and a beer. They found a place to sit and eat. In the distance they could hear somebody sounding like Joan Baez singing *Diamonds and Rust*.

"I have to make an apology," she said to Conan.

He didn't say anything, and she went on. "I guess I'm getting paranoid, but the morning after we came back from the Pelican Inn, I looked for my journal and couldn't find it. I thought you'd come in and taken it from my duffle bag. That's why I growled at you at the council meeting."

"And now?"

"The lady who runs the hostel sent the book to me. I'd left it in the common room. Afterwards, I remembered writing in there, but not at the time. Oh, Conan, I thought you'd drugged me, and came in when I was sleeping to take my diary. I'm so sorry."

He laughed. Then he was serious. "I wouldn't do that."

"I know that now."

"And I wouldn't drug you. You just had too much to drink, and I don't think the brandy agreed with you."

She nodded. "Am I forgiven?"

"You are."

Later, Conan walked her home, and asked her if she'd like to help him at his art booth the next day.

"It would give me a chance to walk around and see everybody else's stuff," he said.

"I'd love to. And I'd have something to do besides sit around worrying what calamity will happen next."

That night she lay awake restless and fearful. When she finally slept, it was fitfully. She'd wake up, sweating, knowing she'd had a bad dream, but couldn't remember what it was.

~

On Sunday when the art fair was over, Gwen and Conan helped load Megan's car to take back the pots which hadn't sold. She'd done very well, but there was always left over inventory.

Conan had a booth too.

"How did you do, Conan?" Megan asked

"Fair. I sold a few."

When the work was done, the grounds cleaned up and all their personal stuff out of there, Megan invited her friends over for barbecued chicken, which Chad was making in the backyard.

All the hard work of preparing for the fair, and striking it at the end was over. It was time to celebrate their successes, even their disappointments.

Chad had tapped a keg of beer, and it wasn't long before everyone was feeling pretty good.

About half-way through the party Megan called Gwen into her bedroom. She was holding an old yellow envelope.

"I thought it was time you have this," she said, handing it to Gwen.

"What is it?"

"Papers that belong to you, now you're grown up. From your mother."

Gwen stared at Megan. Hands shaking, she opened the sealed envelope carefully. She extracted four sheets.

The first, and most important was her birth certificate. Megan had always insisted she didn't know where it was, and Gwen had had to get something from the church to satisfy requirements for date of birth to get her first driver's license and social security card in Michigan.

Megan was babbling on about why she kept it from Gwen, but all Gwen could see were the words: Father of child: Richard Thurman. There it was, right in front of her, recorded on paper. She stared at it. *The councilman.* Her heart was pounding so hard she thought she'd faint. Waves of shock passed through her.

The other papers had to do with custody of Gwen when she was being turned over to her aunt in Michigan. The one that interested her was her birth certificate. She finally knew who he was—the councilman she'd spoken up to at the meeting. Embarrassment surged through her.

Then evil thoughts went through her head. What a mess she could make of his campaign if she exposed his nefarious past to the press. Fathering bastards was not acceptable in the sixties—not even in Sausalito. That would be the end of his political career. It was fun to fantasize such deeds, but she knew she wouldn't carry them out.

"As long as you're forthcoming, Megan, why don't you tell me why you lied to me about baby-sitting the day mom didn't come back."

Megan was flushed with too much beer, but it had also loosened her tongue. She took another gulp of the foamy stuff.

"I didn't see any point in complicating things. I had other things to do that day, and I asked Eric to take care of the two of you. I was afraid you might even suspect *me*, if I told you I wasn't home, and I couldn't stand that."

Gwen nodded. She could have told her that she did suspect her because she'd lied.

"And why didn't you tell me you knew who my father was? You lied about that too."

"I didn't! I didn't know. That envelope was sealed, Gwen. I told you before, she'd never tell me. I had my own idea of who he was, but she never confirmed it."

"You mean Thurman?"

"Yes. He was here several times. In the week before she died, she gave me this envelope, and told me that if anything happened to her, to give this to you when you were of age.'"

"But I am twenty-one, and you kept it from me!"

Megan twisted the glass in her hand. "I've been confused. I didn't want you to get involved in all this painful history. I didn't know what to do."

"It wasn't your decision to make!"

Megan gulped more beer, then sat quietly. "You're right, of course. I'm sorry."

Gwen could see sweat running down the face of the older woman.

Sorry wasn't good enough. But Gwen let it go for now. She felt Megan had more to say, but this wasn't the time to press. Party people were still hanging around. If there was more to reveal, she wanted to discuss it in private.

Gwen still thought that Megan might possibly have a motive— jealousy or something, but she wasn't eager to pursue that vein. She left the room, and rejoined the party outdoors.

Eric had come to help strike the fair, and carry things home for Megan. He flopped down between Megan and Gwen with his beer, and started telling funny stories about some of the things he'd seen and heard at the fair.

"Well, it's over, and I'm glad," Megan said.

"Another year, another dollar," Conan added.

Louis joined the group, when all the work had been done. He was teased for this.

"Hey, give me a break. I had to take down my own tent, and nobody helped me."

"OK, OK, you're forgiven."

Louis made figures out of metal which he sold at the fair. Some were very animated and amusing; some appeared to be likenesses of famous people like FDR or Mark Twain, complete with mustache made of fine wire.

He helped himself to the potato salad, baked beans and chicken.

Gwen joined him. "I thought your figures were very whimsical."

He smiled.

"And well-crafted."

"I wish I could make a living at it. I really want to get out of the insurance business."

She laughed. "Too straight?"

"Yeah. And it's not something I want to do for the rest of my life."

They chatted for awhile. He said he had to leave, but he hoped to see her again.

When Megan got up to refurbish the food, Eric said, "Did you know Conan was in love with your mother?"

"No, I did not."

"Ssh. Keep your voice down."

"Nobody told me that either. Is this the Day of Revelation?" Gwen said.

"Well, she didn't love him, so it didn't go anywhere," Eric said.

"When was this unrequited affair—before or after I was born?"

"After."

"How old was I?"

"I don't remember."

"If she rejected him, could he have gotten angry enough to throw her off the cliff?"

"Oh, I hardly think so."

"Well, somebody did it. It's as good a motive as any," she said.

~

"You'll never guess what Megan gave me," she said to Denise, coming in the front door.

"Guess."

"You know I'm no good at that."

Gwen handed Denise her birth certificate.

After studying the paper, the gasp that escaped Denise's mouth was quite audible. Her eyes were larger than ever.

"The guy who's running for office?"

"Yes, he's an incumbent. He's already on the council. And I stood up and identified myself at the meeting. He knows who I am."

"Oh, my God!" Denise said.

"I feel like such a fool. Now he knows who I am. But I haven't met him."

"Well, that's not so terrible. You don't think he had anything to do with your mother's death, do you?"

Gwen shook her head. "No. Not really. Why? He may have wished her to abort her pregnancy, but her demise came ten years later."

"Right. But why hasn't he come forward? He knows you're in town."

"Maybe he's too ashamed."

"Of what?"

"I don't know. Not getting in touch all these years? Not marrying my mother?"

"He was probably already married."

"That's what I think."

"What did he look like?"

"I don't know. I wasn't paying that much attention."

Denise was thoughtful. "I can't believe it. I mean I can't believe Megan withheld this from you all this time."

"She said she was confused—didn't know what to do. Said she'd never seen this paper."

"Right."

"All that work at the bank for nothing."

"Well, we can call a halt to that job."

"You don't suspect *her* of anything … serious, do you?"

"I don't know. I don't want to. I think she's trying to protect me from myself."

"But it wasn't her call."

"No. It wasn't. I think I'm getting paranoid. I suspect everyone I know. Except you, of course."

"I can't blame you."

"What are you going to do?"

"I don't know."

"Maybe you could get to know him on the council. Join his campaign committee, or something."

"Oh, Denise. I couldn't."

"Just an idea."

"I know. I appreciate the thought."

They sat in silence for some time, sipping their wine.

That night Gwen lay in bed thinking about this man. He was her father? Then she remembered another man—the one who'd appeared at the memorial service. Could they be one and the same? She hadn't really seen his face, bent over as he was.

Well, at least she could go to another council meeting and get a good look at Richard Thurman. But she wouldn't speak up this time. She'd sit in the back and make sure he didn't see her.

In the meantime, she found some of his campaign literature. Like the others, his bio appeared on the inside. He was an attorney in Marin County, had served on the Legal Aid Committee for four years, and the Sausalito City Council for two. The brochure included a picture of him with two boys, a wife and Golden Retriever. Such a nice family man. She felt her heart close. The boys were all clearly younger than she. Did that mean that he'd married after she was born?

Then she remembered the woman, Pip, who'd told her the 'boyfriend' was a lawyer. It all fit.

Chapter 12

Fall rolled around. Gwen felt incompetent—certainly as an amateur private detective. Her friends started calling her *Sleuth.* Meant as a compliment, but in six months all the questions that she'd come to California with were still gnawing at her. Those questions and more.

Gwen missed the color she knew she'd be surrounded by if she were back in Michigan—the beautiful maples, and birches glowing with all shades of magenta, yellow and orange, against a background of evergreens. Native color in Marin was rare. She had called the surrounding hills brown, but Eric told her that was not politically correct.

"We call them golden," he corrected with a wry smile.

Marin had some color—at least where the vivid liquid amber had been planted in neighborhoods and around shopping centers. And there was something about the sky that she loved, whether here or in the Midwest—a certain shade of blue, and a hue not seen in any other season, especially in late afternoon.

Pumpkin patches pre-ambled the advent of Halloween. Unlike Michigan, where pumpkins for sale were generally found only overflowing the sidewalks outside large grocery stores— in Marin farmers rented a small area, fenced it in, set up scare-crows and haystacks, and sometimes other attractions to bring in the customers. Then they filled the space with pumpkins.

Denise had been invited to a Halloween party.

"I'll wait 'til after the trick-or-treaters have come and gone," she said.

"No, I'll take care of them. You go to the party when it starts."

It wasn't hard to persuade Denise.

Before it was really dark, little ones pounded on the door. Seeing them in their colorful costumes of magicians, goblins and spacemen reminded Gwen of being on the other side of the door. Yes, right here in Marin. Mom waited on the sidewalk with a couple of other moms, while she, Alex and a couple of other kids ran up steps and rang doorbells. It had all been such fun, and the memories flooded back.

As the hour grew on, so did the age of the kids. No little sacks— these guys were carrying pillow cases.

By nine o'clock the traffic had slowed down, and by nine-thirty it had stopped altogether. Then at ten o'clock the doorbell rang again. Gwen debated whether to answer it. She thought it pretty inconsiderate of anyone to come so late, and she was sure it wasn't the little ones at the door. But then she thought the big kids might get nasty if she didn't give them a handout. They might soap the windows or throw eggs at them—even break a window. She couldn't let that happen to Denise's home.

She went to the door. Opening it, she saw one person in a harlequin costume, who screeched out, "You will die!"

The person ran down the steps. It was a man, she could tell that much.

She closed and locked the door, leaning against it and shaking until her knees felt so weak she had to sit down.

Was it the same person who had said that at the frenzied art fair dance? She imagined it was. Someone who deliberately changed their voice and their gait.

She didn't wait for Denise to get home. After a cup of hot chocolate and toast—her aunt's remedy for everything— she crawled under the covers and tried to sleep.

In the distance, she could still hear party-making and fire crackers. It was a long time before slumber overcame her like a welcome fog.

When she awoke, she could smell coffee which Denise had prepared. Luckily it was a weekend, and neither of them had to hurry off to work.

Gwen told Denise what had happened the night before. Besides offering consoling words, Denise made French toast and bacon for them.

"Comfort food," she said.

"And it's appreciated."

"Who do you think this creep was—you have any idea?"

Gwen shook her head. "No, but there was something familiar about him."

~

In the following days Gwen was restless. She started taking long walks during the day time. At first she restricted herself to Bridgeway or other populated streets. Then Megan showed her some of the pathways and stairways in the town. They went together up some arduous ascents.

"The climbs are steep but you'll see many amazing views at the top."

Some were hidden or secret in their location. They were fascinating to Gwen. She sought them out and asked how they came to be.

"Most of the towns in Marin had them," a friendly woman at the Visitors' Center told her. "But usually they got deeded to the property adjoining them. This didn't happen in Sausalito. So there is still open access to these delightful byways, if one takes the trouble to find them."

When Megan said she had to spend more time getting ready for the Christmas fair, Gwen continued her pilgrimage alone on weekends. With little else to do, she eagerly sought out these paths, often climbing as many as one hundred steps. But the view at the top was always worthwhile. Depending where she was standing, and what trees lay in the way, she could often see Richardson Bay, the marinas, Angel Island, and two bridges spanning the Bay. Sometimes she could see the old Alcatraz, recently closed as a prison.

"This is the most fascinating city in the world," she told Alex.

"Maybe. But you'd better be careful. Mom worries about you."

"Do you?"

"Do I what?"

"Worry about me," she teased.

He turned red. "Well, yeah, sure."

One day she was climbing Excelsior Lane, which then crossed to Bulkley to Harrison, and on to San Carlos, where some of the steps were not paved. It had rained recently and turned these stairs to mud.

It was bounded on both sides by thickets of dense sage. The path took many turns, as it bypassed groves of bay laurel, live oaks, and overgrown brush. She heard a branch crack and knew someone was behind her. Well, of course, other people used these paths and stairs, but she couldn't take a chance. She increased her pace until she was around the next bend, and then dove into the guardian thickets of thorny blackberry bushes.

She was probably just being overly suspicious, but it seemed the safest thing to do. Here she was able to remain unseen. Very shortly she heard someone rush by on the path. She sank down in the wet weeds and waited for him to pass. Twice he crossed back in front of her hiding place. She could only see his feet. Surely, he would figure out where she'd disappeared. Finally, the sound of steps ended. Who was he? Why was he stalking her?

Looking over the hill she decided that she could descend without going back on the path. Wild herbs grew out of the untamed hill, their scent mingling with the wet, seeping earth. Struggling through the madrone bushes with its red bark, high grasses and stubble of all sorts, she wound her way down the hill, slipping in muddy places, having to rethink her route as small creeks crossed her path and large patches of thorny bushes blocked her way.

It seemed hours later, before she reached the bottom of the hill. A little park was nestled in at the bottom where she rested for awhile, oblivious to the cuts and scratches she'd incurred. And then the long walk home. Only when she threw herself on her bed, did she begin to feel the sting of the many offenses she'd received in this journey. She was too exhausted to get up and tend to them, many of them muddy from when she'd fallen. They'd just have to wait.

Asleep, she dreamed of someone chasing her through a tunnel, round and round in a continuous loop, where there was no escape.

~

Gwen rode over to Megan's to pick up some of the things she'd left there. She wasn't very comfortable seeing Megan after their last interaction, but she'd see what played out. There were lots of unanswered questions that gnawed at her.

Megan was in the shower. Gwen packed up the clothes she wanted, and waited for Megan to emerge. With her entrance there also emerged a great cloud of steam.

"I didn't know you were here."

"Sorry. When no one answered I let myself in. Do you want your key back?"

"No hurry."

While Megan got dressed Gwen looked at the newspaper. There was a picture of each of the candidates for council, and their platform below. Gwen read with sickening heart that Thurman wanted to oust the waterfront community.

"There's no heart in the man," she thought.

She said as much when Megan came out. "I can't believe—"

"What?"

"That he's the father who's been sending me money all these years."

"Every coin has two sides."

Megan ran a comb through her hair.

They went out to the backyard and sat on the swing.

Megan looked at Gwen's arms. "Where did you get all those scratches?"

"Nothing, really. Just an encounter with a thorny bush."

"Where were you?"

"Out for a walk."

"By yourself?"

"I'm not a child, Megan."

"No, but you could be on someone's 'to do list'."

"Oh, don't say that."

"Gwen, I'm glad you came. I have some pictures for you. I've been looking all over for them. I finally found them in that old cupboard in the garage."

"You have pictures of Mom?"

"A few, yes."

Megan went into her bedroom and returned with a stationery box which held the photos.

Gwen took them and began to look through them.

"Oh, my gosh, here's one of me on my tricycle."

"There are several of you. Look at this one of you and Alex."

They were at the beach and Alex was kissing Gwen on the cheek. It made Gwen laugh.

"Aw. We must have been about three then."

"That sounds right."

"Did you know we got married?"

Megan looked startled until she saw Gwen's grin. "It doesn't surprise me. He worshipped you."

Gwen picked up one of her mother holding her in her lap. She looked at it for a long time without saying anything. Then she went on to the next. There was one of her mother dancing with her in the living room.

Several were of her as a child, and many with her mother.

"You two were very close." Megan blew her nose. "She loved you very much."

"I'm so glad to have these. Aunt Marie had practically nothing."

The next picture she picked up was of a group of six people.

"Who are they?"

"The people she worked with at the bank."

"The bank?"

"Don't you remember? I told you that she worked until near the time that you were born."

"At a bank? I thought she was a waitress."

"Only for a little while."

So, let's see this was when—at least twenty years ago."

Gwen studied the old photo. It wasn't taken in very good light. She could make out her mother, but it was someone else's face that caught her attention, someone who looked familiar.

She put her finger on the black woman's face. "Who's this?"

"I don't know their names, dear. I never met any of them."

Gwen turned the photo over. The names of those in the photo were listed on the back. And there it was—Denise Carter.

~

She had intended to confront Megan about the lies she'd told previously, but this piece of news was so shocking, she couldn't say anymore. She wanted to be alone. She thanked Megan for the pictures, and cycled all the way to Rodeo Beach. The skies confirmed it was mid-November. Gwen put on her windbreaker, stumbled down the incline, and along the beach, fighting against the wind with every step.

Once again she tried to unravel the confusing facts. Another betrayal? Why hadn't Denise said anything to her? Why the hell hadn't she said she knew her mother? What were the secrets here? For God's sake, couldn't she trust anyone?

A ring of silence and secrets was closing in on her.

The tears came, and she didn't try to stop them. They ran in fast rivulets down her cheeks. She saw no one else on the beach. The waves bashed as they broke against the shore. No one would hear her on this forsaken shore. She let loose, sobbing to the wind, to the waves, who would keep her secrets.

After walking for an hour, she sat down on a large log that had washed ashore, and thought about what to do.

Defeat was hard to admit, but everywhere she turned, she felt overwhelmed. She couldn't stay here. It was time to admit she'd been licked, and go back to Michigan where it was safe, where there weren't likely to be any threatening surprises. She'd enroll in school the next semester—her last before graduation. It all sounded very predictable, reassuring and secure.

She decided not to tell Denise anything, except that her aunt needed her. "She's broken her hip," Gwen lied.

By the next day she had everything packed.

Chad drove her to the airport. His quiet temperament calmed her.

"You know you can always come back," he said. "I hate to see you go." He glanced at her face. "But it's best for you." He squeezed her hand.

"I'll always remember yours and Megan's hospitality and friendship. I couldn't have made it this far without you."

As the plane left the ground, Gwen could see sailboats on the bay.

She wondered if she'd miss Marin.

Chapter 13

The cold winds of November stung as Gwen approached the street outside the Detroit airport. Surely, Novembers hadn't been this cold when she'd lived here. Always her least favorite month of the year in this state—the colorful leaves were gone, the snow had not yet come to offer a white frosting to the darkened ground—it was just plain depressing. Grey skies, and dark, bare branches on huge oaks, reaching— for what?

Her aunt was glad to see her, giving her a powerful hug and hustling her and her luggage into the warm car.

As they drove back to Royal Oak, the next thing that impressed her was how flat Michigan was. No switch-backs, no twisting roads, not even a hill, at least not around here. She noticed a flock of Canadian geese stenciled against the sky. Seeking warmer climes, the geese knew which way to go.

She realized that at the moment she was feeling sour about everything, not the least of which was returning empty-handed.

"Are you satisfied?" her Aunt Marie asked in the evening. "Can you leave it alone now?"

"No, I'm not satisfied. But I'm leaving it alone, at least for now."

Later, Gwen asked, "Did you really not have any birth certificate for me?"

"I didn't. I checked the Marin hospitals. It seems you were born at home."

"At home?" Gwen was puzzled. Megan had never mentioned that. Perhaps she didn't think it important.

Aunt Marie continued. "No, my sister didn't give me anything. I think she must have had a lot of anxiety near the end to have overlooked something as important as that."

"Well, I have it now. It was in a sealed envelope Megan had, to be given me when I was 'grown up'. Megan didn't know what was in it. She waited 'til recently to present it to me. She must have thought I wasn't a *grown-up* yet," Gwen said bitterly.

The days went by slowly. There was frost on the ground by mid-November, and a three inch snowfall greeted them Thanksgiving morning.

Aunt Marie's church had a potluck dinner for anyone who wanted to participate. Marie had suggested they attend rather than cook a big meal at home.

"Sounds good to me."

A suffused, weak winter light surrounded The First Congregation Church, a small model of a British Cathedral, with an imposing tower. Gwen didn't know any of the people, but they were all friendly. There was loads of good food, and nice to have only had to make one dish— her favorite sweet potato recipe.

She had resisted getting in touch with Brad, but the temptation was too great. If she were going to resume her former life it might as well include him.

The day after Thanksgiving she called him. They agreed to meet that evening by Walgreen's. When Gwen left the bus, the wind had whipped up, and Brad was nowhere in sight. The drug store had closed. She stamped her feet against the cold, and blew on her hands. Where was he? Icy air lacerated her lungs with every frantic breath.

When she could stand no more of the punishing cold, she caught the next bus back to Marie's.

In the morning Brad called.

"Where were you?"

"Where were *you*?"

"I waited at Walgreens."

"That's where I waited."

"*Which* Walgreens?"

So that was the problem. She let out a deep sigh.

"Shall we try again?" he said.

"Back to the buses?" she giggled.

It was frigid—well below zero, she knew.

"Nope. I've got the whole room to myself for a few days."

"Whoopee!"

By that evening she was in his arms.

"It's so good to have you back, Gwen."

They teased and tantalized each other. She loved being encompassed in his warmth, feeling the swell of muscles in his arms and back. Other places too.

She felt such a rush of passion, he finally said, "Hey, slow down, Sweetie. We've got all night."

It seemed like it was supposed to be the other way around. Wasn't it the guy who was always in a hurry to get to touchdown?

She made herself take some deep breaths and slow down. She began to appreciate the finer movements he was making on her neck, her spine, her belly.

When he finally made the move to mount her, a vibration of ecstasy danced the entire length of her body. For being so young he was very good at the art of love-making.

It was the best thing about being in Michigan.

~

Three days later Gwen received a letter in the mail. She studied the envelope. It had first been sent to Megan's place, then forwarded to her aunt's. Her hands shook, as in the corner she read R. Thurman.

She sat down by the window, with the morning's light coming through. Thinking she was still in California, he'd written, "Dear Gwen, I know this is awkward for both of us. Of course I recognized your name as soon as you spoke up at the city council meeting. Until then, I had no idea you were living in Sausalito. Perhaps by now, you know who I am. If not, I'd like to introduce myself. I am your father, and I too, live in Sausalito. I would like to meet you. Perhaps you moved here to find out more about your mother. I read in the paper that her remains had been discovered and you identified them. I would like to help you, if that's possible. Please know you can reach me—"

She threw the letter down, as bitter tears coursed her cheeks.

"Too little, too late," was all she could think.

She looked out the window as lazy snowflakes fell softly to the ground.

Why had he waited so long to identify himself, to reach out to her? And what did he mean by 'help her', to do what? Did he know she'd tried so hard to find the killer that everyone she knew looked like a suspect? And how did she know he wasn't the culprit?

Yes, he'd been providing for her. But that might have been remorse payment. Maybe he'd killed her mother in an instant of wild passion, and regretted it later. Maybe he still felt some responsibility for his daughter.

She picked the letter up. He'd given her an office phone number. Of course. He didn't want her disturbing his happy home.

She had to think. What was she going to do about Richard Thurman?

She went for a walk in sloppy snow. She didn't have boots with her. They were probably still in Ann Arbor. The snow was slick and slippery, but she trudged on anyway. The slush worked its way into her sneakers and socks until they were squeaking in complaint.

A second later she was on her butt. Damn! She hadn't been watching her steps. Well, at least she wasn't hurt. Dark clouds were forming in the sky. She got up, and walked back to Marie's, as a snow storm loomed above.

~

In the following days, many scenarios danced through her mind: She would write a scathing letter asking why he'd kept his identity a secret from her for so long. Or she would go back to California, meet with him and confront him with that same question.

Maybe she'd call him from here and see what he had to say. Or she'd just show up at his office. She could ruin any chances he had for re-election by exposing this letter publicly.

She realized she held a long black bag of resentment toward this man. She had been wistful about him before. Now anger was foremost in her mind.

But there were times when she thought *maybe he really could help.* There were bound to be things he knew about that long-ago time that she didn't.

She had been determined to put California behind her, but as each day passed, she felt a stronger pull to go back. Part of her felt she should talk with him on the phone first, but the whole subject was just too delicate to handle that way. She felt sure it had to be in person.

Christmas was only two weeks away. She wouldn't leave Aunt Marie to face it alone. She'd wait until the holidays were over, before deciding what to do.

If she went back, where would she stay? She had burned all her bridges. Temporarily, she thought she could stay with Denise. Denise only knew she'd gone home to help her aunt through a bad spell. She didn't know Gwen had suspicions about her too.

She called Denise, who was happy to hear from her.

"Of course you can come back here."

"I don't know how long I'll be staying."

"That's OK."

She wrote Richard, telling him she'd gone back to Michigan for the holidays, but planned to return the second week in January. She didn't say she'd given up and gone home in defeat.

He wrote again, saying he looked forward to meeting her.

Aunt Marie wanted to invoke an old tradition they'd had—drive around the rich neighborhoods, like Gross Point, and look at all the colored lights and outdoor spectacles created just for this time of year.

Gwen agreed to humor her. She was glad she could give her this little bit of fun before leaving her. The woman had been her surrogate mother. She knew she was really very lucky to have her.

The day before Christmas nature provided a winter wonderland Gwen had never expected to see again. The snow that had fallen softly on the tree branches the night before had stayed there, no wind blowing it off. Then as the sun rose in the morning, it turned the snow to ice. For almost an hour the sun shone brightly on them, making each tree and every tiny branch appear to be made of crystal, shining in the sunlight.

Gradually the sun melted the ice, and sent it dripping to the ground. But for one shining hour, Gwen and others who appreciated nature's wonders, could enjoy the magnificent splendor. Gwen took pictures. She'd have to show folks in California that Michigan had its wonders too.

Saying good-bye to Brad had been difficult. He actually begged her not to go back. He seemed so sincere Gwen almost believed that their relationship meant more to him than just the fun of the moment.

In any case, she'd have to wait for him to grow up.

But as their last evening ended, she watched him walk away from the car she'd borrowed from Aunt Marie until the shadows swallowed him and she could no longer hear his footsteps. She could still feel his warmth on her face.

The day she left Michigan was bone-chilling with a wind factor well below zero. Her lungs constricted in the biting cold. She was glad to be leaving this frigid climate.

Chapter 14

Denise met her at the airport.

"How's your aunt doing?"

Gwen had almost forgotten that she'd told Denise her aunt had broken her hip.

"She's doing well. She's a strong lady."

"I'm glad to hear it."

They stopped for dinner at Fredo's on Caledonia. Warm and cozy, it was nice to be at a place where the help recognized you.

They ordered pasta with shrimp and a glass of white wine.

She didn't know how much she should tell Denise. She still was confused if not distrustful of her. She had previously told Denise everything, and Denise had even helped her find the identity of her father. Why hadn't she told her anything about knowing her mother, or other details she probably knew about her? Who else in that crowd did she know?

Gwen decided to keep the conversation light tonight. She talked about Michigan, the cold, her aunt's request to go on their old hunt for the best outdoor decorations in the area.

"Some houses were so totally over the top—really garish."

"Did you see your old boyfriend?"

"Oh, yes." She rolled her eyes. "I'm going to miss him."

"He's that good?"

Gwen was taken by surprise. Had she been so obvious? "Yes," she exclaimed. "And what did you for the holidays?"

"I went to Lake Tahoe for a few days with some old ski buddies."

"Do you still ski?"

"Sometimes, but the real kick is a bunch of us skiers get together up there at Christmas time every year."

"Sounds like fun."

"It is."

It would be nice to just go on like this, saying nothing to upset the cart, just keep pretending that Denise was her best friend.

~

Gwen ran into Eric downtown. "I'm back in town," she chirped.

"I see. I had a bet with someone you'd be back. "How was Michigan?" he asked with a bright smile.

"Cold. But it was good to be back there for awhile, and spend the holidays with my aunt. How about you?"

"Went up to a cabin at Lake Tahoe with some old ski friends. We still meet every Christmas."

Gwen felt the blood drain away. Could this be the same gang, the same haunt that Denise had talked about? She didn't dare ask. Instead, "Do you still ski?"

"Yeah, not as much as I used to. It comes back, like riding a bike."

She felt something like jealousy or resentment pass through her. She didn't really know what it was.

"The snow was the best powder *Heavenly's* had in years."

She wasn't listening.

"Did you find out anything in Michigan that enlightened your search?"

"No, I didn't. Eric. I have an appointment. I hate to rush away like this, but I really must go."

"I understand."

She hurried off. She didn't have anywhere to go, but old demons crawled through her again, re-igniting her suspicions of Denise. If Denise knew Eric, why hadn't she said so? Had they been at the same place in Tahoe?

She decided she must becoming absolutely paranoid.

~

Every time she thought about contacting her father, Gwen got cold feet. Finally she decided there was nothing to be gained by procrastinating. She made the call.

He insisted on taking her to lunch. They met at d'Angelo's in Mill Valley.

After introductions, in which he held her hand for a long time, he asked if she'd like a drink.

She declined. She needed a clear head for whatever transpired.

"So, I finally get to meet you," he said.

She imagined he was memorizing every pore and blemish on her face. She, in turn, studied the strong structure of his face, though she could see a muscle in his jaw contract, relax, contract. At about forty-three, he was attractive in an urban sort of way—brown hair well-trimmed, suit and tie. She figured he was close to six feet tall. She couldn't see any resemblance to herself, except maybe the eyes, green, like hers.

There were a hundred questions burning to be said, but she would have to pace them carefully, and not spill all today.

"Where are you living?" he asked.

"With a friend." She wondered if he knew Denise. At this point she didn't feel inclined to let him know too much.

For awhile they engaged in safe small talk.

Then, as she was studying his face, his hair, the line of his chin, she realized she hadn't heard the last thing he'd said.

"You did know that," he finished.

"I'm sorry—know what?"

"That I wanted to marry your mother."

"No. I did not know that."

"What did you think?"

She was embarrassed. "No one knew anything about you. We assumed you were a married man."

He laughed, and she noticed the smile that seemed to emerge from his eyes.

"No. We were both very young. I was certainly single then."

"Why didn't you—get married?"

"Your mother didn't want to marry me."

"Why?"

There was a pause. Gwen took a sip of her water, waiting for him to say more.

"She was wild then—a hippie. I was too straight for her."

"Really?"

There was another pause. Then he said, "She had a whole troupe of friends. She said I didn't fit in." He was thoughtful for awhile. "We argued a lot. We had a very passionate love affair, but couldn't seem to be in alignment on much of anything else. I loved her deeply. But neither of us was willing to give in to the other."

"What were the major divisions about?"

"Politics, for one. I believe in an orderly society; she did not."

Gwen gave a muted nod.

"And religion. That was the biggest issue. I'm Catholic, and would have wanted you raised in the Church."

"Wanted, or insisted?"

He shrugged, as if to say she'd found him out.

"Was she, did she have any religion?"

He made a wry smile. "If you can call it a religion. Something pagan, not even Christian. Goddess worship. She didn't feel I respected it."

"Did you?"

"To be honest? No. And I kept pushing Catholicism on her. I was young and impetuous. Big mistake."

"Apparently, she didn't let anyone know about you—about who my father was."

He nodded thoughtfully. "She was afraid if something happened to her I'd get custody. And she definitely didn't want you raised as a Catholic."

"I only last month got my birth certificate. It was sealed in an envelope that Megan had. She didn't know what was in the envelope, only that she was to give it to me when I grew up."

"Did it name the father?"

"Yes. You."

She thought she saw a small smile of satisfaction. "Did you have a copy of my birth certificate?"

"No. And she didn't file one at the court house. She told me she did, but after she died and I checked, there was none."

Gwen winced.

"She really didn't want you to have me if anything happened, did she?"

He shook his head.

"Were you still seeing her, up until her death?"

He hesitated. "Yes."

"Did you see me when I was little?"

"In the beginning. It was always sad, never knowing when I could see you again. And then, after she vanished, I wasn't allowed to see you at all."

She wanted to ask why he'd never gotten in touch with her in all these years. But judgment told her not to overwhelm him with questions today. They were silent, until he broached the next subject.

"What were you studying at the University?"

"Journalism." She smiled self-consciously. "For someone in journalism, I made an awful mistake here—getting the paper to post an article I wrote, seeking anyone who knew anything about Patricia Harris to come forward."

"I saw it."

"And did you see the other news item which I *didn't* post?"

"About the service. Yes, I did. I came, but I was late."

She caught her breath. "So that was you. I saw someone outside."

"That was me."

"I'm sorry. We were afraid there might be gawkers. We wanted something small and intimate."

"So you changed the time."

She nodded.

"Like the three little pigs."

She laughed. "Exactly."

"I'm not the wolf, Gwen."

She lowered her head in embarrassment.

Something about that reminded her of another incident.

"One day I was walking on one of the stairways up the hill and someone was following me. I was really scared."

"That was me, Gwen."

"Really?"

"Yes, I thought I recognized you from the street and followed you up. But then you disappeared."

"Well, it's a great relief to know it was you. Whew."

"It was after you identified yourself at the council meeting. It was a clumsy and spontaneous move—"

"You didn't also grab my purse one night, did you?"

"No, that wasn't me."

"Or yell, 'you will die' at the fair and again on Halloween?"

"How could you think—"

"I'm sorry. So many creepy things have happened. I'm just trying to clear the record."

He nodded, then smiled. "I can't blame you." When they parted he walked her to her car.

"May I give you a hug?" he inquired.

She submitted to a tentative embrace. In a moment he was holding her close.

She thought she'd heard a sharp intake of breath as he released her. He pulled away suddenly, and left.

She had such a potpourri of feelings as she left him; she opted for the one that made her feel almost numb. It was overwhelming meeting him after all these years, saying things to catch up, but withholding so much of what they felt.

He hadn't said anything about seeing her again. Perhaps it was due to the emotion he'd displayed at the end of his embrace. She'd have to see what unfolded next.

~

They met again four days later in the Trident, owned by the Kingston Trio. Right on Bridgeway, it was one of the nicest restaurants in town, jutting out into the Bay.

While eating their salads, he asked, "Do you like opera?"

"I'm not sure. I've only seen two."

"I have tickets to *Falstaff* in the city, if you'd like to go."

"That sounds like fun. I know it's a comedy. When is it?"

After they'd had their meal and pleasant conversation, Gwen said, "Tell me about my mother. What was she like, what were her passions, what attracted you to her— given all your differences?"

She could hardly believe she'd said all that in one mouthful.

"Well, where shall I start? I was attracted to her endless energy, her vivacity and passion for living. Maybe opposites attract. I don't know, but it was love from the start."

"How did you meet?"

"At a fund-raiser, health care for the indigent."

"Hmm. So she was politically active."

"Oh, yes." He removed a bottle of medicine from his pocket, and took two pills. "And you were on the same side?"

He smiled. "In that matter, yes."

"I understand you offer free legal aid."

"Yes."

"I think that's commendable."

He nodded his thanks.

"Can you think of any reason someone would want to kill her?"

"Only hunches." He shifted in his chair.

She leaned forward. "You have hunches? That's more than I have."

"As I said before, she didn't let me into that group of— hippies. It was as if she were leading two lives—one with me, and one with them. I imagine someone in that crowd would have a far better idea than I of what was going on at the time."

"You would think so. But everyone acts dumb. They don't know anything."

Richard nodded. "You've met them?"

"Yes. Tell me about your hunches."

"Not much. I just have a feeling she knew something she wasn't supposed to. Something nefarious that threatened someone."

"And who was this person, do you think?"

"I don't know. One of her companions, I suppose."

"Did she share her concern with you?"

"No. As I say, it was as if she led two lives. She told me as little as possible about her other life."

"After she disappeared, did you try to find out what happened to her?"

"I did. I was finishing law school then. I was devastated and dropped out for a term— spent my time trying to trace the events that led to her disappearance."

"Go on."

"I didn't get anywhere. Not being part of that tribe of hers, no one was willing to tell me anything. Not until her remains were found did I even know her fate."

"Didn't she tell you anything about what she was up to, or who her friends were?"

He shook his head sadly. "Megan was the only one who revealed anything, and she was pretty buttoned up."

"Something bothered me about what Megan told me regarding that day," Gwen said. "She told me she'd been taking care of me the day Mom disappeared. But later Eric told me he was watching her boy, Alex, and me. I don't know why she'd lie." She paused. "Don't misunderstand me. She's been very good to me. But that disturbs me."

"Of course." He shook his head.

"Did she ever mention the artist Varda to you?"

"Briefly, why?"

"Eric said he took us to Varda's boat, the *Vallejo* that afternoon. I gather my mother had been there too."

"Yes, I believe they were friends."

She waited for him to go on, but he said no more. Was that another loose end, or did it mean something?

"Richard, do you think you could help me find some answers?"

"If I can."

If only she could trust him.

Chapter 15

Gwen had not been in San Francisco at all. It seemed strange, considering she'd been right across the bridge for so many months. Richard picked her up in downtown Sausalito, and they drove across the bridge, through the city, down Lombard, and then Van Ness. They parked two blocks away from the War Memorial Hall. As they walked along Van Ness Gwen looked across the street.

"What's that building?"

"City Hall."

"It looks like a wedding cake. It's beautiful."

Show-cased with masked lighting indeed it was an architectural pride of the city.

Gwen felt like a little girl. Inside War Memorial Hall, she took in the chandelier, the balconies, the velvet seats that curved around embracing the stage. Why had she never come to San Francisco before and tasted its delights? Had she been so single-minded as to think of nothing but her mother's murder?

Richard had brought opera glasses which he gladly shared with her. She was amused and entranced by the story and the music, and afterwards realized it was her first real absence from thoughts of the murder.

When the opera was over, he took her across the street to *Inn at the Opera* for a drink. When her first Margarita was gone, she had another. Emotions schooled to be withheld burst forward. She was on her third Margarita when she spoke up.

"Why didn't you ever come to see me? Or even write to me?"

"I didn't know where you lived, except that you'd been taken to Michigan."

"And you did nothing to find out?"

"Your aunt wanted nothing to do with me. This information was given me through Megan Denison. I went to the department of Vital Statistics. No birth certificate had been filed in court. I declared I was your father and wanted to know your whereabouts. I was told that they did not have that information."

"There must have been something you could do to find out."

"I talked to your mother's friends. No one seemed to know what had become of you. Only Megan, and as I said, she was mum."

"So you just gave up." She made a motion with her arm that caused her drink to spill.

Richard lowered his glass and dropped his eyes. "I guess you could look at it that way."

"I never heard of a father not being able to find his child." Her voice was becoming slurred. "Even after the abolition of slavery, some former slaves were able to find wives, children they'd been separated from." Tears were running down her face.

"I'm sorry I let you down. Really, very sorry." He swallowed two pills quickly. His breathing was becoming erratic.

"Like you're sorry I didn't get a Christmas present one year? I *never* got a Christmas present from you."

Richard said nothing.

"Were you ashamed of me?"

He reached across to take her hand. She jerked away.

"Of course I wasn't."

"This illegitimate child of yours? You must have been ashamed. It could ruin your career."

She was raising her voice. Others were watching.

"Gwen, please. I think it's time to go."

"Oh. OK. If Daddy says so."

Richard paid the bill and rose to leave. Gwen struggled with her coat, and he came around and tried to help her with it. She was clearly drunk.

She was wearing high heels, and it was difficult for her to navigate the walk to the car. He held her arm firmly, although she tried to jerk away. He opened the door for her, but as she just stood there, he had to practically push her in.

They drove back to Sausalito in silence.

"Where do you live?" Richard asked.

She shook her finger back and forth. "I don't tell that to anyone," she slurred. "Not even you."

"You must. I can't let you off downtown."

"Yes, you can. I'll take a cab."

"Do you remember your address?"

"Of course."

He gave in at last. He told the cab driver that she'd had too much to drink, and gave him ample money for the ride.

"Please walk her to the door, and make sure she gets inside."

~

In the morning she had an even worse hangover than when she'd been with Conan. After using the bathroom, she crawled back into bed. Memories of the previous evening flashed through her mind—first pleasant ones of being taken to the opera, the opulent surroundings and the joyful music. And then the truth of the scene she'd made in the bar came down on her like a torrent of toxicity.

Why had she done it? He'd been so nice to her. What an awful way to show her appreciation. What was she drinking, anyway? Oh, yes, Margaritas. They went down like lemonade, so delicious, so beguiling. And she'd made a total ass of herself. What had she said? She couldn't remember, except that it was very confrontational.

Why had she behaved like that, even if she were drunk? Old resentments came flooding forward. She was angry. She'd not only lost her mother as a young child, but her father remained incognito for the rest of her life. What did he say his excuse was? She couldn't recall. It couldn't have been very good.

It took deep concentration to remember how she'd gotten home. At first she was afraid she'd let him bring her home. No, that wasn't right. Where was her car? Oh, she didn't have a car; what was she thinking? She fell back into a murky fog.

It was almost noon when she awoke again. Her mouth was totally dry. She drank a whole glass of water, but it didn't take that feeling away.

Three hours later she walked downtown in the fog and cold. Fog horns sounded their frequent wailing, as she fought the wind all the way. She couldn't see Angel Island, the bridge, or anything at all in the Bay. It was like looking out at the ocean instead of the Bay.

Now that my head is clear— What shall I do about Richard?

~

Gwen debated for three days how to approach her father. She was so ashamed of her behavior. What must he think of her? She went over in her mind different ways she could apologize to him. Maybe he'd never want to see her again.

She was amazed when she heard from him. Again a letter sent to Megan's house had been forwarded to Denise's. It had been written the day after they'd been together.

He was apologizing to her! He said he didn't blame her at all for her feelings, and was glad she'd been able to express some of them, albeit not under the best conditions.

She felt the chastisement.

He went on to ask her to get in touch with him.

It would be hard to face him, after their last time. But she did want to see him. She called his office, and they set another time to get together on the weekend.

In the meantime, she missed seeing Conan. On Saturday she went to the houseboat area called Gate 6. The tide was out; the stench of dead fish accosted her nostrils. Barges and assorted vessels squatted in mud.

"Sorry about the stink. That's the downside of living here."

"I just lost my appetite."

"You get used to it."

"You have this every day?"

"Low tide, yeah. Not usually so smelly, though."

After she'd been there for half an hour Eric came by. The men talked about some huge fish that someone had caught the previous day, a subject which didn't hold much interest for her.

Finally Conan turned to her. "I heard you went back to Michigan."

"I did, for awhile."

"What made you come back?"

"My father got in touch with me."

He whistled.

"Did you guys really not know who he was?" she asked.

Conan shook his head. "We knew she was seeing somebody, but she'd never say who. That seemed to be a separate part of her life. And she wanted to keep it that way."

Eric said, "So who is he? Do we know him?"

"You might. He's Richard Thurman, the councilman."

"Oh, no," Eric laughed. "No wonder we didn't know him."

"He's anti-houseboats," Conan added.

"I know," Gwen said wryly. "I didn't choose him."

"Have you met him?" Conan asked.

"Yes. He's trying to be very nice. He claims he was unable through Megan or the courts to find out where I'd been sent to live."

"Do you believe him?"

She shrugged. "I guess so."

"So our little sleuth has found her kith and kin," Eric joked.

The men smoked a joint, while Gwen had a beer. When she was ready to leave, Eric said he'd walk out with her. They crossed the open space of land between the water and the street and he stopped.

"Go easy with Thurman, Gwen. He's hurt you a lot. Don't jump in his arms."

She nodded. What was he trying to tell her?

~

She met Richard downtown again—this time just for coffee. It was difficult to look him in the face.

She mumbled, "I behaved terribly the other night. I really did enjoy the opera, and I am very grateful for your taking me to it. I certainly didn't show my appreciation properly."

"You're forgiven. I do want you to be able to express yourself. I think you must have built up a lot of anger over the years."

She couldn't deny it. "I guess I have. It's not just you. I just don't understand the collusion to keep me in the dark so long."

"No. Nor do I. I was in the dark, too."

"Why so many secrets? I just don't get it."

She sipped her coffee. It was still too hot, and on the bitter side.

"Richard, did you ever know someone called Denise?"

He shook his head. "Why?"

"I've been working at the bank with this woman, and she'd become a good friend. She never mentioned that she knew Mom, but then Megan showed me a bunch of old photos—mostly of me as a kid, but one was of Mom with her staff at a bank, and Denise was one of them."

Richard shook his head. "I've no idea. Why don't you ask her?"

"I guess I've been afraid to."

"Why?"

"I don't know. It seems like she must have some reason for keeping it a secret and it might not be a very nice one." She tried her coffee again. Cooler, but the bitterness hadn't gone away. "And what makes it worse— I'm living with this woman."

He raised an eyebrow. "I'd ask her. No point in tormenting yourself over this."

She nodded. "I'll think about it."

The next week he invited Gwen to come for dinner at his home. It was in the hills of Sausalito and not easy to find, so he said he'd pick her up.

"And your family?" she asked.

"I'm alone at the moment. I'll tell you all about it when you come."

She'd finally given him her address and phone number. He came for her at six-thirty on Friday night, and drove up Princess Street, turned on Bulkley, then made three more turns before reaching his home.

"You can see how it could be hard to find."

"Yes. The streets wind around so much up here. Who laid them out—the deer?"

"That's possible," he grinned.

His house was not as large as some they'd passed, but it was tastefully built in an art deco style of the thirties.

"I thought you were married. Where's little wifey?"

She bit her lip, immediately regretted having said that.

"We've been separated for some time. Not divorced."

"Is that because of being Catholic, or because it wouldn't look good on your resume?"

Another mistake. Why was she being so rude? She emitted a small laugh to make light of it.

"Both, I suppose. No, we won't get divorced."

"And your boys? Where are they?"

He proffered an uneasy glance at her. "You mean the publicity photos."

"Yes."

"They're my nephews. Karen and I didn't have any children."

She was shocked. *Did this mean she was his only child?*

She thought the pictures deceitful. But she could only say, "And the dog?"

"My brother's."

A long period of silence.

Later, she couldn't remember what he'd served for dinner.

Chapter 16

It took Gwen two more days to get up the courage to speak to Denise. Then she asked her point blank one evening after supper. "Denise, you knew my mother, didn't you?"

Denise frowned and looked puzzled. "Your mother? What was her name?"

"Patricia Harris."

Denise looked confused. Gwen showed her the staff photo. "You're in this picture."

Denise studied it. "Well, so I am. Which one is your mom?"

Gwen flashed a look of disbelief. She took the picture from Denise and looked at the back again. For the others, she'd written their names, for herself, Patricia just wrote 'Me.'

Gwen pointed to her mother's face. "You didn't know this woman, standing next to you?"

"Yes, I knew that woman. Her name was Pat Austin."

"You're kidding."

Denise shook her head. "Honest."

Austin. That was her grandmother's maiden name.

"I can hardly believe it. Why would she use an assumed name?"

Denise shrugged.

"How well did you know her?"

"We were friendly at work, but that's as far as it went. I don't think we ever went out together."

"Well, I guess that solves one mystery and creates another."

Denise rose to clear the dishes, and Gwen followed suit.

"Did you know my mom died—I mean before I came?"

"I knew Pat disappeared." She thought a minute. "Those were *her* bones?"

"Yes."

"Oh, my God. I never put it together."

"How could you, if she was using a different name?"

"Do you know what happened to her?"

"Only that she was apparently pushed off the cliff on the way back from Stinson Beach. That's really what I'm looking into—who could have done such a thing."

"You're sure it was murder?"

Gwen hesitated. "No. But it looks that way. I have to know."

"So finding your father was secondary?"

"I guess so. Both important."

"I had no idea."

Gwen buried her face in her hands. "I'm so sorry, Denise. For awhile I thought you were keeping some secret from me. I'd gotten so I didn't trust anyone."

Denise put her hand on Gwen's arm. "That's understandable."

"I just didn't know who to trust. I thought Conan drugged me and stole my diary. I even wondered if Megan pushed my mom off the cliff."

Then they both started to laugh. Not sure why, but the tension had dissipated, and there was a sense of relief, if only temporary.

~

Gwen decided it was time to visit Megan again. She hadn't seen her for several weeks. She parked a block away, as there was nothing closer. As she approached the porch she could hear arguing inside. It was January, but quite warm, and the windows were open.

She recognized the voices—Megan and Conan.

She stood still and listened.

"I don't think that's any of your business, Conan."

"Why did you wait so long to give her that envelope?"

"What do you care?"

"Maybe she'd have found him sooner, been satisfied and gone home," Conan said."

"Why do you want her to go home?"

"She's not happy here. And she could have at least found out who her dad was a whole lot sooner if—"

"I didn't know what was in that envelope." Megan's voice was escalating.

What gave Conan the right to confront Megan about Gwen's affairs?

Too many questions. She went down to the waterfront and found Eric. She told him what she'd just overheard.

"Let's go outside," he said.

A newbie musician was trying to learn the guitar, beginning the first few bars of a song over and over. A few feet away a woman was washing herself in the outdoor communal shower in view of God and everyone. The smell of marijuana and other drugs permeated the air. A man nearby snorted up a line of coke. *I could get high just hanging around here,* she thought.

"Do you know anything about this?"

"Sounds like a family fight," he said.

"Family?"

"Brother and sister."

"Megan and Conan are brother and sister?"

"You didn't know?"

"No. Why didn't anyone tell me?"

Eric shrugged. "Thought you knew, I guess."

"I remember a lot from when I was a child here. I barely remember him."

"He was in love with your mother, you know."

"So you told me."

"But she wasn't in love with him."

Gwen chewed on the fact that Megan and Conan were siblings. More surprises. Then she asked Eric what he thought the argument meant.

"From what you said, it sounds like he believed you should have been given that envelope a lot sooner."

"Yeah, but that part about me going home. It sounded like he wanted to get rid of me."

"Or just solve the question for who your dad was sooner. So you *could* go home."

Gwen nodded. She left Eric soon after that. There was just too much to think about.

~

Winter rains had deluged the Bay Area for two weeks. Finally, it cleared up in March. Flowering trees came into bloom, some as early as February.

"Have you seen any of Marin's waterfalls?" Richard asked.

"No, I haven't."

"The rain we've had should make them pretty impressive now."

They had breakfast at the Depot, a café at the hub of Mill Valley. Then driving out Throckmorton, they turned on a side street, and drove through a grove of old redwoods.

"This is amazing," Gwen said. "These two towns—Sausalito and Mill Valley, right next to each other, and so very different. Sausalito—all about water. Then you drive a couple of miles and you're here—in a redwood forest, with a mountain for a backdrop. Fantastic."

Richard smiled at her. "Marin's a wonder, alright."

He knew where he was going, and pulled into a small parking spot. They walked a hundred yards back into the woods, past a gurgling stream and there it was—a thundering waterfall, cascading over a promontory, and down into the creek beside them. They crossed a little wooden bridge to get a better view.

"Wow. Are there more like this?" she wondered.

"All over Marin. You just need to hike in the hills—behind houses, in neighborhoods.

"It's beautiful."

They stood in silence for several minutes, listening to the explosion of water, and the play of sunlight on the cascade of the falls.

"Did you and mother come here?"

"How did you know?"

"I didn't. Just thought of it."

"We liked hiking the hills of Mill Valley."

"And none of her hippie friends saw you," she smiled up at him.

"That's right."

"Where were you living then?"

"A shared apartment in the city, with another law student."

"How did you—"

"Get privacy?"

"Yes."

"We spent a lot of time outdoors."

Gwen laughed. "I thought you were too straight for that."

"We didn't have a lot of choice. I didn't have any money. Sometimes when my roommate was away, we grabbed a few hours, even a weekend occasionally."

"Actually, it sounds romantic—making love outdoors. In tune with nature and all that."

He pointed to the cliff above the waterfall.

"I think you were conceived up there."

"Really?"

"Really."

What an intimate thing for him to tell her. She smiled. She'd have to hike up there some day.

~

She hadn't seen Varda in many months. He'd said she was welcome anytime, so Gwen decided to take him up on it. She knew he was having a dinner party Saturday night, and decided she'd invite herself.

"May I come?"

"Of course, dear one."

Varda was a wonderful cook and again prepared some Greek or Turkish dish with spices Gwen was sure she'd never tasted before. It was a small affair compared to the big party she'd gone to before. There were about twenty people, and Gwen didn't know any of them. She talked with an older man on her left, and a younger, gorgeous woman on her right. It seemed Varda knew everyone. It was a very artsy group— a couple of poets, some painters, a local philosopher, and two nuns. Even the nuns were poets.

When he mentioned they'd be coming, Gwen showed her surprise.

"I like an eclectic group," he said.

This time she had more opportunity to study his work, which was shamelessly posted everywhere. She didn't think it was the sort of art she'd buy for herself, if indeed she could afford any, but it had a certain original charm that she admired.

When she had a chance to speak to him she asked, "Do you sell much of your work?"

"Goodness, yes. Several galleries in the city, Sonoma, Napa—all over the Bay Area. I don't like to ship them—too much trouble to package them correctly. And some have gotten damaged in the past."

"How do you get so many pieces done, if you're running around to the galleries?"

"Oh, I have help with the deliveries."

"I have a friend who has one of your pieces— Conan Galbraith. You know him?"

A dark shadow crossed his brow. A woman with too much make-up and too much to drink tapped him on the shoulder. He was soon engaged in conversation with other guests.

What was that about? She felt hurt that their pleasant chat was cut off so abruptly. Then she remembered that Eric had told her that Conan and Varda had had a falling out. Oh, why had she put her foot in her mouth?

She left the dinner party wondering what the rift had been about. And how long ago had it happened?

~

Megan was making chili. It was a cold day—cold for California, anyway. Her fresh, hot cornbread was already made.

"Help yourself," Megan said. "The chili will be ready soon."

"Thanks, I'm starved."

"Chad will be watching TV all afternoon—football. So we can have girl talk."

"I thought the games were over."

"He records the ones he misses, and watches them later, or again."

After the chili was ready and eaten Gwen told Megan how good it was. Then she said what was really on her mind. "I just found out you and Conan are siblings."

Megan looked a little startled, but then she said, "Oh, I thought you knew."

Gwen shook her head. It could have been an innocent oversight.

"I've been looking out for that little brother of mine for years."

"It must be nice to have a brother, though."

Megan looked compassionately at Gwen. "Yeah, tough to be an only child. But siblings aren't all sweetness and light."

"What do you mean?"

"Oh, I don't know. Look, do you need any more of the stuff you left here?"

Megan rose to take the dishes to the sink. Gwen followed to help her. "No, not now. Is it in your way?"

"Not at all. How are you and your dad getting along?"

"Really well, at the moment. He knows he can't make up all those years, but he's trying."

"Bring him round some day, will you? I'd love to meet the mystery man."

Gwen rinsed the dishes, then filled the sink with water. Megan had no dishwasher.

"I don't know if he'll come. He thinks you withheld information that could have helped him."

"Yup, I did. He must know I was in touch with your aunt."

"Even though you told him all communication was through a third party."

Megan nodded. Gwen changed the subject.

"Guess what we did last week."

"Tell."

"We went to the waterfalls where I was conceived."

"You what!"

"I don't know why, but he wanted to let me know that."

"Don't you think that's weird?"

"Yeah, in a way. But he's trying to be really nice, even though I got drunk in the city and let him know what a jerk he was not to locate me."

Gwen let the soap bubbles wash over her hands. She watched them break slowly. It seemed that each bubble that broke was a day lost in her childhood.

Megan said, "Patricia made that almost impossible. She never filed the birth certificate, so he had no proof of paternity. And nobody could vouch for him."

"She must have been absolutely determined that he not get hold of me and turn me into a good little Catholic."

"Your mother was adamant that you not be raised Catholic."

"Even if it meant my having no parent."

Megan squeezed Gwen's hand.

"Of course she didn't know she was going to die," Gwen added.

"But she did."

Gwen turned a startled face to Megan. "Knew what?"

"Knew she was going to die. She had cancer, Gwen."

"Cancer? You never told me."

"I didn't think you needed any more sad and ugly things to deal with right now."

"She was my mother. I had a right to know."

"I'd have told you at some point. I *am* telling you."

"What kind of cancer? Was it incurable?"

"Breast cancer. She had treatments. There was hope for awhile. And she was in remission, but her prognosis that last year wasn't good."

"Oh, my God! So she'd have died anyway."

"Probably. That's why she gave me the envelope for you."

"What was she doing on a bike?"

"She never gave up. She had her good days. As I said, she was in remission."

They were quiet. When the dishes were done Gwen walked back to her old bedroom where she could be alone. For a few minutes numbness swept over her and she felt almost nothing. Then a deep stab of pain coursed through her for the mother she'd lost, for the suffering her mother had endured, and for all the years they hadn't had together.

Chapter 17

She enjoyed Eric's company. If they'd been closer in age, she might even have fallen for him. He looked the quintessential sailor of another day with his beard, pipe and sailor's cap. She wondered why he'd never married.

They talked about fate of the houseboat community. They went to council meetings together.

Since she now knew where her father stood on the subject, she tried to keep her mouth shut on this subject when they were together. Although she was developing some feelings for him, she felt disconnected when it came to their differing views on the waterfront community. How could he be so heartless?

"So that's your dad," Eric said.

"Yeah."

"Why don't you get him to come down and see just how industrious we are?" Eric tried to put a note of joviality into this question.

"I could try," she conceded. "Don't hold your breath."

~

The next time she and Richard were together, they climbed the Excelsior steps from Bridgeway up the steep hill. She felt safe this time since she was with her father. She remembered with irony that he'd been here the time she was so frightened, too.

"Richard, I know your views on the waterfront community," she started.

"And I know yours."

"I was wondering if you'd go with me there. I know some of those people. They work really hard. I think you might change your mind if you could meet them."

"Gwen, I'm sure some of them are very nice. But do you realize there is no sanitation plan there? They loop electric wires from one boat to another. They take free water from the city in five gallon jugs, pay no taxes, no utility bills."

Gwen swallowed, not having realized all this.

"Please go there with me for a visit."

"That area is an eyesore."

"Please?" she begged.

He sighed. "Alright. But don't expect me to change my mind."

She told Eric he would come.

"Then, let's have a barbeque for him."

"I doubt if he'd like the publicity."

It was arranged that he'd come on the next Sunday afternoon.

A friend of Eric's made her own version of paella. Ribs were being slowly cooked on the grill.

The word had gotten out that a councilman was coming to visit. Although skeptical, everyone's hopes were raised. At least this guy was willing to have a look. An attempt was even made to clean up the place, but a welter of objects bedecked the area, from rusty oil drums to leaky, worn water hoses. There was far too much disorder to make it ship-shape in such a short time.

Eric greeted them when they arrived, and introduced him to several people. Some of the residents were friendly; some were reserved or stayed away. The more assertive ones engaged him in political conversation. No one was rude.

Richard greeted everyone warmly, and listened attentively to what they had to say. When they asked his opinion, he deferred, saying he was only here to listen and observe. Like any good politician, he had lots of smiles to give away. He even held someone's baby.

Eric led him around, and showed him some improvements that had been made. A photographer snapped pictures.

Richard mumbled to Gwen that he'd have preferred a more discreet visit.

When it was time to eat he said the ribs were the best he'd ever had, and Gwen believed him. They were wonderful.

Still March, it began to get very chilly as the sun fell below the western hills. Gwen and Richard thanked their hosts and bid them good-night.

On the drive home, Gwen gave her father a big hug.

"Thanks, Richard. You were great."

Richard was quiet and thoughtful.

"Your friends were very gracious."

"I'm glad you liked them."

She waited to see if he'd say more. When he didn't, she said, "So what did you think—about their situation?"

"I'll have to mull things over. I'd rather not make any statement now."

"You sound like you're talking to the press."

He smiled and took her hand.

Eric and Gwen were eager to hear what he had to say at the next council meeting. On Wednesday they met at City Hall.

When the subject was brought up, Richard announced that he'd had the privilege of being invited to the waterfront community, and they had hosted him in grand style.

Eric and Gwen smiled at each other.

"I was really impressed with the warmth of the community and their hospitality. The aroma of slow-cooking ribs mingled with that of marijuana. The ribs were excellent. I didn't partake of the other substances. Want good ribs?" he joked. "Get invited to the waterfront community."

There was polite laughter. Then Richard got serious.

"Regretfully, I cannot change my opinion about the living conditions. They are abysmal." He repeated what he'd said to Gwen. "Unless and until proper sanitation, electric connections are brought up to code, and a host of other issues are addressed, I maintain that this part of our great city should be dismantled and cleaned up."

Gwen and Eric exchanged looks of defeat.

The hill people exchanged looks of victory, and coughed out great cheers.

Not surprising, the press was there, and the next day the papers were carrying pictures of Richard at the waterfront, along with his statements at the council meeting.

Sally Stanford had stood up to him, and her remarks were included, but when she spoke there were many boos.

Eric and Gwen were irate, as were others.

"The wild fires will continue for awhile. But eventually there will be outright war," Eric stated.

"*War?*"

"Houseboat wars with the 'authorities'."

"How could that happen?"

"We won't leave voluntarily. And they aren't going to let things stay as they are forever."

~

Gwen had been at Richard's house before. Now, if she could only find it.

She studied the map she'd gotten at the Visitors' Center. She decided to walk, rather than try to bike these high ascents. The roads up the hills were a warren of twisting, turning lanes with frequent dead ends and one-ways.

She had no problem with the first two turns, but realized she'd made a mistake after the third. She was glad she'd brought her flashlight. February days were short. The streets were poorly lit, and often only wide enough for one car, with ditches of a foot or more deep. In lieu of shoulders, she thought wryly.

She came to a fork. Which way? She went to the right and soon came to a dead end.

Oh, my God, I should have at least come in the daylight. The howl of wind against dead branches was scary. A skunk followed her. She must do nothing to alarm him.

After another half hour of frustrating wrong turns, she finally discovered Richard's street, but it was not the end of her tribulations. A car came toward her. Realizing she was wearing dark clothing and might not be seen, she stepped to the edge of the road and her foot dropped six inches into a muddy crevice. Ten minutes later, with a rush of adrenaline she arrived at Richard's unannounced.

"What a surprise," he said, gesturing her in.

"I feel betrayed," she said standing just inside on the polished slate.

"I told you it was unlikely I'd change my opinion."

"My friends and others were so nice to you—"

"Yes, they were. That doesn't change the fact that their living conditions are worse than some refugee camps."

"They're happy. Why can't you live and let live?"

"Because they're part of Sausalito, and we're carrying them."

"What do you mean?"

"Who pays for their electricity, their water? Do they pay their share of taxes? Gwen, be realistic."

"No, I won't listen to you." She stormed out, realizing she'd left a small mud puddle in his entrance. Too bad. Well, he'd just have to clean it up.

"Gwen, Gwen! Don't leave like this!"

She felt a hand grip her arm like a vice.

"Let me go!"

"You can't leave like this."

Even in the poor light, she could see the fire in his eyes. She was frightened.

"Richard you're hurting me!"

Finally, she jerked away from him.

She looked back, but could see no one.

She stumbled her way toward home. The lights below from Bridgeway provided a guide for her, as she made her descent. But it had started to rain. She hadn't thought to bring an umbrella. As the water fell forcefully from the sky, she was drenched with it.

When she did reach home, still shaking, she took a hot shower, climbed under the covers feeling stupid, but in a strange sense avenged.

Chapter 18

In the days to come, she helped Sally Stanford's campaign, distributing brochures and knocking on doors, engaging people in discussion. She was determined to defeat Richard's platform.

Returning home exhausted after a day's work at the bank and an additional two hours of campaigning, she wondered how much of her grit was about her political stance, and how much had to do with her father. Was she still resentful that he'd never managed to find her as a child? Still, she forged ahead—for Sally, she told herself, and the things they both believed in.

~

Varda was having an opening of a new exhibit in a local gallery. Gwen went, hoping to receive a friendlier smile than the dark look he'd given her at the end of their last encounter when she'd asked about Conan.

The gallery was full of people—both from the hill and lower town. There were even some boat people there.

Most were holding glasses of wine. The pleasant bouquet of eastern food again tantalized her senses. She discovered the bite-sized delicacies, still warm from an oven located on the premises, and devoured three of them. Filled with meat, vegetables and spices, they went down easily with the wine. Someone adorned in Greek costume was offering them along with some Greek words no one understood, but for which everyone smiled graciously.

Her appetite satisfied, she vied with others to see the works of art.

There were so many people there; it was difficult to appraise them without dodging heads. Still, she reveled in the sights.

"You like?"

She turned suddenly to see Varda.

"The food or the art?" she quipped.

"Both."

"I like them both. You are very talented," she said.

"I know," he replied.

They laughed.

"Can I get you more wine, dear Gwen?"

She was surprised he remembered her name.

"Thank you."

He raised his hand and snapped his fingers in the direction of a man circulating with a tray of drinks.

When her glass had been refilled, he said, "You must come and see my permanent collection on the Vallejo."

"I have seen it."

"Oh, but there were so many people, so much confusion then."

"Perhaps," she said.

"Tomorrow," he pressed.

She was curious, not only about the man and his work, but why he had darkened at the mention of Conan in their previous encounter?

"You will come for lunch. Just the two of us. And I will surprise you with a small feast."

"Oh, no. That isn't necessary at all. A sandwich will do."

"A sandwich," he scoffed. "Oh, you Americans. In a sandwich there is no sensuous blend of flavors."

She laughed. "I suppose not."

"All of the senses must be stimulated, nursed to their fullest," he went on. "Only then can we appreciate the gift of the gods."

She smiled as his eyes sparkled in the delight of his own words.

The next day she had mixed feelings about going to see this man. She thought he'd been blatantly sexual the previous evening. And he'd made it clear it was just to be the two of them. Puzzling—how did he attract so many women? No young goat, he was overweight and pompous. What was his magnet?

She wanted to find out. She agreed to go.

He had indeed prepared a small feast. He was showing off his cooking skills as a toreador might show off his agility and swordsmanship. He had prepared a five course meal. Although she protested, he forged ahead, until she'd eaten so much, her stomach complained.

She knew he had many friends—many female friends. No wonder, if he treated each like a queen.

When they'd finished eating, he served very strong coffee. She didn't want to hurt his feelings, but she just couldn't get it down.

"It's alright, dear Gwen. You will get used to it."

A chill ran down her back. He'd implied that she'd be coming back.

She did come back. Two days later she was there again.

"I've watered down the coffee for you. But you will learn to drink it full strength."

When they'd finished, he said, "Come. Let me show you something you haven't seen."

She didn't know what was so compelling about him. He was twice her age, if not more, but seemed to exude an easy authority, and she felt drawn to him in a strange way. What was she letting herself in for?

He led her through a narrow hall and into a small room. More art work was displayed on the walls.

"Is this yours?"

"No, none of it. This is the work of others whom I admire. Some are not great artists, but have been friends of mine."

She walked slowly around, noting the artist's name, where legible, on each piece. Some she admired. Some she thought were the work of deranged madmen.

Suddenly she stopped, when she saw in the corner of a delicate water color, "P. Harris."

Varda came up behind her and put his hands on her shoulders. She almost collapsed in his arms.

"Your mother."

"Did you know her?"

"Of course. She was the brightest star in my universe."

As she could no longer stand, Gwen sat down on the little sofa.

"I didn't know. Did you know when you first met me that I—?"

"I suspected. I asked around."

"Did you know what happened to her?"

"Yes. But not the details."

"I'm trying to work that out."

He nodded.

"How well did you know her?"

"Not in your biblical sense, though not for lack of trying. She was in love with someone else. I don't know who." He stroked his chin. "Somehow she was able to resist my charms." He paused, as if trying to figure out how that could be.

"Patricia had such vivacity. Such courage. She was a most lovely woman. Yes, we became very good friends."

She had misjudged his interest in her. She was glad for that.

Gwen felt her eyes tear up, but she would not let them overflow.

"What do you mean 'courage'?"

"You knew she had cancer?"

"Yes, I only just found out."

"She went through several chemo rounds. They'd tell her it was cleared up, and then it would come back. She got terribly sick from the treatments, but she kept going. She wouldn't give up. She had you. She said she had to live for you."

The tears would not be held back. First they came silently. Then they were accompanied by great sobs. Varda sat beside her and held her in his arms.

"Let the tears come, my dear."

And she did.

Chapter 19

G wen was not only fiercely caught up in Sally's campaign, but would have nothing to do with her father. She wrote her own letters to the editor, and encouraged her waterfront friends to do the same. She offered to type them up, correct grammar and spelling, if need be. Denise had a typewriter. Someday there'd be personal computers, but they were not in the hands of many laymen yet.

On weekends, if she wasn't out knocking on doors, she was working in the printing office, getting out more brochures.

"Do you think this flyer effectively states my platform?" Sally asked her one day.

"I do, as I understand it. You feel public facilities should be offered near the shops and near the houseboat community. And you feel that that community should be supported, not shunned. They are part of what makes historic Sausalito interesting. It gives us character."

"That's about it, Honey. You tell 'em."

Although Denise was on her side, she was caught up in her own goal, taking classes to further her career.

Gwen went out in all weather. She often got very wet, working "Hurricane Gulch" on the south end of town; the winds came through Golden Gate and over the hill from the ocean with a vengeance. She ducked her head into the gusts and forged ahead. After two weeks of this, she knew she was getting sick. "Just a cold," she thought, and plunged ahead. But by Friday, she had a fever. The bank was sending Denise to a seminar for the weekend.

"I wish I could stay and take care of you," her friend said.

"It's OK. I'm not helpless."

Within an hour of Denise's departure the doorbell rang. Gwen hesitated. She really didn't want any visitors or religious proselytizers, but it might be something important. She stumbled to the door. Opening it, she faced Richard.

"No, no. You shouldn't be here."

"But I am here."

"Please leave."

"No, I have to take care of my little girl."

"I'm not your little girl."

He marched her back to bed. "Stay in bed."

Her face was so hot he got her a cold cloth for her forehead. He brought a bowl of ice water and kept changing the cloths as they warmed up.

"Have you had anything to eat?"

"I'm not hungry."

"You must have something to keep up your strength."

He found some orange juice in the fridge and got her to drink part of it.

"We can't let you get dehydrated. You need several glasses of liquid a day."

"Seems l've heard that before."

"More important than ever when you're sick."

"How did you know?"

"Your roommate called me."

Thanks a lot, Denise. I don't want to see him!

"How have you become so rundown? What have you been up to?"

"Campaigning,"

"Neither rain nor snow?"

"Something like that."

Her throat was so sore she could hardly swallow.

He came back with salt water. "Gargle this."

She turned away, but he insisted.

"If you don't get better, I'm calling the doctor tomorrow."

"And if I'm not better by the end of the week you'll call the priest for last unction."

"None of that now. But you've got to take care of yourself."

"Why are you doing this for me?" She spoke with effort. "Aren't you afraid you'll make me well, and I'll get out there and beat the pants off you? Shouldn't you be trying to keep me sick so I'd be no threat to you?" There was a sardonic smile on her lips.

"Yeah, you're right. Still, my highest priority is getting you well. Taking care of my girl."

"I'm not yours, Richard."

She saw him open his mouth to speak, then close it.

"I think I'd like a piece of toast," she said more to dispel the talk of possession, than from hunger.

In a few minutes he was back.

"Here's hot tea to go with it. Toast and hot tea. Would you like some milk toast?"

"What's that?"

"An old remedy for sore throats. Pour hot milk over toast, add a pat of butter—makes it soft—"

"Soggy," Gwen laughed, but it hurt her throat and she started coughing.

"No thanks." But she dipped her toast in her tea until it was soggy.

After an hour she was nodding off.

"I'm going to leave. Is there anything you need before I do?"

"Sleep," she murmured. "Just sleep."

"I'll look in on you later. He left. Gwen drifted off to sleep, dreaming about someone taking care of her, making sure there was nothing to frighten her, ever.

Richard came back around six o'clock and insisted on feeding her.

"I brought some chicken soup. It's still hot, at least warm."

She didn't resist. The warm liquid felt soothing on her throat, and warm all the way down.

"You really don't need to do this. I've managed alone when I was sick before."

"I'm sure you're very capable," he said.'

They were silent for awhile. When she spilled a bit of soup on her pajamas, he got a towel to help clean it up.

Finally, she said, "You're being very kind, but it's not going to change my views about the waterfront."

"I know that. But we don't have to be enemies because we don't agree on all issues. Do we?"

Her mouth twisted. "I wonder what we really have in common. Not politics. Not religion."

"How about the arts? Do you like theatre, music and art?"

"Yes."

"We can do those things together."

She gave a noncommittal motion of her head.

~

Varda had been on her mind before and since her illness. She had given him her phone number, and he called her.

She knew he could hear the stuffiness and her deep bronchial cough when she talked.

"My dear, what can I do for you?"

"Nothing. I'll be fine in a few days. I don't want to see anyone."

The next day there was a package for her. She opened it and found a book of poems by Rumi. A note was enclosed which said, "For good health all the senses must be nourished. Varda."

So she made a feast out of reading the Persian's fine poetry. He couldn't have chosen a better gift. It took her mind off her sickness, off the campaign and off her mother's demise.

She had never paid much attention to poetry before, but found she could relish some of the phrases, the philosophy and the beauty.

"Out beyond ideas of wrongdoing and rightdoing there is a field. I'll meet you there." Rumi.

~

In another week she was well enough to leave the apartment. Varda had asked her to come over as soon as she felt well enough.

"No big meals. Nothing, really," she'd insisted.

"Agreed."

He'd prepared some sort of strange tea she'd never tasted before. It was thick and sort of sweet with a cinnamon taste. Something else too, which she couldn't identify.

"You must drink all of it, my little bird."

"Why do you call me that?"

"I want to take care of you."

"What are you talking about?"

"I am your godfather."

"What! No, I don't have a godfather."

"Not before. But now you do. I appointed myself your godfather." He leaned back, proudly, stretching both arms out against the back of his sofa, a big grin on his face.

"When?"

"Just now."

She laughed. "You are outrageous."

He was serious. "Not really. Your mother, when she knew she was dying, asked that I take an interest in your welfare. I am afraid I've been very remiss in carrying out her orders."

She shook her head in astonishment. "First I have no father. Now I have two."

"Two is good," he said.

"You knew my father and I have … become acquainted."

"Yes. And is that going well?"

"Mixed. He's trying. But we're on opposite sides politically."

"Ah, he's *hill people*. I did hear from fellow Water Rats that he'd visited our fine community."

"Yes, and they treated him very well."

"A pity a man has to shove his small philosophy in a shoebox and keep the lid on tightly. Where is the adventure in that?"

Gwen offered a weak laugh. "May I ask you something?"

"Of course."

"When we were talking the night of your party, I mentioned Conan Galbraith. You frowned. Can you tell me why?"

Varda pursed his lips, ran his hand through his hair, and looked out the window.

Finally, he said, "He is a friend of yours?"

"Yes."

"He was a friend of mine, too, a student. He was in a class I was teaching here on the Vallejo. A private class for half a dozen students. Your mother was in it, too. That's how I got to know her."

"When was this?"

"Oh, it must have been fifteen years ago."

"Anyway, I needed someone to wrap and deliver my work to galleries I had consignment arrangements with. He was glad for the work. I was glad to have that task off my hands. For two years he did this. He kept very good track of the inventory, the receipts, payments from the galleries. I trusted him completely."

Gwen listened to every word. "And then?"

"The day came when I could no longer do so."

"What do you mean? Did he cheat you on payments for paintings that had sold?"

"No, not that." He rubbed his face. "I don't want to go further into it now. Nothing that would turn someone into a murderer. It has no bearing on your mother's fate."

"Tell me anyway."

He shook his head. "The crime I'm thinking of—I have no idea if Patricia or anyone else found out about it. In any case, as I said, it wouldn't be worth killing for."

"Please?"

He shook his head firmly. "No. It would be gossip. Evil gossip. I can't do that. If you find out more on your end that connects the two, I might be able to collaborate then. Not now."

Gwen sat up straight in frustration. "How will I ever find out anything if no one tells me anything?"

Varda gave her a sympathetic smile.

"Now, my dear, will you dine with me? Nothing fancy—just some lentil soup."

"If you insist."

"I do."

The soup smelled heavenly, but like so many Eastern foods, she found it too spicy for her palette.

She waved her hand in front of her open mouth.

"I'll get you some water."

He brought back water and some Greek bread. With the help of these supplements she was able to finish her bowl of soup.

Chapter 20

She hadn't been with Louis for weeks. Suddenly he called her at Denise's and asked to see her.

"I'd like that," she said. "Where would you like to go?"

It was an unusually warm and sunny day for March. At least Gwen thought so, though perhaps the residents were used to this early spring. She had to admit that this part of California was breathtaking and made it a very desirable place to live.

They met at the "Elephant" Park downtown.

"Good to see you again, Gwen." He gave her a hug.

"Thanks. You too."

They were close to the ferry.

"What do you say to a ferry ride to the city?"

"That sounds like fun. What will we do there?"

"Walk around. See stuff you probably haven't seen."

They caught the next ferry, passing San Quentin not long after leaving the dock.

"Seems like the best piece of real estate on the Bay is reserved for prisoners," Louis remarked.

Gwen agreed it was one of the best.

Not far out she caught site of Varda's sailboat. It had an unmatched presence on the water. Glorious, with the wind behind her, the colorful spinnaker was ballooned out fully over the bow. Gwen longed to sail on it.

Before long they were disembarking at the Ferry Building.

"We could walk up the street to Moma, if you like. That's the Museum of Modern Arts."

"Fine."

Gwen enjoyed some of the art, couldn't understand a lot of it, and laughed at the decorated toilets.

"This is art?"

"Whatever cooks your goose."

When they'd had enough of the museum they stopped for a meal at a little restaurant on Fourth Street.

On the way back to the ferry they were drawn to jazz music inside a small bar.

"Want to go in?" he asked.

"Sure."

They heard something like Dave Brubeck. It wasn't Brubeck, but at least it was his music. The slow jazz put them in a romantic mood, and soon Louis was holding her hand.

He told her he was thirty years old, divorced from a sweet girl who didn't like sex, didn't have any kids, was tired of the noose-and-jacket society, dropped out and joined the water rats.

"So you've given up selling insurance? What are you doing now?"

"Trying to find myself, I guess. Hanging around the docks. Helping out. But that isn't a future."

"What does a future look like to you?"

"I don't know."

Maybe he was a bit lost, but Gwen knew he was very intelligent, the knowledge he revealed talking about art, and later science.

When he brought up the black hole, she said, "I really don't understand that concept."

He squeezed her hand. "We'll discuss it someday."

When she'd first met him, she thought she was only interested because he might be able to provide her some clues about her mother. That didn't pan out, but she realized now she was attracted to him.

He wasn't the tallest man she'd ever dated—a good three inches shorter than Brad. Damn, she wished she'd stop comparing. Louis had beautiful blue eyes, highlighted by very thick brown eyebrows. His hair was dark brown, and the contrast with his blue eyes was stunning.

On the return ferry ride, they walked out on the deck and realized they were the only ones there. He put his arm around her, and for several moments they just looked at the moon play on the water, and watch the wake churn up the water, creating a black and white motion picture in the night.

When he drew her into his arms to kiss her, he met with no resistance. His lips were soft and full, and so very sensuous. She was reminded of what Varda had said—one must taste all the senses to experience the gifts of the gods. She was enjoying this one. His hand slid down her back and she felt it arch in response.

Another couple had come out on the deck, but neither of them cared at this point. Besides they were in the dark, except for the moon.

When they returned to Marin, Louis wanted to go home with her, but she felt things might be moving too fast. Instead she invited him to breakfast in the morning.

"You can meet my roommate," she warned him.

They kissed good-night under the ever-watchful elephants and reluctantly parted.

~

At eight a.m. Gwen hurried out to buy fresh croissants. When she returned Denise was just getting up.

"We're having company for breakfast," she said.

"Who?"

She made coffee as she relayed the short history of her friendship with Louis.

"Wow," Denise said. "Think anything will come of it?"

"Oh, I don't want to think past today—really."

Denise raised her eyebrows.

"I've made the mistake of fantasizing about what's around the corner a couple of times before. Even listening to how my first name sounded with his last name. You ever do that?"

Denise smiled. "Yup."

The doorbell rang.

"I can disappear."

"No, don't. I want you to meet him."

Gwen sailed to the door and let Louis in. He held out a bag of melon and strawberries.

"I passed a fruit stand on the way."

She thanked him and introduced him to Denise.

She cut up the melon he'd brought, added a few strawberries, and served it with the croissants and coffee.

Denise engaged him in conversation about insurance, saying she really needed to get health insurance at least.

Gwen managed to turn the conversation to the art they'd seen the day before, and when it came to the toilets, Denise wanted a full description.

"While we're eating?" Gwen asked.

"Well, they were clean, weren't they?"

They all started laughing.

When they'd finished eating, Louis suggested a walk along Bridgeway on her end of town.

They strolled hand in hand down to scenic walk along the water. When they were downtown by the shops Louis ducked into one of the almost hidden stairways, pulling her after him.

He kissed her hard and long. When he finally took a breath he said, "I've been wanting to do this all morning."

"Me too," she admitted.

After a long walk, and a few more partially hidden embraces, they headed back. Denise was out; she'd left a note on the counter. "Won't be back until evening. Have fun, you two."

Louis read the note over Gwen's shoulder. They turned to each other and laughed. They started on the sofa, but hormones and passion led to further exploration in the bedroom. However, Gwen wasn't ready for 'going all the way', as she called it, so after a stimulating, but frustrating hour for both of them, she climbed out of bed.

"Not ready, she explained.

"I can wait. I think."

When he left, she realized she knew very little about him. Well, that would come with time. She wasn't going to get serious with anyone, anyway.

CHapter 21

The next time she was with Megan, Gwen wanted to know more about the goddess circle, and if her mother had been part of it.

"No, she wasn't. It was formed after she was gone. You've met several—my husband, Alex, Eric, Conan and me."

"Men in this circle?"

"Yes. You'd be surprised how many men worship the goddess around the world. It doesn't mean they've lost their masculinity or given up authority in all arenas. But, like us, they're looking for some balance."

Gwen nodded.

"Have you ever been involved with anything of the sort?"

"I've read a few books. Once I went to a wiccan circle."

"A coven! You surprise me."

"I never believed all witches were wicked. The same energy that creates evil can create good. It's all in your intention. When you gather together and create that energy you can send it anywhere. That night we sent it up to help release Hungary from the claws of Communism."

"That is wonderful."

"I really did feel something when we raised the cone of energy."

"Good for you."

"But all the ancient spells about wart of toad and eye of snake—I didn't believe that."

"But it must have helped create the cone."

"Only because that's what they believed. I think if we'd all believed we had to be naked, that would have worked too."

"Or had to have two shots of whiskey first."

"Exactly!"

Megan hesitated. "Would you like to join our circle, Gwen?"

"Oh, goodness. I don't know. I can't say I believe in goddesses."

"That's OK. We're really kind of a study group. Right now we're learning about Mary Magdalene. We believe she was probably a primary disciple of Jesus."

"Interesting. Let me think about it."

"Of course. Our next meeting is Friday evening, if you want to join us."

It was Sunday. That gave her almost a week to decide.

~

Gwen was frustrated that she still hadn't gotten any answer to why her mother was murdered. She decided the only person who seemed to know anything about Patricia Harris was Varda.

She called to ask when it would be convenient for her to come over.

"You needn't cook a thing."

"Then what kind of host would I be?"

"I don't want you to be a host—just a friend."

Nevertheless when she arrived she could smell the food. She refused to eat. So they sat on soft cushions in one of the salons.

"Varda, I'm still trying to find the reason someone would want to kill Mom. Can you help me?"

"How?"

"I don't know. But you knew her well."

Varda rubbed his face with his hand. He squinted. Gwen didn't know if he was trying to recall something, or deciding how to tell her he didn't have any ideas.

"My father suspects she knew something she wasn't supposed to know. Something that put the killer in jeopardy."

Varda turned toward her quickly as his dark eyes flashed.

"Who?"

"He had no idea. Do you?"

Varda turned away.

"You do know something, don't you?"

"I don't think there's a connection," he mumbled.

"But I need to know," she protested.

Varda started pacing, and running his hands through his mop of tangled white hair.

"Tell me, please tell me what Conan did ten years ago to make you stop trusting him."

"Alright. It may be important now. I don't know. There's probably no connection."

"Tell me."

Finally, he rumpled his hair and sighed deeply. "OK. As I said before, Conan used to deliver my work to galleries in San Francisco, Napa, Santa Rosa. He took care of billing and receipts."

"Yes."

"One time some friends of mine went to Lake Tahoe for a holiday. They visited several galleries, and saw about ten pieces by 'Varda'. At the time I wasn't doing business with any galleries in Lake Tahoe. But my friends didn't know that. They came back and told me how good it was I had so much of my work there."

"So where did all these pieces come from?"

"What do you think?"

"Are you saying that he ... *forged* your work?"

"Yes."

"Maybe it was someone else."

He shook his head. "I went there, to those galleries. They showed me the invoices, the same ones we were using all along, and with his signature, as my representative."

Gwen could hardly believe it. Varda's monolith was swaying side to side, moaning, making grinding noises. The wind whistled through spaces that were not airtight. She started to feel dizzy.

"Here, you must lie down, little bird. This is too much for you? I tell you too much."

"No," she protested. "I want the whole story." She took some deep breaths and felt better. The room stood still.

They were sitting in the main salon of the Vallejo, where many of Varda's pieces were exhibited.

"Look, here." He got up and removed a piece from the wall and brought it to her. "You see this little mark?" He pointed to a small diagonal line about a third of the way down on the left side. "It's not conspicuous. It's not meant to be. But it is the way to know for sure it is Varda's work.

"So I take a trip to Lake Tahoe, and see all these pieces by 'Varda'. Not one was mine."

"What did you do?"

"They were 'on consignment', which means that the artist gets nothing until the work is sold. The galleries had sold a total of six pieces, and I got the names and addresses of the buyers. It was a lot of work. But both the shops and the buyers were reimbursed."

"And you fired Conan."

"Yes."

"Was this before or after my mother died?"

"After."

"Then he could have killed her, if she threatened to expose him."

"I don't think he would go that far. And I doubt your mother knew about the forgeries. She would have told me."

"Did you report this to the police?"

"No. I warned Conan, and told him if there were any further misdealings, I'd report him to the authorities. So he stopped. At least for awhile."

"He has a painting of yours." She corrected herself. "At least one that looks like yours."

Varda shook his head. "Enough. Let's get some fresh air."

They walked out to Bridgeway, and south, toward town. He described with great enthusiasm and gestures his upcoming exhibit in San Francisco. But there was no more talk about Conan.

~

Although she didn't have any particular beliefs one way or another, Gwen decided that exploring the subject of the goddess couldn't hurt. She wasn't afraid of being swept away.

And besides, despite discovering her father, she felt rather isolated. Being a part of this group would make her feel more like she had family. She hadn't realized what a strong need that was until so many emotions were awakened after she'd come to Sausalito. Old ghosts kept coming out of their hiding places.

It was Friday. Gwen phoned Megan that she'd be there.

She wasn't surprised that the place was alive with candles when she arrived. Gwen could smell incense too. Chad, Megan, Alex, Eric and two women she didn't know were already gathered in the living room. They had rearranged the furniture, and put the coffee table in the middle of a circle of chairs. On the table were small things the others had brought for the altar.

Gwen was upset with herself that she'd forgotten to bring anything. There was a small photograph of someone's mother, an antique gold locket, a small bouquet of feathers tied with a green ribbon.

She was introduced to the women. The group sat quietly waiting for more people to come. Before long, another woman and Conan entered.

They sent up a prayer to the Goddess, blessed the Divine Feminine in everyone, and asked if anyone desired hands-on healing.

Gwen felt somewhat uncomfortable with this ritual. It ended with Chad circulating with smoking sage and a ribboned feather. He wafted those present with the cleansing of smoke—an old tradition in many cultures, he explained.

When it was over, Alex said, "Let's take a walk. I have a confession to make."

"Alright."

They'd gone for about two blocks, before he spoke.

"Share this with me?" He lit up a joint, and held the smoke a long time.

She accepted the toke and held the smoke, but she didn't feel any different. She had only tried it twice before, but it never seemed to have an effect. Maybe because she'd only taken one or two tokes.

"Remember when some guy yelled at you a couple of times, "You will die?"

She looked at him wide-mouthed in amazement.

"That was me."

She gulped. She couldn't believe it, but how else would he have known of it? She felt a potpourri of feelings from betrayal to relief.

"Why? Why would you do that, Alex?"

"I wanted to scare you into going home. I mean I didn't really want to scare you, but I thought if you were frightened enough, you'd leave."

He took a deep breath. "I thought it worked. You did go home. But then you came back."

"Why would you want me to leave?"

"Cuz I don't think this place is safe for you."

"Why not?"

He took another deep drag on his joint. "You're on a dangerous trail. I'm afraid something awful might happen to you."

"Did you do anything else to frighten me?"

He said nothing.

"Well?"

"Yeah. When you put that article in the paper, I called to say I had information, but needed to meet you personally."

"Was that the call your mother took?"

"Yes. But I can easily change my voice." He took another hit while Gwen tried to absorb what he'd said.

"It scared you enough to make you move, but not to leave Marin."

She was trying to hang on to what he was telling her.

"One more thing. Do you know who put the announcement in the paper about my mother's memorial service? Was that you?"

He colored. "Yeah—same reason."

Gwen was quiet. She supposed she should show appreciation for his concern for her, and for his honesty in confessing. But she was angry, too. She'd been terrified by those words—twice.

"I care about you—sis."

Sobs wanted to come. She held them back and squeezed his hand.

Good God. She was surrounded by lies and love.

CHapter 22

Gwen continued to see Louis. He was funny and sexy. And he helped to keep her mind off her mother, when she was at a loss of what to do. She deliberately didn't bring up conversations of politics and religion. There was enough of that with Richard and Sally. She just wanted to have fun with Louis, nothing serious.

They rented a kayak, went swimming in a nearby lake, and even tried roller skating. He made her feel happy and strong. She had been in her head so much; it was good to be in her physical body, even if she felt unfulfilled sexually. Time, she thought. Maybe in time.

Richard, too, wanted to see more of her. He took her to the ballet in the city. She was surprised when he suggested it. She'd never known any men interested in ballet before. But of course, she knew he enjoyed the arts. She did too, so she had to admit they had this much in common.

They saw Swan Lake with the San Francisco Ballet, and Carmina Burana which the College of Marin dance department put on in San Rafael. She loved the sensuous pulse of the latter, which she'd heard on the radio, but had never seen in dance form.

Both times, when they went out afterwards, she was careful not to drink too much. One glass of wine was all she would allow herself.

After *Carmina* Richard said, "Want to go slumming?"

She answered with a puzzled smile.

He took her to a little bar on Second Street, called the Flat Iron, so named, she surmised because it was shaped like an iron, coming to almost a point near the corner. The floor, weathered and warped by a flood or plumbing disaster, was uneven, and gave Gwen the feeling she'd already had enough to drink. A juke box was playing a Johnny

Cash song. The bar stools were filled by men of various ages drinking in solitude, as they watched a baseball game on television. All heads were turned to the box on the wall. She picked up a fetid odor as they passed the stools and headed for a booth.

Since the bartender was totally focused on the game, Richard stepped up to the bar and asked him for two glasses of white wine.

When he returned with the drinks he said, "I'm glad you're feeling better. Hope you're not soliciting out in the rain, anymore."

"Soliciting! No, Richard, I don't even do that on moon-lit nights," she laughed.

"I think you know what I mean."

"Yes." She wanted to avoid the subject of politics. "I don't think I ever thanked you for all the financial help you sent over the years. I don't know how I'd have managed without it."

The announcer was blaring out the plays of the game. "And another home-run for the Giants" he bellowed.

The occupants of the stools cheered and stomped their feet.

Richard looked puzzled and dismayed. "I'm not sure I heard you."

"Thank you for the financial help you've given me all these years," she yelled over the TV.

"Financial help?"

"Yes."

"Gwen, I never sent any money to you or your aunt. I didn't know where to send it."

"What!"

He shouted back, "I never sent you money." For the moment the TV announcer was quiet; folks turned to look at Richard Thurman shouting.

He looked at her with incomprehension.

"And so it looks like the Giants are taking down the Tigers," the announcer roared.

A huge whoop arose among the fans.

"Then who was sending it?" Gwen shouted.

"I have no idea."

Gwen was stunned. Another bomb. And if whoever was sending it had found a way to get it through, then surely her father could have, if he'd tried.

He reached his hand over to hers. She had all she could do not to pull hers away.

"Did you really think I was supporting you all these years?"

Her mouth twitched. "Yes."

"I'm sorry to disappoint you."

They were winding up the end of the ninth. Everyone in the bar was cheering, raising glasses, and bear-hugging strangers.

Gwen and Richard were silent for several moments. She couldn't look at him; she raised her eyes to the TV. In no way could she join in the joy of the occasion. She rose to leave.

"I'd be glad to help you now if you need money."

"No," she said.

Was it her pride that made this snap decision? Her disappointment in him? She just wanted to get away, and think this through.

They drove to Sausalito in silence.

She realized she'd thought she was receiving some kind of care or love from him all these years. Now it was clear she hadn't. He had never lifted a finger in all that time.

When he dropped her off, she walked down to the waterfront where there were no people and no lights. She took off her shoes, and let the rough brown sand squeeze between her toes. The rhythmic, predictable cadence of the surf was reassuring as her eyes fell upon the deep indigo of the water and the moonlit white foam.

In the distance she could hear the lowing of the fog horns, as *call and response* was played out in different pitches between the lighthouse and a ship coming through the gate.

Nothing was making sense to her. If her father hadn't been sending her money, who had?

Chapter 23

G wen couldn't forget what Varda had said about Conan and the forgeries. She was desperate to get more information. She knew Varda would not approve, but she wanted to get inside Conan's houseboat and look for the *faux Vardas*. She couldn't help but feel there could be a connection between his illicit work and her mother's death. If she'd found out and threatened to report it, what would he have done?

She started visiting Conan more. Sometimes she brought food, for which he was always grateful. She even gave him a Beatles album. She knew he was crazy about them. Although the houseboat itself was never locked, the partitioned room which he'd made into a studio was.

She decided it was innocent enough to ask to see his studio. She'd seen others'.

"It's a mess. Sometime, when I get it cleaned up."

"I don't care if it's cleaned up. Aren't artists' studios supposed to be a mess?"

"Not as bad as mine. You can hardly find a footpath in there." He smiled. "Some day."

"Well, can you show me some of your recent work?"

"What do writers call it—'writers' block'? Artists have blocks too."

"You haven't been working?"

"Not much."

She changed the subject. She didn't want him to get suspicious. But *she* was suspicious. If he were so reluctant to open that door, she couldn't help wondering what was behind it.

She had seen enough movies and television to know that there were ways of opening locked doors without keys. Dare she try?

She was no detective. Varda would have a fit if he even knew she was contemplating such a maneuver. His priority was her safety, and she knew it should be hers, too.

She wished she could ask Denise or someone to help her, to at least cover her back, but it wouldn't be fair. She knew what she was planning was dangerous.

Since the space one entered into on his houseboat was never locked, she had waited for him there in the salon more than once. It wouldn't be too suspicious, she reasoned, if he were to find her there. She'd just have to hope he didn't catch her in the act of trying to enter his inner sanctum.

She confided her plan to Denise.

"Are you nuts?"

"Oh, please. I didn't come here for a lecture. I want to talk it through with you, make sure I'm approaching it as intelligently as possible."

"I can already tell you you're not."

"OK." Gwen got up to leave the room.

"No, don't go. Tell me how you plan to carry this off."

Gwen explained that it was alright with Conan that she go aboard and wait for him in the parlor, so that part wasn't too dangerous.

"What I need is something I can slip between the door and the doorjamb to release the lock to the studio."

"Jesus," Denise sighed. "Like in the movies."

"Exactly."

"You want to get yourself killed, girl?"

"No, I want to do what I have to do as safely as possible."

Denise shook her head. "Sometimes they use a strip of metal or plastic. Or some kind of pick, I think. I'm no expert."

"Do you have a credit card, Denise?"

"Yes."

"That might work."

"Might. Is might good enough for you?"

Gwen went to the kitchen and poured herself a glass of water. "Want some?"

"No thanks."

"We could try it on *your* door."

"And what would that prove?"

"If it works on your lock, it increases the chances it will work on Conan's."

"You're hopeless."

But Denise got up, retrieved the new credit card from her purse.

"OK," she said. "You go outside. I'll lock the door, and you see if you can unlock it with this." She handed the card to Gwen.

Gwen was both doubtful and excited. She took the card outside, and heard her friend lock the door.

"I can't see," she shouted.

The porch light came on, which helped marginally.

Gwen took a deep breath, positioned the card between the door and the jamb, and attempted to slide it up and down, or to catch it on something which would release its hold.

Finally, Denise opened the door and stepped out. "Here, let me try."

Gwen handed her the card, went inside and locked the door. She could hear Denise fumble with the card and the lock.

In a few minutes she heard Denise say, "It's not working. Open up."

Once inside, they studied the lock.

"This is a heavy-duty bolt," Gwen said. "I don't think Conan's lock is anything like this."

Denise shrugged. "Have you looked at it carefully?"

"Probably not well enough. But it's not a bolt."

"Next time you're there, take a look."

Gwen knew that Denise wasn't eager to let go of her precious credit card. VISA cards were fairly new, and not many people had them yet. For single stores, yes, there were credit cards, but not the kind you could use almost anywhere.

She felt that there was a ticking bomb, and hated the delay, but she made another trip to Conan's. He wasn't home. That gave her a chance to look at the lock. What a perfect opportunity to test it with the card, if only she had it. She looked around the space she was in to see if there was anything remotely possible to use. She tried a table knife—too tight.

She remembered the metal nail file in her purse, and tried that. No luck. She studied the keyhole, and thought maybe there was something that would release the lock, if she poked around in it. She found nutpicks in Conan's utility drawer. No, the opening was too small.

Conan still hadn't come back, so she wrote him a note and left.

She was discouraged, but as she walked away she thought of going to a locksmith. *I'll tell him I lost the key to my closet, and did he know if there was a trick I could use to release it.*

She looked 'locksmiths' up in the phone book. The closest was in San Rafael on Second Street.

She waited by the exit to Gate 6 to see if anyone she knew who had a car was heading north. Soon Philippe, who had been one of the barbecue servers stopped and asked which way she was going.

"North, San Rafael."

"Hop in."

All the way there he played some kind of Motown music loud enough to explode her eardrums. But she was grateful for the ride.

Philippe was going on to Novato, so she got out at the Central Exit in San Rafael and hoofed it to the shop.

"Look, I can be back and pick you up in an hour and a half. There's coffee shop on Fourth Street called "Bloomers". I'll pick you up there, OK?"

"That would be wonderful, Philippe."

The locksmith shop was tiny, easy to overlook. The light was poor, and Gwen wondered how the man worked in such dim light.

He introduced himself as Loch the Locksmith. A red beard accompanied his curly, red hair. About five feet five inches Gwen figured he weighed around one hundred ten pounds.

She told him her problem.

"The best thing," Loch said, "would be for meself to come out and change the lock."

"And the most expensive," she smiled back at him.

"What kind of lock is it, if ye don't mind me asking?"

She wondered if he were an Irish elf.

When she hesitated, he gestured to several styles on the wall.

"It's most like that one," she pointed to one of several Master locks.

"Well, depending on how much space there is between the door and the jamb, it shouldn't be too difficult to break the catch, God willing."

"What do you suggest I use?"

He rubbed his chin, and pulled on his beard. "A credit card. Or a piece of wire, if it don't bend too easy."

"Thank you," she said, moving to the door.

"If that don't work, glad I'd be to come out and replace the lock meself."

Oh, sure, she thought. *Just the thing.*

~

"You positive you want to do this?" Denise said.

"I am. I wish I'd had your card this afternoon."

She told Denise about being alone a long time at Conan's and then going to the locksmith.

"He thought a credit card would work."

"Well, next time you want to be foolish, come borrow it, but bring it right back. I can't let you have it for any length of time."

"Of course not." But Gwen wished her friend weren't quite so protective of this little piece of plastic. She knew her laminated driver's license wouldn't work. It was too thick. She'd looked at plastic wares in the hardware store, but none were flat and stiff enough, even if she cut them.

The following Sunday when she knew Conan would be out until around four o'clock, she borrowed Denise's precious VISA, and made an early visit to Conan's. Her heart was beating twice as hard as usual as she approached the locked door. With sweaty hands, she pushed the card between the door and the jamb. She could feel it start to go in, but then stop. No click, no release of the catch. She fussed with it for five minutes.

Then she threw herself in disappointment on Conan's sofa. Her head back, in a few minutes she realized she was staring right at the open sky through his skylight. Skylights, of course! Suddenly she remembered—there was another one over his studio. She'd seen it from the outside. Was it possible …?

She left, and as she walked away she looked back at the houseboat. She could clearly see the other skylight over the studio. It was open. But how would she get into it?

Gwen gave Denise back her credit card. She reported its failure, and subsequent awareness of the second skylight.

"Oh, my God! You are plumb crazy, girl."

"Maybe. But I came here on a mission, and I haven't accomplished it. Not even close."

"What makes you think these forged paintings have anything to do with anything?"

"My mother could have found out about the forgeries, threatened to report it, and out of fear, Conan could have killed her. He was one of her bike buddies."

"Possible. How could you prove it?"

"I don't know. That's why I have to see what's in his studio. Besides, why does Conan keep his studio locked—not his residence, just his studio?"

Denise listened.

"So now do you see?"

Denise raised her voice. "What I see is that you're putting yourself in a lot of danger."

Ignoring her, Gwen said, "It would have to be done at night. I'd need a flashlight—"

Denise cut her off. "You'd need a lot more than that."

"I think it would be easiest to access the roof by going up from the inside, the one in the parlor."

"Ah, and how do you hope to do that? Are you going to drag a ladder over there?"

"Help me figure it out, instead of being such a nay-sayer, Denise," Gwen begged.

Denise only shook her head in despair.

Gwen brightened suddenly. "He does have a little step stool. I could use that."

"To get through an eight foot ceiling?"

"I don't think it's that high. Anyway, I'm a karate expert."

Denise burst out laughing. "That's going to get you up there? A few kicks and punches?"

"I didn't mean that. But I'm strong. I could jump from the top step of the stool. Maybe."

There was a long silence as Gwen puzzled out the best way to proceed.

Finally, Denise said, "Let's say, by some miracle you were able to get on the roof, and by another miracle found the skylight over the studio open, and by a third were able to drop into the studio without injuring yourself—now let's suppose you found your quarry. How are you going to get out?"

Gwen was stunned. Why hadn't she thought about this?

"I guess I'm not cut out to be a sleuth."

"I guess not."

"But," Gwen said in a cheery voice, "it's the role I've been cast in, so that's how I'm going to play it."

"You haven't answered the question."

Gwen pursed her lips. "How am I going to get out? Open the door. When I shut it after me, it will be locked, won't it? Isn't that the way locks work?"

"Not all of them."

Finally Denise said, "If you do this crazy thing, take a camera, or you won't have proof of anything."

"Oh, right! I knew you'd be helpful." Gwen gave her a kiss and dashed out the door.

"Get a guy to go with you!" Denise yelled after her.

Chapter 24

Get a guy to go with me? Who? Denise had presented enough obstacles for Gwen to realize it would indeed be difficult to pull it off by herself.

She didn't want to involve Louis. She wondered if Alex would go with her. That would pose other risks, she mused. Alex wasn't accustomed to just popping in the way she was, especially not at night. If Conan were to come home… she didn't want to think about it.

She asked Alex to go for a walk with her. Then she presented the situation to him, and the game plan. He listened patiently. He didn't poo-poo her ideas.

Finally he said, "When were you thinking of doing this?"

"Sometimes he goes away for the weekend. That would be the safest. I'll pay attention to what's coming up." She turned to him. "You mean you'll do it?"

"Let me think about it."

A few days later he asked, "What did you plan to do with the information if you do find forgeries there?"

"Let Varda know."

"Let's keep it to ourselves for awhile."

"Why?"

"Do you want my help?"

Gwen colored. What kind of deal was this? It sounded like *My way or no way.*

She frowned. "I don't know, Alex."

He shrugged and walked away.

"OK," she yelled after him.

~

It was the first weekend in May. Gwen had known for only two days that Conan was going away. He said it was a fishing trip with some guys he knew from Sacramento. She'd found out he was leaving Friday and coming back Sunday.

"Bring me some fresh fish?" she asked eagerly. She was becoming so deceitful.

"If we get them frozen in time."

She and Alex decided to go for Friday night. He brought some rope and she remembered to bring her Brownie camera with the removable 4-use turning flash bulbs.

When they got to the ark they found the outer door locked.

"No!" she said in dismay. "How could this be?"

Alex shrugged. "Guess when he goes away for a whole weekend, he locks up."

"All our carefully laid plans up in smoke."

"Let's sit on his deck and watch the moon."

She was very frustrated. Alex lit a joint, took a hit and offered it to her. She shook her head.

"Relax, there's got to be another way," he said.

Gwen stood up and leaned over the edge of the houseboat. "There's nobody tied up on this side. Nothing but darkness."

"We'd need a fucking boat to get up from that side," Alex commented.

"The rubber raft!" Gwen exclaimed. "On the other end of this barge."

They walked past the front entrance and to the far end of the craft. Alex studied what he saw there.

The deck in the aft was used mostly to store things. The raft, a tool box, several feet of water hose, a gas tank, and miscellaneous other things were tied down here.

"Let's leave now," he said. "Think this through, and come back tomorrow night."

Disappointed, Gwen agreed.

On their walk along Bridgeway they discussed various means and obstacles of getting to the top of the arc.

Suddenly Gwen had another idea. "Maybe a credit card would work in the *front* door. We haven't attempted that."

"I doubt it. But we can try."

They decided against any entry from the dark side. At least for now. Too many obstacles, a wobbly rubber raft for one.

The next night they approached the front door with Alex's credit card.

Holding her breath, she waited while Alex slid it around between the door and the jamb.

"Voila!" Gwen squeaked. The catch released, and they were in.

She fetched the three foot step stool. Placing it under the skylight, she reached up as high as she could. Not high enough. She climbed down, and Alex got on the ladder. At five feet, eleven he was able to reach through the ceiling.

"Do you think you can hoist your way through to the roof?

"I don't know."

Gwen could see that the opening was small. Maybe it wasn't big enough for him.

He grabbed the metal frame of the skylight and hoisted himself. This looked like a trial run to Gwen, as he quickly lowered himself. The next time he was serious. Taking a deep breath he hoisted himself up until he got stuck in the narrow space, with his legs suspended in the air.

"I can't get up or down," he whispered in veiled terror.

Gwen suppressed a giggle. She couldn't help but think of Winnie-the-Pooh getting stuck in Rabbit's hole after eating too much. But it was no time for humor. She took hold of his legs and pushed. No good.

Finally, she heard him say, "Can't do it. Pull me down."

After considerable effort on her part, Alex was back on the ladder.

He climbed down to the floor. "You'll have to do it. I'll push you through."

She climbed up on the stepladder.

"Here," she said, "you keep the camera and flashlight until I let you in." She handed the items to him.

Alex pushed her from behind. She was able to get her arms over the skylight's framework, and with another push from below, she was on the roof.

She let out the breath she hadn't realized she was holding. She crawled across the roof to the other skylight. The opening was too small, as the window was only partially opened. With the squeak of rusty hinges she made it larger. Peering down into a totally dark abyss, she sat by the opening wondering if she dare jump down into that pit of darkness. What if she landed on an upturned saw, or worse? She wished she'd kept the flashlight.

"What are you doing up there?" Alex called up in a stage whisper.

"Sitting."

"Well, get on with it."

She looked down the hole again; it hadn't gotten any brighter. But she lowered herself through the opening, then closed her eyes and let go. There was a loud thump as she landed on the floor of the studio. She inhaled and released a deep breath of relief. She wasn't hurt.

She skated carefully across the darkened room toward the crack of light under the door leading to the parlor. She opened it and Alex joined her in Conan's sacred space, as dark as a cave. They dare not turn on the overhead—that could bring attention to their presence. Scanning the room with her light, it was still difficult to make out what was there. Lots of stuff was leaning against the walls, but most of the room was bare.

Alex approached one side and began looking through the piles of artwork.

She approached one of the stacks leaning against the opposite wall and turned it over. It was definitely Varda style.

"Alex," she called softly. "Over here."

He joined her and together they spread out a stack of eight pictures.

With her flashlight she looked for the little diagonal line Varda had told her about. No such marks. Each was signed *Varda*. She spread the paintings out on the floor, and took flash pictures. After the first bulb had made its final revolution, she replaced it with a second bulb, and took the other four photos.

"Look what else I found," she said, showing Alex an address book. "These are addresses of galleries—Pilson Gallery Phoenix, Monroe Gallery Santa Fe—"

"I think we should get out of here," Alex said.

"Just let me get a couple pictures of the address book, or should I just take it?"

"No, leave it here. He'll notice it's missing."

She changed bulbs again and took pictures of the addresses. "There's probably more forgeries over there," Gwen said, pointing to another wall.

"I'm getting nervous. I think we have enough to make our point."

They put the room back in order, restacking the art works as they'd been, and walked out of the studio. Gwen checked to make sure the door locked after them. It did; that was a relief.

Leaving the premises quickly, they saw no one. Gwen wanted to run, but knew that would only draw attention to them if they were seen. When they got out to Bridgeway, she felt safe.

"I'll take this film in to be developed tomorrow," she said.

"Don't let anyone else see the pictures."

Gwen was dying to show the photos to Varda. Had she really promised not to? Why did Alex not want anyone to know?

"Get copies for me," Alex said.

What did he plan to do with them?

~

The film was developed and Gwen picked it up. She was happy with the results. She gave Alex his set, and he smiled in satisfaction through his dope-induced stupor.

Chapter 25

Alex's drug problem was becoming worse. When Gwen went to see Megan two days later it was obvious she'd been crying. "What is it?"

"It's Alex. We tried to cover it up for a long time. I think we didn't want to believe it."

"You mean ..."

"The drugs. When he had an accident a few years ago, he got hooked on morphine. I think they let him have it too long, and he became an addict. Then he went on to other drugs. Not just pot. He'd had a taste of stronger stuff, and craved it." In a whisper she confided, "Even white powder,"

"Cocaine. I'm sorry."

"Last year before you came back, he went through a rehab program. He was clean for about six months, and then he started in again."

"Was that after I got here?"

"Yes."

Megan wiped her eyes and looked out the window. The sun was shining brightly. Flowers were in bloom—tulips and peonies.

"I don't know why he does it. It's as if he's hiding something."

"Do you have any idea what?"

"No."

"Has he had any counseling?"

"Oh, yes. More than once."

"Did something happen today, Megan?"

"He was here, stoned. Usually, he's quiet when he's—that way. Or ridiculously happy. Today he was surly with his father, then rude to me. He finally marched out of the house. I don't know where he went."

"He's a big boy. I'm sure he's OK."

"I think something's terribly wrong," Megan said.

"Did he mention anyone, or anything?"

"No."

~

Gwen decided that her loyalty to Varda was stronger than what Alex had said. She wasn't sure he'd want to see the photos. She could tell he didn't want to think ill of anyone. But she felt she had to let him decide what to do about them.

After she'd had her tea with Varda, she said, "I have a story to tell you!"

"And what might that be, little bird?" he asked with a smile.

"I don't think you're going to like it," she warned.

Gwen withdrew the photographs from the envelope.

"I took some pictures of work in Conan's studio." She paused. "Are you ready for this?"

He had a stricken expression on his face, as though he knew what was coming. He nodded, and she handed him the packet. He studied them carefully. He looked up with great sadness in his eyes.

He stared at the pictures for a long time. Finally, he asked, "How did you get these?"

"I took them myself."

"How?"

"In his studio. And I have this," she said, showing him photos of the address book.

Varda looked uneasy. "You'd better tell me everything, little bird."

And so she did. His face was as white as the clouds outside. Gwen could see that he was very chagrined at what Conan had done.

"You weren't sure he stopped altogether," she said.

He looked down at the photographs. "No." He started pacing again, and tapping his forehead in that way of his.

"This time," he said, "I will go to the police."

~

Conan was quite shocked at being arrested. Gwen heard from Chad, who'd attended the trial that he came close to striking an officer. Apparently he didn't have a clue that anyone had been in his studio. She was told that when the pictures were shown to him he demanded to know who had taken them. The police didn't know, as Varda refused to reveal that information.

The district attorney had gotten in touch with the galleries listed in Conan's address book. All acknowledged having ordered works of Varda. When confronted with this fact Conan had no defense.

Conan's trial was over by the end of the week. Chad reported that Varda was on the stand, explained his little secret and had shown a genuine *Varda* as 'exhibit one'. Then the falsified ones had been displayed, many of which had been confiscated by the authorities from Conan's studio. When the evidence was presented, Conan crumbled, and admitted he'd been making Varda forgeries for some time. He was convicted and sentenced to a two year term of imprisonment.

Gwen thought with irony that the reason Conan didn't have any new work to show her wasn't that he had *artist's block*, as he'd said. He'd been very busy indeed.

~

Gwen got a call from Megan, who was very worried about Alex. He'd been gone for three days. Due to his behavior the last time she'd seen him, she finally reported him to "missing persons".

"Can you come over?" Megan asked.

"Of course."

They called the people they knew who knew him. No one had any idea where he'd gone. And no one knew who was supplying him with drugs.

Gwen could tell Chad was worried as well, but he tried to reassure them that Alex was OK.

Gwen said, "He's got to work something out, Megan. He needs some time on his own."

"I guess," Megan said.

She looked so mournful, Gwen said, "Megan, do you want me to stay with you? Move back in for a few days?"

"Oh, would you? That would be wonderful."

"I'll still have to go to work, but then I'll come here."

"You are precious."

How could she ever have doubted Megan?

Gwen explained to Denise that she'd be at Megan's for a few days.

"I understand," Denise said. "Is there anything I can do?"

"I can't think of anything. Keep track of my phone calls, maybe, and my mail?"

"Of course."

Denise drove her and some of her clothes back to Megan's.

"I'll see you at work."

Eric reported that he'd hunted everywhere for Alex, but couldn't find him. "He hasn't been at the *No Name Bar.*"

"I haven't seen him at the waterfront, and either has anyone else."

"What about his drug associates?" Gwen asked

Megan closed her eyes and shuddered.

"I wouldn't know who they are. I'll keep asking around," Eric said.

~

A week later, Gwen saw a small article in the paper saying that an unidentified body had been found in the water by the headlands—white, male, between twenty and twenty-five years old. Anyone with any information should contact the coroner's office.

Gwen showed the article to Chad.

Chad exposed a stricken face to Gwen. With trembling hands he called the coroner's office.

"We have pictures," the coroner said.

"I'll come up," Chad said.

He turned to Gwen. "No point in worrying Megan with this unless…"

"I'll go with you," Gwen said.

Coroner Holmes greeted them and urged them to sit down.

He opened a file on the desk. He extracted two pictures. They were both headshots, cut off at the chin. Chad saw the photos first. Slowly he looked up and gave a painful nod to Gwen.

There was no doubt whose pictures they were.

"What was the cause of death?" Chad asked.

"We'll have to wait for an autopsy report, but the victim was murdered."

"Murder!" Chad gasped. "Who'd want to murder him?"

"I'm sorry," the coroner said.

"What is the evidence?" Chad asked.

"He was strangled."

Silent screams reverberated around the room.

"If you wish, I'll show you another shot which includes his neck."

Painfully, Chad nodded, and the coroner passed another photo in his direction.

Gwen watched Chad glance at the photo, then push it away.

The coroner added, "The body was wrapped in a length of canvas."

"What kind of canvas?" Gwen asked.

"That hasn't been established yet."

"Were there any fingerprints?" Gwen asked.

"If there were, they were washed away by all the time the body was in the water. We didn't find any."

"I don't suppose you've come up with a date of death," Chad said.

"The legal date on the death will be the day his body was found, washed up on a sandy cove by the tide."

"But do you know—"

"I'm afraid not specifically. Bodies take on the ambient temperature of where they're found. In case of the ocean, that's pretty cold," Mr. Holmes said.

"That's right. In these waters it would take a long time for that to happen."

"Why is that?" Gwen asked.

"Are you sure you want this information?"

When they nodded, the coroner forged ahead. "You see, the temperature determines how long it takes the body to decay. When it does decay, the corpse forms gases. It is the gases that cause the body to rise and float."

"So the body wasn't bloated, and never came to the surface to float?" Chad asked.

Gwen swallowed. "Then how—"

"The waves and tide brought the body ashore. So it's difficult to determine the date of death."

"Aren't there other indicators?"

"Yes, but none too reliable. Stomach contents can indicate when the last meal was in some cases. Rigor mortis is an indicator if death was between six and eight hours prior to discovery. After that, the muscles relax and rigidity reverses. So establishing the date of death is a very inexact science. Unless the body's discovered within those limited perimeters."

Gwen tried to forget they were talking about someone they knew.

"As I say, we'll have to wait for the final autopsy report," the coroner added.

Chad nodded. "Where is ...he?"

"At the Reardon Funeral Home in Mill Valley, where the autopsy is being performed."

"Do they always do an autopsy?" Gwen asked.

"In suspicious deaths, that is the procedure. It may also give indications of toxicology. And hopefully, some idea of the date of death."

There was a long silence, as the coroner allowed them to process the information. Gwen looked out the window at the flowing hills. She said to the coroner, "You have a beautiful view, with the hills beyond."

"Yes, if it weren't for that lovely pastoral sight I don't think I could put up with this job."

Coroner Holmes turned to Chad. "I have to ask you what you want done with his remains."

"I'll get back to you on that, after I talk to my wife."

The coroner had compassion, Gwen thought. He gave them whatever time they needed to take in the horrific facts he had to impart.

When they left, Chad and Gwen drove most of the way in silence. Before they got back, Chad said, "How will I tell Megan?"

"She'll know, just to see your face."

"Why would anyone want Alex dead? It doesn't add up. He never hurt anyone."

Gwen heard him choke on the last word.

As soon as she saw their faces, Megan knew something was wrong.

"What? Where have you been?"

Chad explained that they'd identified Alex's body by some photographs. Megan screamed, and went into her room, where they could hear her sobbing.

Gwen and Chad sat in silence in the living room, trying to process the shock that Alex was dead, and the awful way he'd met his end.

In about an hour Megan came out of the bedroom, and asked her husband what the coroner said.

"Are you sure it's him? You didn't see a body did you?"

"He showed us photographs. It's Alex."

Megan covered her mouth and emitted a sob.

"Shouldn't you look at the body—to make sure?" she choked out.

"I don't think that'll be necessary."

There was a silence. Then Megan asked, "Did he drown?"

"No. He was put in the water after …"

"After what?"

"After he was strangled," Chad managed to choke out.

"Strangled! No. You mean he was murdered?"

"It looks that way." He took his wife in his arms.

CHapter 26

The days that followed were difficult for everyone. The Denisons had to make practical decisions, while still trying to grasp the fact that their son was dead, and constantly asking who could have done this, and why. They decided to have the body cremated. And they wanted a memorial service. It was decided they'd do as they had with Patricia's ashes—have a goddess ceremony outdoors. The service was held on the national Memorial Day.

Besides the usual things that were set out, a table outside the circle was spread with photos of Conan from babyhood through his high school graduation. Lots of silly pictures from high school, but there didn't seem to be any after that.

The fragrance of lilac and roses was overcome by the sage and incense Chad was burning.

But Gwen couldn't help feeling miserable about the whole thing— her childhood friend's death, her sympathy for his parents, and the reminder of a similar ceremony last year.

Neighbors brought refreshments over. They didn't come to the ceremony, but had been invited to the reception indoors.

There was whispered talk of the cause of death. It was the coroner's opinion that Alex had been strangled, wrapped in canvas, and then transported to the Headlands where the body was dumped off the cliff.

In the kitchen Gwen could hear talk of what a sweet kid Alex had been, and how could anything so terrible ever happen to him.

When almost everyone had left, Gwen, Eric and the Denisons were left.

"You two go rest. We'll clean up this stuff," Gwen said to Megan and Chad.

As they washed the cups and dishes, Gwen and Eric talked about how the murder could have happened.

"It had to be related to the drugs," Eric said.

"I wonder if he owed some dealer a lot of money," Gwen said.

"It's a very pricey habit." Eric agreed. "He didn't make a lot at the post office, and he was into some heavy stuff. Coke. Maybe even heroin."

It sounded reasonable. But she wondered if it had anything to do with the break-in she and Alex had committed. Had Conan killed Alex because of that? But that couldn't be; Conan was in prison when Alex was murdered. Anyway, it had been three weeks between the break-in and Conan's arrest.

She also considered the possibly of a connection to her mother's death. She ran the idea past Eric. Since her mother's death was over ten years ago, he didn't think it likely.

~

It had been a week since Alex's death had been reported. Detective Harbison was questioning Megan in the living room. He had already spoken with Chad. Gwen sat beside Megan for moral support.

The man had thinning sandy colored hair, although he appeared to be only in his thirties. His eyes were pale, but held a look of intensity. His most memorable trait, Gwen thought, was that he possessed a constellation of moles on his left cheek. She wondered if he'd given them a name. Then she chided herself for such irreverent thoughts at such a serious time.

"I'm sorry, Mrs. Denison, to put you through this, but I have to ask you some questions."

Megan nodded numbly.

"You were the last person to see him alive. Is that correct?"

Megan mumbled.

"Will you speak up, ma'am?"

"I guess so," Megan said.

Gwen said, "We don't know who might have seen him after he left here."

Detective Harbison nodded, and pulled on his ear lobe.

"You said he was in a foul mood when he left. Do you recall anything he might have said in your last encounter?"

"He said 'You bastard'—a number of times."

"Who do you think he was referring to?"

"I have no idea. I don't believe he meant either my husband or me."

"It sounds as though someone had it in for him." The detective scribbled something in his notebook with one hand and pulled on his ear lobe with the other.

"Do you have any idea who his enemies were?"

"Enemies! He didn't have any," Megan protested.

"Have you been able to get any leads, Detective?" Gwen asked.

"About what time did he leave your house, ma'am?"

Gwen thought he must be a newbie at this job, but not so new as to know who should be asking the questions.

Megan sighed. "I don't know. Maybe four o'clock."

Gwen intervened. "Did he report for work that evening?"

Megan looked at her. "He's supposed to be at the post office by six o'clock. I don't know."

Detective Harbison stood. "We'll be in touch if we need more information."

When he'd left Chad came into the room.

"He really wanted to know who Alex's drug buddies were. He came back to that three times. He thinks I know something I don't. He's sure that's what this is about."

"Well, what else could it be?" Megan said. "Of course we don't know who his drug buddies were. He wouldn't bring them here."

"Well, I'm going to find out!" Chad announced.

"How?"

"I'll go to the bars, find out who knows him. Who sells the goddamn stuff."

"Oh, Chad," Megan murmured. "Be careful."

"There must be places where dealers hang out eager to make sales. I'll pretend to be a customer."

Twice he thought he found a possibility, but neither panned out.

"I'm too old," he said. They don't trust me."

~

Gwen had thought at first that Conan was the most likely candidate for causing Alex's demise, but now that didn't seem to hold up, since he was arrested before Alex's probable death. Maybe the killer was his drug dealer. Isn't that how they punished the debtors and warned their other customers? After all, no one knew how Alex could pay for those drugs. He was probably deeply in debt.

Gwen decided she'd try to get into the drug crowd. Chad had failed, but maybe she would have better luck. She didn't tell Alex's parents or Varda; she knew they wouldn't want her to take this risk.

She biked to a couple of low-life bars in town, where no one knew her.

She asked in these places where she could get some stuff. The air in the bars was blue with smoke. One of them was so cloudy she began to feel queasy.

When they just shook their heads, she said, "Come on guys. I'm not an under-cover cop. I'm a student, on vacation from University of Michigan. Give me a break, huh? I can pay."

This was the line she used. Finally it worked. On Caledonia she walked into a small dive. She could hear the pinball machine and see a small black and white television on the wall before she could make out anything else. She approached the bar and ordered a lager. Beside her sat a white and a black man together.

"I'm looking for some stuff," she said to the black man.

"What kind of stuff?"

"Watcha got?"

Like any job, she guessed she'd have to start at the bottom, build trust, because all he offered her was marijuana.

"Gee, haven't you got anything stronger?"

"No, lady."

She paid for it, waved and said she'd be back.

~

She didn't know how to judge marijuana. She took the plastic bag to Eric's boat, and asked him to try it.

"This is shit," was the grade he gave it. "They either pegged you as a newbie or a snitch."

"You mean it isn't the real thing?"

"You have to understand. Marijuana comes in different qualities. A seasoned user can tell the difference."

"How are they different?"

"They cut it with useless stuff."

They smoked some of it anyway, but it didn't give either of them a high.

"Take it back. Tell them you want 'gold'."

"That's the good stuff?"

"The best."

"Have you been able to find out anything leading to Alex's death?"

"No."

"Where do you guys in the boat community get your drugs?"

"Well, most of us only use grass, of varying qualities. A couple of guys here sell it, but I wouldn't call them dealers."

"Why not?"

"They only provide the community. They're not out on the street trying to get teen-agers on it." He tipped his Budweiser up. "A lot of folk's choice is still alcohol. Mostly beer."

"How about coke?"

"Cocaine? Only a couple of guys here I know are into stronger stuff."

"Where do they get it?"

"I don't know. I'll ask around."

"Thanks, Eric."

Gwen took the bad grass back to the bar where she'd met the guys. The bartender said, "You lookin' for Useless?"

"Who?"

"Useless—he's the guy you –"

Just then she saw him, returning from the men's room. She threw the bag on the counter and repeated what Eric had said. "This stuff is shit. What'd you take me for?"

The black guy grabbed the bag and looked apologetic. "We must have given you the wrong one. Sorry about that. Wait here. I'll be back in a minute."

While she waited the white guy he was with pretended she wasn't there. He never looked at her, just kept raising a bottle of Sierra Nevada to his mouth.

Useless came back, and slipped another plastic bag to her surreptitiously. She started to open it, to smell it.

"Not here," he cautioned. "At least wait until you're outside."

She nodded. "This stuff better be real."

She was halfway down the street before she remembered she was supposed to ask for 'gold'. It was too late now. She thought she was lucky to have made the exchange. She could tell by smelling it that it was stronger than the last batch.

CHapter 27

Varda had been on a teaching assignment for two weeks in Santa Fe. Gwen had eagerly awaited his return. When he did get back, she called him, asked if she could come over.

"Of course, dear one."

It was a fog-laden windy day. As she approached the shore she could hear the huge crashing of waves before she could see them. When she climbed on the gangplank, she heard it gnashing at its hinges. The wind blew her to one of the side rails, and for a moment she lost her footing.

Nature was so noisy that her knock couldn't be heard. After three attempts, finding the door unlocked, she let herself in.

He apologized for not hearing her, and brought her one of his special herbal teas.

"Something is very wrong. I can see that," Varda said.

"Yes."

Gwen told him of Alex's murder. She explained that the family thought it was drug related.

"This is terrible." He put his hand over hers. "He was friend of yours, no?"

She nodded. "We grew up together, until..."

Then she confessed, with some embarrassment, that she had attempted to buy drugs in order to insinuate herself into the drug community, and get information, as to who his killer might be.

He shook his head and his finger. "Bad move. Much too dangerous."

He looked frightened by what she'd told him. Suddenly, he reached out and hugged her. When he released her, he said, "Did he owe money?"

"Probably. He was into really heavy stuff, and he only had a job sorting mail at the post office. None of us knows where he got the money for his habit."

Varda pursed his lips, rubbed his face and frowned.

"What is it?" Gwen asked.

"Is it possible he was blackmailing someone?"

"To keep a secret?"

"Perhaps."

"About what?"

"I don't know. But little bird, don't get mixed up in this. You're putting yourself in much danger. The fact that you stirred things up no doubt has already reached the drug community and whoever killed Alex."

Gwen felt sick.

Varda scratched his head. She could see the worry in his face. "I have to help you."

"How?"

"Give me a minute."

Gwen watched while Varda got up and paced the floor, all the while, tapping his forehead with his fist.

"Conan is, was his uncle, right?"

"Right."

"I wonder if there's a connection."

"Like what?"

"Shsh. Let me think."

He kept pacing, and Gwen waited, not entirely patiently.

Finally, he said, "It's wild—my thoughts. I don't think they make sense."

"Please tell me what you're thinking."

"You mustn't do anything foolish. Like food, we must marinate theories. Let them stew in their own juices until they come to a boil, then simmer for some time."

"What are you talking about?"

"It's possible Conan is somehow involved."

"How?"

"Is just a theory. He is the dead boy's uncle. And I know from before he isn't honest. I'm not saying he is the killer, but—" Suddenly he stopped and slapped his forehead. "No, no, he was in prison." He shook his head as though negating the words he had just spoken.

~

The detective came by a couple of more times, and questioned Gwen too. The sheriff's department didn't seem to be getting anywhere in solving Alex's murder.

Chad was impatient. "They don't seem to know a damn thing."

"Let's go to them. *We'll* do the questioning," Gwen suggested.

When they got there, they demanded to see who was in charge. Then they demanded to know what the department had found out, if anything.

"I'm sorry, sir. We're doing everything we can."

"Have you questioned the 'usual suspects'?" Chad asked.

"He means the drug dealers," Gwen clarified.

"Yes. You understand they won't talk."

"Don't you guys pay out for squealers?" Chad asked.

The supervisor pursed his lips. "We'll let you know as soon as we have a lead."

~

Gwen stopped by Denise's to pick up more of her clothes, and check on phone calls.

"Yeah, your dad's been trying to get a hold of you."

Gwen had a sickening feeling. She felt somewhat ashamed of it. After all, what was money? Was that how she was judging love? But somehow, she realized she thought less of him. It had been a real downer to realize he hadn't done anything tangible to find her in all those years.

She remembered with embarrassment that she'd even kissed some of those checks when they'd come in—not because they were money, but because they were regular reminders that he remembered and loved her. At least that was what she'd believed for years. Now there was a big hole in that fabric.

"I think you'd better give him a call."

"OK," she sighed.

She agreed to have dinner with him, and they drove to a seafood restaurant in San Rafael. The eatery was on the canal which eventually wound out to the Bay. Customers could arrive here by land or by sea, so to speak, tying up at the restaurant's dock.

It was a warm summer evening, so they ate on the patio overlooking the canal.

She ordered lobster, and focused on cracking and collecting its delicious tidbits.

She waited until she was finished eating to tell Richard about Alex.

"I read about a body being found. That was Megan's son?"

"Yes."

"I'm truly sorry."

"I've been staying with her again because she needs my support. He was her only child. And he was murdered."

Richard whistled. "Have the police come up with any suspects yet?"

"No, they haven't. It's in the sheriff's hands. He was killed somewhere else, and then dumped off a cliff in the Headlands."

"When do they think this happened?"

"They don't know. His body was well preserved, because the ocean's so cold."

"Nasty business. Any clues?"

"We think it was drug related."

Richard raised his eyebrows.

"Yes," Gwen said. "He was into the heavy stuff—deeply."

"How could he afford it?"

She shrugged. "He had a job sorting mail—the bottom of the food chain. The family thinks he might have owed his dealer a lot of money, and couldn't pay up, and so…"

Richard took her hand and extended sympathy through touch.

"I had one other thought," Gwen said. "It's probably crazy. Don't laugh."

"I wouldn't laugh at you."

Gwen pursed her lips and gazed at the canal. At eight thirty it was still light out. She watched two sailboats motor quietly back to their berths, as their wake slapped against the retaining wall.

Then she looked at Richard and said, "Do you think there could be any connection to Mom's death?"

Again, he raised his eyebrows. "How do you figure that?"

"Oh, I don't know. I don't have a clue. It's just a thought that keeps popping up."

"Let me think about it."

Heading back to Sausalito, they were stuck in traffic. As police cars and ambulances raced by they knew there must be an accident ahead. Highway 101 became a parking lot.

At first they sat quietly and chatted, but after a short time Richard began to show his impatience. His body movements became jerky, and soon he was swearing.

"Hey, Richard, it's OK. We're not in a hurry, are we?"

"I hate this. I hate not having control."

"Just pretend we're chatting at a beach."

"Oh, right." He took out the little bottle she'd seen before and swallowed a pill.

She wondered if he had heart trouble.

Gwen didn't like this side of him. But then again, it proved he was human. If she could get drunk and make a scene, and he'd forgive her, then she could forgive a little temper.

~

Gwen returned to the bar where she'd obtained the marijuana. She found Useless sitting by himself.

"Look, now that you know I'm not a snitch or anything, could you please sell me some hard stuff?"

"Ma'am, I don't get into that. Only grass."

"Well, could you put me touch with somebody who does?"

"What you want with that stuff anyway? You don't look the type."

"Never mind analyzing me. You sell? I pay." She couldn't believe how tough she sounded.

"I'll have to make some contacts. Come back next week. I'll let you know if I got a lead."

Maybe she was wasting her time. Maybe she'd settled for too light a dealer, who only had pot. Or so he said. Maybe, even if she got hard stuff it wouldn't lead to any information, and that was what she really wanted.

Chad and Eric hadn't been able to make any contacts. What made her think she could? She didn't even know the lingo. She didn't come across as a cokehead. This angle didn't seem to be paying off.

Nevertheless, she met the pot dealer at the same time the next week.

"Let's go outside."

They stepped out in the windy evening.

"What shall I call you?" she asked.

"*Useless* is fine."

"How did you get that name?"

"Short for Ulysses," he smiled.

"It doesn't bother you?"

"Naw. Not any more."

"OK, what did you find out?"

"I have to be careful. The party I spoke to knows I don't use, and knows I don't sell, so he's kinda suspicious."

"So where does that leave us?"

"With a big price tag."

She couldn't believe what he wanted for a tiny amount.

"Would I be dealing with him or with you?"

"Me. I really don't want to get into this. And you seem like nice a lady. So you think it over, and if you're still interested, come back next Friday."

Gwen sighed in frustration. "Thanks."

She left him, and biked back to Denisons. Not only could she not afford this stuff, but it started to seem like a foolish trail, one that probably led nowhere.

She wished she could talk to someone about it, but she knew that everyone who cared about her would think she was nuts to put herself at risk like this.

Maybe she should be more direct—ask specifically for information, even if she had to buy it. That would be more dangerous, but might be more profitable.

The next week she went back. She ducked her head in the door, and saw Useless.

"Hey, your lady friend's back," the bartender said to him.

Useless turned and saw her. He got off his bar stool and came toward the door. They stepped outside.

"Look. I'm going to level with you. I think I can trust you. What I'm really after is information—not drugs."

"What kind of information?"

"A friend of mine was murdered. He was a drug addict, unfortunately. The family thinks he probably owed a dealer a lot of money, and that's why he was killed."

"You talkin' 'bout the guy that washed up off the Headlands?"

"Yeah. Alex Denison. Ever hear of him?"

Useless shook his head. "Cops working on it?"

Gwen nodded. "But they've come up zero so far."

"So you're playing amateur detective?"

Gwen dropped her eyes. "You could say that."

"Wish I could help you, but like I say, I don't deal with the hard stuff."

"You think the contact you made might know something?"

Useless shrugged.

"Look, here's my phone number. If you find out anything, I'd appreciate a call."

She handed him a piece of paper with her first name and Megan's number.

He accepted it, and nodded.

~

There were two slots open in the June election, and four candidates running.

Gwen had almost forgotten about it since Alex's murder. The night before the election she got on the phone again and reminded people to vote.

"It will be what it will be," she said to Megan before going to bed. "I did what I could."

"You did a lot, and Ms. Stanford should be very grateful to you."

When the votes were counted the next day, both her father and Sally Stanford were winners. Well, that should make for an interesting battle, Gwen thought.

Sally had a victory party that night for her supporters at the Valhalla.

Although tired, Gwen went to show her support. She would just put in a brief appearance.

The crowd was ecstatic. A lot of river rats were there, rejoicing with an open keg of beer. Also some of the storekeepers who were in support of public facilities. When Sally was ready to speak, she put two fingers to her mouth and blasted out a whistle that got everyone quiet.

She gave a victory speech which ended with, "And this isn't the end of the ride. You wait and see. My next victory speech will be 'from Madam to Mayor'."

Cheers could have been heard a block away. Hugs were given to friends and strangers alike.

Chapter 28

The next day after work Gwen was eager to tell Varda about the election results. When no one answered the door, she let herself in.

"Hello," she called.

He appeared suddenly in a simple bathrobe, tying the belt around his waist. He looked upset.

"My dear, I am occupied."

Almost paralyzed with embarrassment, and feeling herself color from chest to cheeks, she backed off.

"I'm so sorry," she mumbled, dashing out the door.

She certainly had heard enough about his lovers, but had never met any of them, or stumbled into such an embarrassing situation. It just had never been an issue before.

She raced down the gangplank, jumped on her bike and sped down Bridgeway. How stupid she felt. She was beating herself up so much for such a social faux pas that she didn't see a car turning the corner as she was crossing Nevada Street. The car's brakes squealed as it came to a halt, but not before the impact knocked her off her bicycle.

The driver got out to see if she was alright, and helped her up. He apologized profusely, but she said it was her fault.

"I don't think you can ride this," the man said, examining the bent wheel.

She had a cut elbow and skinned knee, but otherwise was unhurt. He offered to take her and her bike wherever she wanted to go. While feeling wildly disoriented by the preceding events, she debated whether to go south to Denise's or north to Eric's at the waterfront. Eric could fix the bike, she knew.

She decided on the latter, and climbed in the stranger's car. The man loaded her bicycle into his trunk and drove her to the waterfront. He took the bike out of his car and followed Gwen to Eric's place."

She thanked him. As he walked away, she realized she'd never asked his name.

"What the hell happened?" Eric asked as she presented her tear-stained face to him.

He brought her inside, heard her story, then went to examine the bicycle, and bring it up on the deck. When he came back he poured her a glass of whiskey, which she didn't like.

"Drink it, he said. "I think you're in shock."

She told him about the humiliating incident at Varda's.

He laughed. "So he had a lover."

"But I should never have gone there uninvited," she protested, sipping the distasteful beverage.

"I'm sure it's not the first time his amours have been interrupted."

"Still…"

"Still what? You should ride that tin lizzy of yours more carefully."

"Can you fix it?"

"You know I can. Right now we're going to fix you."

He left and came back with a soapy wash cloth, alcohol and bandages. He cleaned up her elbow and knees with the cloth.

"Now be brave."

"What?"

"This is alcohol. It's all I have."

She hadn't had a skinned knee since she was a kid. She'd forgotten how much they sting.

He dabbed it on the scrapes, as she gasped.

"You're lucky you didn't break an arm or worse."

She gulped down the rest of the whiskey, as Eric applied bandages.

"Now, just rest."

She was sitting on the sofa. When he said that, she turned and lay down, pulling the afghan over her.

She awoke realizing she'd been asleep for a long time. Eric was smoking a pipe and reading on the other side of the room.

Alarmed, she said, "I have to get home."

He shook his head. "I called Megan. Told her what happened, and that you'd be spending the night here. She'd going to call Denise and tell her not to expect you at work tomorrow."

"I can't miss work." Why did her head feel like a watermelon ready to burst open?

"How would you get there?"

Dimly, she remembered the accident with the bike. And that Eric had no car.

"I could take a cab."

"Stay with me and help me fix your bike."

It was hard to reject this proposal.

She nodded, and was soon in the arms of slumber again.

In the morning, the sound of sizzling bacon awoke her. Then she could smell it. And the coffee. She rose in her crumpled clothing, and headed for the john. A primitive affair, she wasn't sure she knew how it worked. She washed her face, combed her hair with Eric's brush, and rubbed some toothpaste around her teeth.

When she'd done what she could for her appearance, she followed her nose to the food.

"How did you sleep?"

"Great."

He laid two aspirin beside her plate. "For your hangover."

"Thanks." She swallowed them with some fresh orange juice.

"And your bruises?"

"They're not bothering me. You're a good nurse, Eric."

He placed two eggs and five pieces of crisp bacon on her plate.

"I can't possibly eat that much bacon!"

But she did.

"Ah, the lady has an appetite."

"I guess it's because I didn't have supper. And because this bacon is so good."

When they'd finished their second cup of coffee, Eric asked if she was ready to tackle the bike."

"Sure, if you tell me what to do."

On the deck, Gwen could feel the morning sunshine on her face.

"You don't mind if I do a few Yoga stretches first," she said.

"Go ahead. I'll get some tools."

In a few moments he came back with an assortment of items in a canvas bag. "You carry this. I'll bring the bike down."

They found a dry spot near Eric's sawhorse to begin the task.

He removed the tools from the bag and placed them on a makeshift table made from a piece of plywood and two sawhorses.

"I don't have all the equipment a bike shop has, but I think I can straighten this wheel. While I play doctor, you play nurse," he smiled. "Hand me the hex wrenches."

She didn't have a clue what hex meant but she knew what wrenches were, and took a guess.

"Good. I'll hire you."

She watched while he removed the wheel.

"I should probably be doing this in the shop, but it's so nice here."

"Now we'll have to undress the young lady." He stripped the tire from the wheel.

He held the errant wheel out in front of him, closed one eye, and studied the alignment, or lack thereof.

"It's worse than I thought. We'll have to go back inside to use the vices."

They picked up the tools and the wheel, and entered the end of the dwelling he'd made into a shop. Gwen had not been in this part before. All about were tools, boat parts, and a workbench that embraced one whole wall. Two vices were attached to it.

He picked up the electric drill.

"Drill bit," he requested.

"Where?"

"There."

She handed him one.

The telephone rang.

"Too small." He chose the one he wanted.

The phone kept ringing. Eric ignored it.

"Screws."

She handed him a large compartmentalized box of screws. He chose the ones he wanted.

She did indeed feel like a nurse in the O.R. while the surgeon barked orders at her.

She watched with curiosity as he attached a piece of two-by-four to the bench vertically. Then, to that, he fastened another vice. Now she could see his intent. The three vices were placed in a triangular pattern. Into two of them he guided the crooked wheel.

He leaned so he could see the edge of the wheel. With his hands, he started bending it, carefully, slowly, pushing the bent side toward the third vise to achieve his goal. He kept fine tuning his patient, until it was straight.

Finally, he said, "I think this is as good as it gets." He removed the wheel from its grips. "Operation over. Now, let's get her dressed."

Together they wrestled the tire back on the wheel. Eric placed the wheel back on the Schwinn, and tightened the bolt.

"Eric?"

"Hmm?"

"Who do you think was supplying Alex with drugs?"

Eric was silent, and Gwen thought maybe he hadn't heard her. He kept spinning the wheel on the bike, studying its alignment.

"Don't know."

Eric stopped working, and wiped the sweat from his face and neck with his sleeve.

He set the bike upright. "I think she's ready to ride."

Gwen suddenly felt dizzy. Everything was spinning inside her head. She looked at Eric helplessly, and would have fallen, had he not caught her.

"What's wrong?"

"I don't know. Everything's whirling around—the world, my head—"

"Are you dizzy?"

"Yeah."

Eric helped her back in the salon to a chair.

"How now?"

"Still going round and round."

She turned her head to follow him as he went to get her a glass of water. The spinning got worse.

"I'm taking you to the hospital."

"No, let's wait."

"Let's not. I'll go borrow a car, and you sit tight." He started out the door. He turned back to say, "And that's an order."

He was gone. Gwen closed her eyes and the spinning continued. Her stomach was upset too.

About ten minutes later Eric returned, jingling some keys. "Got 'em."

He slowly and carefully helped Gwen into the 1955 Buick.

As they rumbled along, Gwen thought she might throw up. The car was making all sorts of noises, and to Gwen at least, it seemed to be lurching.

"Stop farting," he said. Then he turned to Gwen and said, "Not you—the car."

"Can you go slower?" she whined.

He didn't hear her. "I'll give this old girl a tune-up. She probably hasn't had one in a decade."

They reached Marin General Hospital in San Rafael and Eric pulled up to the Emergency entrance. He helped Gwen inside and seated her in a vacant wheelchair. In a few minutes she was wheeled out of the reception room, as Eric called, "I'll wait out here."

She was placed on a gurney in a tiny space between two 'shower curtains', as she thought of them. In about twenty minutes, a nurse came in, took her temperature, blood pressure and asked a ton of questions. She left abruptly, leaving Gwen to wonder what was next.

About forty-five minutes later a man came in. About five feet six, with longish grey hair, his manner was swift and to the point. Built like a bull, his short-sleeve white garb revealed tattoo covered arms. He, too, asked a lot of questions.

"When will I see a doctor?" Gwen implored.

"I am your doctor—Flash Gordon."

His look must have revealed her suspicion.

"*Doctor* Flash Gordon."

He turned her head to one side, then the other.

Gwen groaned with discomfort, as the room went round and round.

"Rocks in your head."

She would have jumped off the table if she could. She thought he meant she didn't know what she was talking about.

"The condition you have—rocks in your head. If you want the medical term, it's benign positional vertigo."

She liked the benign part. "What does that mean?"

"The short version is that it occurs when small pieces of calcium break free and float in the tube of the inner ear. This messes with your mind—sends the brain confusing messages about your body's position. Do you want me to fix it?"

"Can you?"

"Maybe. You'll have to trust me."

"What would it involve?" she asked skeptically.

"I will lean you back against my arm, then twist your head quickly to the side."

She winced. "And that's it?"

"If it works. Doesn't always."

Perhaps to stall for time, she found herself looking at his tattoos. One was of a Harley motorcycle.

"Do you ride motorcycles?"

"Yup. Race them too. Ever go to a motorcycle race?"

"No, can't say as I have."

"Nothing like it."

As strange as he was, he was allowed to work in this hospital, so he must be legitimate. Besides, what other choices did she have?

"OK, I'll do it."

"Come to the race Sunday?"

"No! The procedure."

He knew what she meant. Before she could have second thoughts, he pushed her back against one of his brawny arms and torqued her head aggressively side to side. Then he propped her back up.

"How do you feel now?"

After catching her breath, Gwen moved her head gingerly, then more assertively.

"It's gone."

"Happy?"

"Well, yes. It's great!"

"It could come back, and if it does *you'll* come back." He handed her his card.

When she returned to the lobby, walking confidently across the room, Eric rushed to her with concern.

She smiled. "I'm fine."

She relayed the experience to him.

"*The* Flash Gordon?" he laughed. "He's one of Marin's characters. He plays pool, and roars down the freeway naked on his bike like a madman."

"What!"

"No, no. Did I say that?" He stopped to guffaw. "What I meant to say was he swims naked in the ocean, and roars down the freeway like a madman." He burst out laughing and Gwen joined him.

"But he's a good doctor."

"Glad to hear it," she smiled.

They pulled up to the Denison's house. Together they transmitted the chain of events to Chad and Megan, from yesterday's bicycle accident to the hospital.

"Sounds like you had quite a carnival of experiences," Chad said.

"It was no carnival, Chad."

"Well, we're very glad you're alright now," Megan said. "Can I get you something?"

She brought out a pitcher of lemonade, just as the telephone rang. Chad answered.

"Gwen, it's for you," he called. "It's Denise."

"What's up?" she asked her friend.

Denise sounded anxious. "Last night a guy called for you. Maybe I shouldn't have, but I gave him Eric's number. Did you get the call? Have you heard from him?"

"Who? What are you talking about?"

"I know this is crazy, but it sounds like his name is *Useless*. It's probably another false alarm."

"No, Denise, it isn't! I know this guy. What did he say?"

"He said he had information for you."

"Did he say what it was?" Her heart was throbbing.

"No. He said he'd call back."

"When?"

"He didn't say."

Gwen groaned.

She made sure Chad understood that if a call came for her, please let her know right away.

CHapter 29

She turned and tossed half the night, wishing there were some way to reach Useless. If he didn't call soon, she'd start hanging out at his watering hole.

As she tried to sleep she became deeply aware of the geriatric mattress she was on—probably the same one she'd had as a child.

"I should buy the Denisons a new one," she thought, moving farther to the edge of the single bed to avoid the sag in the middle.

In the morning the phone rang, and she jumped to her feet and ran out the living room.

"It's for you," Chad said.

She almost grabbed the phone from his hand.

It was Louis. She hoped her disappointment didn't show.

"Hey, you're a hard girl to get a hold of. Never know where you're crashing."

"Mmm," she mumbled.

"You sound sleepy. Hard night?" he asked.

"Just hard to sleep. How are you?"

"Really wanting to see you, stranger."

She wanted to see him too. But then she might miss that all important call. But if she stayed home, she'd be twisting her hands all day and he probably wouldn't call. Dilemma.

He said, "Are you still there?"

"Yeah, just thinking. When did you have in mind?"

"Today?"

"If you can give me a few hours."

"Sure."

When she hung up, she thought she could get a couple more hours of sleep. But that wayward sandman wouldn't come. After another hour she got up, took a shower, and had some breakfast.

~

"Why are you so sure that a man killed your mother?" Louis asked.

"Well, what woman would?"

They were sitting downtown in Elephant Park, licking ice-cream cones on a sunny, warm day in July. At least it had been warm in the Banana Belt, but cooler downtown near Hurricane Gulch.

"It's just you shouldn't exclude the 'fair' sex. It wouldn't be hard to push an unsuspecting person off the cliff."

"Well, I haven't met any women in that crowd except Megan and a couple who came to the Goddess Circle."

"Didn't you tell me that Megan lied about baby-sitting you that day?"

"Yeah, but I really can't see her doing that to my mom. What would her motive have been? They were good friends."

"Maybe she had a dark side. You don't know everything about her."

Gwen was beginning to think she was looking for support in a can of worms.

"I'm trying to figure out if there's any connection between my mom's death and Alex's. Do you see anything to link them together?"

"You mean the forgeries? It's possible, I suppose."

Gwen threw the base of her cone to a waiting pigeon.

"I borrowed a car. Wanna drive over to Mill Valley?" he said.

"Sure."

A short drive on the freeway—just one exit up from Sausalito.

She had told him before about the waterfall on a side street off Throckmorton. He asked her now if she'd show him where it was.

"I doubt there'd be any water falling now. It's July. We haven't had rain for months. But it's still a lovely sight."

"Let's go."

She remembered the way. There was a tiny parking area, where they left the car, and walked hand in hand through the wooded path beside the creek.

"I'm surprised there's still water running in the creek."

The waterfall was no more than a drizzle.

"Feel up to a climb?" she said.

"Sure."

It was a steep ascent in places, even though a winding path had been carved out by forerunners.

When they finally reached the top, they were both winded. They discovered that after a level stretch, there was a bluff above which water preceded the one below. It too must overflow with water in the rainy season. They stood where they were and then collapsed on the dry ground.

"Shall I tell you a secret?"

He nodded.

"This is where my father said I was conceived."

"Really!"

"Really. But I only saw it from below."

"So that's why you wanted to come up here."

"Not to conceive!"

Very private, at least for now, Louis wasted no time in enveloping Gwen in his arms. First he removed her headscarf, then her shoes. She started laughing. But as he slowly unbuttoned her blouse, with his eyes on hers, the ardor rose again. Passion rose quickly in both of them. Finally, Gwen was willing to give herself to him, but he teased her, kissing her lips, her open mouth and neck endlessly. Perhaps he knew it would drive her crazy. Her body begged for more.

She was heaving with desire, until finally as he was preparing himself for the final act, she, in a frenzy, discarded her own slacks.

As her pleasure peaked she let out an uninhibited howl. She couldn't help feeling it had something to do with the location. Almost like violating a sacred spot, yet exhilarated by the setting, there was something overwhelming about just being *here*.

But that did not diminish the thrill she felt being with Louis. Even as they drove home on the cozy bench seat of the modern Plymouth, Gwen cuddled up to him, and felt herself getting aroused all over.

~

The telephone rang, Chad answered.

Gwen heard him say, "Sorry, I don't understand what you want."

There was another pause. "Just a minute."

Chad turned to Gwen. "Do you know anyone called Useless?"

Her heart bobbed up to her throat. She grabbed the phone from Chad.

"Hello, it's me, Useless. You the lady I talked to at the bar that wanted information?"

"Yes, yes, that's me." She was out of breath.

"I got the name for you—the dude layin' out the dope for your friend."

"Yes?" She held her breath. It seemed forever before he spoke again.

"Conan."

Gwen gasped. She was so stunned she couldn't talk.

Then the line went dead.

~

The Goddess Circle was meeting again. A large crystal ball adorned the center altar and two candles were burning—one for Alex and one for Conan. Members brought mementos important to them and placed them on the altar. Gwen felt the warmth and peace this group radiated immediately. She also felt the sadness.

After an opening prayer to the goddess, Chad lit the sage, circled the group with a feather, and wafted the smoke on anyone who desired the cleansing.

Everyone in the group felt the absence of Alex and Conan. It was suggested by Anna, a woman with long grey braids, that they spend some time talking about their memories of the two, and pray for them both.

Anna said she remembered Alex as a little boy with longish hair learning to ride his two-wheeler. She remembered one day when he fell off the bike she gave him a popsicle. For the next three days he 'staged' a fall in front of her house, hoping to receive the same kindness. A gentle laughter followed.

Eric was silent for a long time. Then he said, "Conan's been my friend for ages, but that doesn't mean I knew everything about him. I suspected the forgeries for a long time, but I didn't know."

"What made you think that?" Megan asked defensively.

"Just the way he acted sometimes. Secretive, covert."

"Did you ever ask him about it?" Megan said.

"No. Maybe I didn't want to know."

There was silence.

Megan asked if anyone knew who was supplying Alex with drugs.

Anna spoke up. "Please, this isn't a hearing; it's a sacred circle. Please keep your remarks to remembrances, not questions."

Another silence.

A woman named Sara spoke up. "I used to be in love with Conan. But he did not reciprocate. We were good friends, though."

Gwen listened to other memories about the two men. She put her arm around Megan when the older woman began to cry.

Megan reminded the group that the crystal ball had belonged to Alex. She had given it to him when he'd joined the group two years before.

They ended with prayers for both the living and deceased members of their group.

"May the Divine Feminine rise again and raise us to our natural state of power."

When the group broke up and Eric was ready to leave, Gwen said she'd walk part way back with him if he didn't mind.

"Course not. Come on."

They walked down Ebbtide Street, breathing in first the fragrance of flowers blooming in July; then as they got closer to the water, the smell of salt water. It was windy and they could hear the lines on sailboats clanging against their masts in the heavy gusts.

"I found out something since we saw each other. I couldn't reveal it in the Circle; it wasn't the time or place, but…" She stopped, wondering where to begin.

"I'm listening."

"Alex was being supplied by Conan."

Eric stopped in his tracks. "How do you know that?"

"My *informer* told me."

"What are you talking about?"

"Remember the guy I told you who was selling me grass?"

"Yeah?"

"I finally told him I needed *information*, and could he ask around and find out who was supplying Alex with drugs."

"Holy Moly. And he did?"

"I didn't expect to ever hear from him, but yes, the other day he called and that's the name he gave me."

"Do you trust him?"

"I don't have any reason not to. He didn't ask for any money."

Eric mumbled, "How many Conans can there be?"

"That's what I thought."

"It makes sense, though. Once I went to Conan's, and Alex was just leaving. When he was out of sight Conan said, 'Someday I'm gonna bust his crystal balls!' Looking back, Alex could have been blackmailing Conan."

"Blackmailing him about what?"

"The forgeries, I suppose."

"And Conan was paying him off with drugs."

"Right."

After several minutes she said, "I wonder if Conan was selling forgeries in order to get money for the drugs he supplied Alex with."

Eric snorted. "Do more forgeries to conceal the fact he was doing forgeries? Wow."

"How else could Conan afford to furnish the stuff for Alex? His own work wasn't doing well," Gwen said.

"What a mess."

"Oh, m'god!"

They walked in silence for several minutes. Then she said, "That leads to another question."

"What's that?"

"Do you think Conan could have killed Alex?"

Eric took in and let out a long breath. "Oh, God."

"Well, everyone thinks his death is connected with the drugs and the dealer. It makes sense, doesn't it?" Gwen said.

"I guess so. I hate to think it might be true, though. And I don't know how you'd prove it."

"And then there's the time-line problem"

"Do you know what Alex was strangled with?" Eric asked.
"No."
"Can you get a copy of the autopsy report?" Eric asked.
"I think Chad has one."
"It might give us some clues, Sleuth."

Chapter 30

Gwen decided it was time to bite the bullet and call Varda. It wasn't an easy apology for her to make. Easier to do on the phone.

She practiced what she'd say, and it sounded awfully formal. If she listened to Eric, her walking in on Varda was no big deal at all. She picked up the phone and dialed twice before she let it ring.

She was about to hang up when he answered.

Before she could say anything but 'hello', he said, "Why don't you come over?"

"When?"

"At noon."

She hesitated. "Alright."

She rode her bike along Bridgeway on a beautiful sunny July morning, until she came to the behemoth Vallejo. She walked up the gangplank at twelve o'clock and knocked on the door.

After her second attempt to arouse the artist, he came to the door.

"Mon cher, little bird. Come in, come in."

He gave her a big hug, and Gwen felt her whole body relax, knowing everything would be alright.

"Any news?" he asked as he put the kettle on.

"Oh, yes."

"Tell me. But first we must have our tea. It's only civilized."

Gwen had actually come to enjoy the strange concoction Varda called 'tea'.

When this ritual was finished, Gwen relayed that Alex had been blackmailing Conan because he knew about the forgeries. "At least that's what Eric and I think."

"This is most interesting," Varda said. "How do you know this?"

"It's a long story." She told him in summary about her 'friend' who discovered through his contacts, that the person providing Alex with drugs was his uncle, Conan.

"And one time I saw Conan hand over a packet of something to Alex. I was in the house, and they were in the yard. They didn't see me. Then Conan immediately left. I didn't think anything of it at the time."

Varda stood, paced the floor, tapping his forehead with his fist, as was his custom when he was trying to solve a problem.

Then he said, "If Conan was being blackmailed by Alex that gives Conan a motive for killing him."

There was a quick inhale of breath. "Yes."

"I wonder if Alex was blackmailing anyone else."

"Like who, for what?

"Well, with Conan in jail, Alex must have been hurting to get his hands on some drugs. Perhaps he took more chances, went after somebody higher up in the food chain that he had something on."

"Who would that be?"

"I don't know."

"I'm just thinking out loud."

She noticed Varda's hands were soiled with glue and paint.

"I interrupted your work," she said.

"Not at all. You are my favorite pastime."

She smiled. "There's a problem with that theory, though."

"What's that?"

"Alex was found dead *after* Conan was arrested."

"Ah, yes. But his body was in the water several days, is this true?" Varda said.

"We don't really know. I haven't made the numbers work yet. Conan was arrested on April twentieth. Alex's body was found on the twenty-seventh. If he was killed before the twentieth, then it could be Conan, but that means Alex was in the water a long time. The coroner said the body didn't show much sign of decay. But that's because the water was so cold."

"I see. Yes. Do you have copy of autopsy?"

"Eric asked me that. I'll have to try and get it from Chad."

"If the body couldn't have been in the water more than a few days, that means he was murdered after Conan's arrest." Varda said.

~

Gwen slept in late the next morning. She had tossed and turned most of the night thinking of Alex's murder. If Conan really was his supplier, but not his killer, then who was the killer?

She sat alone at the kitchen table with her Wheaties, again going over the facts, the suppositions and theories.

Chad joined her. "I thought I heard you out here," he said.

They chatted for a few minutes. Then Gwen said, "Chad, may I have a look at the autopsy report?"

He looked surprised. "It's not very pleasant reading."

"I know, but it might give us some clues."

He nodded, rose and retrieved the document. He handed it to Gwen and she took the kind of breath that she thought would steel herself against unsavory details.

She read through the material, amazed to find that whoever performed the autopsy found it necessary to dissect his entire body, giving a vivid description of the condition of each organ. She recoiled at the thought of poor Alex being cut up in pieces like a side of beef.

"Why do they do that?" she asked Chad.

"I suppose it's routine in deaths of suspicious nature. And to establish time of death."

"Why would they have to… ." Her hand flew to her mouth as she read more words.

"Have to what?"

She was barely audible. "Cut his testicles."

Chad sighed. "I don't know."

With each disclosure the pathologist performing the autopsy made it clear that the organ in question was still well preserved due to being in icy waters of the ocean. It would decay much faster if it were in the swamps of Louisiana.

She scanned the report looking for the cause of death. Strangulation.

Yes, they knew that. But with what instrument? That's what she was hoping to find out. But nothing was said regarding the method.

"Damn," she said. "I'll call—" she glanced to the bottom of the page for the person's signature. "Ronald Travis, pathologist. Maybe he'll tell me."

Chapter 31

Louis had called three times in the last two days, missing Gwen each time. Finally, she was there to receive his call.

"Hey, Sleuth, what have you been up to? I miss you."

The mellow, deep voice made her remember that she missed him.

"Me too."

"Let's drive out to Pt. Reyes."

Pt. Reyes was a national park northwest of Sausalito. There were beaches, sand dunes, hiking trails, and in the right season whales could be seen changing their residence with the seasons.

"Sure," she said. She needed a break from all the amateur detective work she was doing.

When Louis picked her up in his old Ford she gave him a big smile and he gave her a big kiss.

"More later," he promised with a squeeze of his hand

They drove out Sir Francis Drake through Taylor State Park with all its towering redwood trees, on through grasslands, to the little town of Olema. There they turned right, then after one block turned west, and followed the road through Inverness and on out to the ocean.

On the way Gwen filled him in with what she'd discovered about Alex and Conan.

"Seems like he's your guy," Louis said.

"Yeah, except the dates don't add up."

They waded in the freezing water. Even though it was July, the ocean hadn't gotten the message that it was summer. In fact in northern California, the ocean never warmed up enough to swim, except for the very brave. Louis and Gwen sat on a blanket in the sand and listened to the waves lick and lap the shore. The wind was quiet, so they were able to enjoy the beach and the sun.

Gwen got out the sandwiches she'd wrapped in waxed paper. She'd made them with ham and slices of pear.

Louis peeked inside his. "I only had this kind once a long time ago. Who was I with? Let me think." The sandwich lay in his hands, while he looked upward, trying to remember.

"I thought my mom was the only one who made them this way."

The next bite he planned to take was halted mid-air.

"What is it?" she asked.

"Yeah, it was your mom."

"How well, exactly, did you know my mother?"

"I had a crush on her, I admit it. Puppy love."

"And how did she feel about you?"

"Not the same, I'm afraid. She mostly hung around with Conan and Eric and that crowd. They were older. We only went out a couple of times."

They finished eating lunch in silence.

Nestled into a nook in the dunes, they were in a very private spot. Few people were on that part of the beach.

He pulled her down and began kissing her. She didn't resist, but she was not responding physically.

She wondered if the lips she was kissing had been kissed by her mother.

"What's up?" he asked.

"I don't know. I guess I'm just too wound up about the murder, and Conan."

"Can't you put it aside for awhile?"

"I'm trying."

He sat up and lit a cigarette. She lay quietly on the blanket.

In a few minutes he said, "The wind's come up—it's getting chilly. Shall we go?"

"Yes."

There was little conversation on the way back to Sausalito.

When she got out of his car, she said, "Give me time, Louis."

"Of course."

~

The next day she called Reardon's Funeral Home, and asked to speak with the person who'd performed the autopsy of Alex Denison. He wasn't available. She was promised he would return her call. But the rest of Friday ticked away and she did not hear from him.

On Monday she tried again. This time he came to the phone. She identified herself as the step-daughter of the Denisons.

"I'd like to know if you were able to determine what instrument may have been used in strangling the victim."

"I'll have to look over my report and get back to you. What was the date of death?"

He clearly didn't remember the case. She wondered how many bodies he butchered in a week. It was all so frustrating.

When he called her back on Tuesday, he said it was difficult to tell.

"Can you narrow it down to something as wide as a belt, or narrow as a wire?"

There was a pause. "It would be my opinion that the victim was garroted with a wire."

Gwen choked back her revulsion. "May I ask on what you based that opinion?"

"The neck was incised somewhat—about an eighth of an inch."

"Thank you."

"But time in the water clouded a clear ligature mark."

She was about to hang up when she thought of one more thing.

"Is there any way that the body could have been in the water seven or more days?"

"It's possible. The ocean's very cold."

"You put the date of death as April twenty-seventh in your report."

"Yes. I have to use the date the body was discovered as the *legal* date. We don't know the actual date of death. In that environment it could be anywhere from three days to three weeks or more."

Three weeks or more!

"Thank you. Thank you very much."

That was interesting. But she really didn't know anything more for sure. Alex could have been killed before Conan's arrest, but then again, maybe not.

It was all so frustrating.

Chapter 32

Gwen had become a fair sailor under Eric's tutelage. She could handle the *Wicked Winch* alone now if she had to. She didn't get stuck in irons anymore with no wind. And she didn't capsize.

They had sailed often on warm, sunny days last year, but as cold weather had come she had declined.

"I'm a fair weather sailor, Eric."

Now that it was July again, and the days had warmed up she agreed to go. They talked about sailing and they talked about Conan and Alex.

The second time they were out in the Bay, the wind was high. Eric said he'd better take over.

"Fluky winds."

"What does that mean?"

"It means the wind keeps changing directions—unpredictable."

"I noticed."

They sailed out toward Angel Island on the leeward side of the island and then toward Alcatraz. There the winds were erratic again, and after coming about several times trying to keep up with the whimsy of the wind, they found themselves almost on top of a fishing boat. Technically, they had right of way since the other vessel was motoring, but the fishing boat seemed oblivious to them. Once again Eric maneuvered a quick change of tack to avoid collision, but the Wicket Winch suddenly capsized, spilling them both in the frigid waters of the bay.

Gwen stayed near the boat. She tried to help Eric right it, but like a drowning man, he was pulling her down with him.

"Let me help you," she screamed."

But she kept being pulled under. Finally, she broke away from him, and started swimming for shore which was miles away. How long could she last in these frigid waters? The shock of the cold was paralyzing.

By now, of course, the fishing crew knew what had happened. They spotted Gwen, and came to help.

"Jump in," a voice called.

But she didn't have the energy to do so. She had all she could do to put one arm over the gunwale.

"Here, give us your hands,"

Two strong men pulled her aboard, and dumped her in the hull like a beached whale. She didn't have the strength to move. She was so chilled and exhausted she collapsed. Breathing was her only priority.

"Eric," she tried to tell the men. "Eric." But her words were inaudible.

The last thing she heard was, "She's in shock."

Later, someone was shaking her shoulder, "Where do you want to go? San Francisco?"

She mumbled, "Sausalito."

They took her there, and got a taxi to take her home. By now she was at least alert enough to give them an address. Megan got her into a hot bath, made her soup, and hovered over her like the caregiver she was. It wasn't long before Gwen fell asleep.

Several hours later when she awoke, she could hear voices and wandered out to the living room.

"Are you feeling better, Gwen?"

"Yes."

"Could you tell us what happened?" Megan asked.

Both Megan and Chad were there waiting to hear her story.

She told them about capsizing, swimming and being picked up by the fishermen. Then she asked, "Did Eric make it back?"

They looked at each other. "We haven't heard from him."

Her heart sank. Could he have drowned?

"Can he swim?" she asked.

"I would think so, since he's out on that water all the time," Megan said.

"It would be foolish to sail if you couldn't swim," Chad said.

"Were you wearing life jackets?" Megan asked.

"Not this time. We usually did." Gwen admitted.

She felt their criticism and said, "I've never known him to capsize before. I wonder if he got the boat righted."

"How did it happen?" Chad asked.

"The winds were—fluky."

Chad offered to go down to the marina and see if Eric had gotten back. First, he made the women some tea and brought out the cookie jar.

They sat in silence, sipping their tea and munching ginger bars.

Two scenarios kept running through Gwen's head. One, he was dragging her under because he panicked, and really couldn't swim, or two, he was trying to drown her. She didn't like either one. Both made her skin crawl. If it were the former, she was afraid he might have drowned. If the latter... well, she didn't want to dwell on that.

It was hours before Chad got back.

"He's OK. He finally got the boat up, or maybe someone helped him; and he sailed to shore."

"Why were you gone so long?" Megan asked.

"He didn't come to *our* shore," Chad said. "He ended up by the Yacht Club near Crissy Field in San Francisco. Somebody on the dock felt sorry for him, still wet and shivering, brought him inside to warm up and got him a drink. Then he drove Eric back to Sausalito."

"Where's his boat?" Megan asked.

"Still in the city, I guess."

"Did he talk about what happened?" Megan asked.

"I think he was embarrassed. He was glad to hear Gwen got back safely."

Comforted that Eric was alive, Gwen was nevertheless upset that he hadn't phoned or anything to see how she was fairing.

Megan asked, "Did you find out if he could swim?"

"No, I didn't. If he clung to the boat, and was able to right it, he may have been able to save himself without swimming," Chad said.

~

Gwen woke up with a sore throat, and within a few hours had a fever. Two days later she was diagnosed with pneumonia. Very glad that Megan was here to take care of her, Gwen tried to put all worries out of her mind and just sleep. The doctor had prescribed antibiotics. She felt weak and overwhelmed. Maybe the project she had taken on was too much for her. If she could just stay asleep for a very long time.

On the fourth day, Eric came to the house. Gwen could hear voices in the other room. Then Megan peeked in to see if she was sleeping.

"Eric's here. Do you want to see him?"

Part of her wanted to say *no*. On the other hand she wondered what his story was.

"For a few minutes."

"Alright, I'll tell him."

Eric walked into the bedroom. "I didn't know you were sick," he said.

She felt like saying, "You didn't know I was *alive*."

He was obviously very much ill at ease. "That was some day."

Gwen nodded.

"You got picked up?"

"Yes."

She wanted to ask about him, but she was too angry. They sat in silence, and finally he said, "Megan said I could only stay a few minutes, so I guess I better leave. Just came to make sure you were alright."

Right, she thought. She coughed deeply to let him know she wasn't.

When he was gone, Megan came in to see what he had to say for himself.

"Nothing."

"No apology?"

"Not a whiff."

"Did he explain what happened?"

"Nope."

"I suppose he was embarrassed."

"Embarrassed! Maybe so, because his plan to drown me didn't work!"

"Oh, Gwen, you mustn't say that."

"And maybe he's Alex's killer, and knows I have my antenna out."

"Oh, God! No."

"Did you find out if he could swim?"

"I didn't ask."

For days, while beginning to feel better physically, Gwen was dragged into a downward emotional spiral thinking that someone she'd trusted had either been trying to drown her, or in any case had done nothing to help her. They could have righted the boat together. What was the matter with him?

She stayed in bed longer than she need have, just thinking, puzzling it over and over. And not wanting anyone's company.

~

When she did finally rouse herself, it was to see Varda. He was waiting for her on the deck of the Vallejo when she arrived. She was eager to share her news about the ligature used on Alex, but she had learned to respect Varda's ritual.

It was unusually warm, and the tea was served cold. Not chilled with ice, but probably refrigerated.

Gwen looked south toward the forest of sailboat masts bobbing in the breeze.

"It's lovely out here," she said as she drank the dark liquid and munched on something deliciously flaky made with nuts and honey.

"It's often too cold or windy to be outside, but I appreciate the days when nature accommodates our thirst for warm, sunny weather," he said.

When the tea was finished, Gwen said, "Are you ready to hear my news?"

Varda smiled. "Of course, my dear."

First she told her friend about the boating accident with Eric, her suspicion, and her illness.

"I was almost out of energy from fighting him off, before I had to start swimming to get away from him."

Varda expressed great concern, and they discussed the various reasons Eric may have behaved as he did.

"We will have to keep an eye on him." he said.

"Now I want to tell you about the autopsy. I did get the report, which wasn't very helpful in giving information on the instrument used to kill Alex. However, I was able to speak with the pathologist, and he said it was his opinion that a wire was used."

Varda looked thoughtful.

"That wasn't in the report?"

"No. He seemed hesitant to say that, because it was just his opinion." Gwen went on. "He thought it was a wire because there was a cut in his neck about an eighth of an inch deep in front, and a groove around the rest."

"That points further to Conan, does it not?" Varda said.

"Yes! He had to use strong wire across the back of his art work to hang it. If he killed Alex on his houseboat, wire would have been readily available."

"Exactly what I was thinking," Varda said.

They stared at each other in this common theory.

Then Gwen sighed. "But it doesn't prove anything. Anyone can get wire, and perhaps the killer even wanted it to look like Conan's work."

"Did you find out if it were possible that he was in the water for a week?"

"The examiner told me it could be anything from three days to three weeks or more. So that doesn't prove a thing."

Varda whistled. "But it allows for the possibility that Conan killed Alex." He paced the floor. "Who else had a motive?"

"I don't know. Eric? I don't know what it would be. We know Alex was blackmailing Conan. We don't know anything like that about Eric."

"Except that he may have tried to drown you. Just because we don't know what his motive might be, doesn't mean he didn't have one. Let's not rule Eric out yet."

They sat in silence, listening to the breeze and gentle waves hitting the shore.

"Varda," Gwen said, "do you think there can be any connection between Alex's death and the death of my mother?"

"Oh my. Why do you think so, little bird?"

"I don't know. It's just a feeling."

"I don't see the connection but perhaps I'm overlooking something."

"Eric told me that Conan was in love with my mother. And if she wouldn't have him, well, wouldn't that be a motive to murder her?"

"I loved your mother too. But I didn't murder her."

"No. But if Conan was violent enough to murder Alex, he might have lost his temper before, too?"

"Perhaps. Yes."

Chapter 33

It was time to make another visit to Conan's houseboat. She slid Varda's plastic card in the door and gained entry. At least this time she had no fear of his bursting in on her.

She was looking for a piece of wire that might have served as the instrument of death. She carefully scrutinized the parlor, the kitchen, sleeping area and both decks. She knew Conan wasn't so dumb as to leave it in plain sight, so she had to look everywhere. Dumping the entire contents on the floor, she looked in his trash. There, inside a paper bag she found a wire. It was about eighteen inches long. She looked for traces of blood but didn't see any. Maybe they'd been wiped or washed off. She thought perhaps she'd found the weapon of the crime.

She took her leave of the houseboat, and hurried to show Varda.

"Where did you get this?"

For once, even Varda forgot the formality of the tea.

"In a bag buried in the wastebasket. If it was just a piece of discarded wire, why would he put it in a bag before discarding it?"

Varda nodded. "Even though there are no obvious traces of blood, we must have it examined at a lab for occult evidence of blood," he said.

"Don't you think I should take it to the sheriff's, and let them do that?"

"Yes, of course," he sighed.

~

As she explained why she was there, she had the feeling that the officer at the desk had listened to many stories and had developed, with practice, an attentive look betraying his genuine disinterest. When she presented her finding she was scolded for disturbing the crime scene.

But it wasn't designated a crime scene, she wanted to say.

She was told she should have contacted them before removing anything from the area. She wondered to herself if they'd have thought it proper for her to dump the trash on the floor, and then report a suspicious paper bag, or would it be alright to open the bag? The whole thing seemed ridiculous to her. The authorities hadn't gotten to square one in discovering Alex's killer. If she hadn't touched anything, how could this valuable piece of evidence have been discovered? They should be thankful for her assistance.

The officer took the bag, looking dubiously inside.

"Did you touch the wire?"

She admitted she had.

"Then I'll have to take your fingerprints, miss, so we can disregard them."

She didn't see how they could get fingerprints off that tiny surface, but she didn't argue.

While he took her fingerprints she explained why the wire was significant, the connection to the forgeries, how they already had Conan in custody.

"Will you send it to the lab, find out if there's any occult blood on it?"

He looked at her with a twisted smile. "I'm sure our officers will know what to do with it."

She scribbled her name and phone number on a piece of paper, and handed it to the officer. "Please let me know the results."

She left wondering if her great find would get lost in the shuffle of things or discarded as a worthless item some crackpot had provided. She should have asked to speak to the sheriff himself.

She reported to Varda what had transpired at the sheriff's office.

"I'm sorry you felt he didn't take it seriously. I suppose he deals with such things on a more or less regular basis."

Gwen was feeling discouraged.

"Listen, you're wearing yourself out thinking of nothing but Alex's murder. How would you like to go sailing? I'm taking a party out tomorrow. Would you like to come with us?"

"I thought you'd never ask."

"You could have said you wanted to go."

"Maybe I was afraid of making another faux pas."

He laughed. "You did nothing wrong."

"I'd love to go."

When she left him that day he said, "Bring a jacket. It gets cool on the water."

"Yes" she smiled. "I know a little bit about sailing."

~

The next day, as she approached the boat she could already smell food. Of course, she thought, what kind of party would Varda have without an array of tempting delicacies.

She climbed aboard, noting a sea of people, none of whom she recognized; she did not see Varda. An attractive young man helped her to a seat, sliding in beside her in such tight quarters their thighs were pressed together.

"Where's Varda?" she asked.

"Below, getting the food ready. Is this your first time on *La Joi de Vivre*?"

"Yes. And you?"

"Three times before."

A band of two young men and a woman began to play sea-shanty songs, and the guests joined in singing. The hint of marijuana swirled around her. A few feet away, she saw two young women sharing a toke.

Someone in an old-fashioned sailor's outfit was passing out Bloody Marys from a tray. Another such was serving Mimosas.

Gwen thought it too early in the day to be drinking, but she forged ahead anyway, accepting a Mimosa. This was a special day. The drink went down as easily as orange juice, which it was, in part. She had another.

Finally, they were underway. They motored out of the marina, and south to the larger portion of Richardson's Bay. She learned on the way from her seatmate that it was named after a man who had settled here, and had run a business providing fresh water, beef and staples to the sailing ships in the eighteen hundreds. This was at the little inlet that included the present location of the Vahalla. This cove was also used by rum runners to transport liquor during prohibition.

When they reached the Bay she watched as two fine specimens of the male gender hoisted the sails. It was thrilling to watch as the enormous sails exploded and announced their presence with loud snaps. What grandeur, as a rainbow of color swept across the sky. Soon the sails were tamed, as those minding the sheets had them adjusted perfectly. Now it was smooth and soundless sailing.

Varieties of sweet and savory finger food were passed around, and Gwen was glad she'd skipped breakfast. Not all foreign foods, there were American sweet rolls, which she suspected a guest had brought.

But that was only the beginning. Large plates holding complete Varda-type meals were distributed to the guests. Gwen had to decline; she couldn't eat another bite.

Finally, Varda emerged from below where he'd been overseeing the food, and received a hearty welcome from the guests. The band played and the guests sang, *For He's a Jolly Good Fellow.* Varda walked around greeting various guests, including Gwen, and then took over the wheel.

As she made her way to the head, Gwen saw someone who looked very familiar. It was hard to place her out of context. Leaving the head, she was still mulling over who it could be. She took a circuitous route and passed the woman. My gosh, it was Pip, who'd talked to her about her mother. Somewhat stunned, she kept on walking and sought out Varda at the wheel.

She greeted him, assured him she was having a great time, and then asked about Pip.

"Oh, we've been friends for a long time. It was she who first was willing to display my work in her art gallery. If it weren't for Pip I might not be where I am today."

"You're kidding," Gwen was amazed. "What happened to her?"

"Coming about," he yelled to the crew.

When they were smoothly on another tack, Gwen waited for an answer.

"It's a long story, and not a happy one."

"Tell me. I met her, you know, when I asked for those who knew my mother to come forward. She told me she'd had an art gallery."

"That's right." He took a deep breath. "Alright. Pip loved her husband dearly, and trusted him completely. She didn't have much of a head for finances, and let him manage that part of her business. He died suddenly of a brain hemorrhage. He had serious gambling debts, of which she was only dimly aware, and outstanding loans from several banks. Anyway, they came after her, poor girl, and took everything she had, including their home, the art gallery, even the art. She had not taken all the work on consignment. She'd bought much of it outright. The greedy gremlins took it all."

The band was louder than ever, playing *Do You Know the Way to San Jose?* Gwen was having trouble hearing Varda.

"Sorry. What was the last you said?"

"She lost it all."

"Did she have any insurance?"

"No. He left her no life insurance, and there was no property insurance."

"That poor woman."

"She lived with me for awhile on the Vallejo, then unwilling to take any more charity—she was a proud lady she was—moved into a 'share' home, and lives in a very frugal manner. We see each other now and then. I do what I can for her, and she loves to come sailing."

"That's so sad."

"Yes."

"She said she had my mother's work in her gallery."

"And it was swept up with everything else."

Gwen moaned.

"I gave her one of the ones I had of your mother's. She still has it on her wall, I believe."

Gwen felt the tears well up.

"Why don't you go talk to her? I think she's pretty lonely, there by herself."

Gwen summoned her courage and approached Pip.

"Hi, I don't know if you remember me—"

"Of course I do. Sit down."

Gwen sat. Looking straight ahead at the waves beyond, the woman grasped Gwen's hand and held it.

There seemed to be no need for talking.

Chapter 34

Gwen decided it was time to move back to Denise's. Megan was sorry to see her go, but accepted Gwen's decision without argument.

"I'm just so thankful you stayed as long as you did."

"You're welcome."

"Stop by—when you can."

"I will."

She packed up her clothes, and Megan drove her back to Denise's. After they got them in the house, she gave Megan a heartfelt hug.

She felt a surge of relief as Megan drove away, as though some heavy burden had been lifted from her shoulders.

Denise welcomed her with open arms. She had prepared salmon and asparagus for supper.

"This is great. I'll do the meal tomorrow night."

"I'll take you up on that."

They discussed the events that had transpired in recent weeks.

She told Denise that Conan seemed to be the obvious suspect for the murder of Alex, but how the dates were puzzling.

"So if the condition of his body indicated that he could only have been dead for a few days, there's another possibility."

Gwen was flummoxed.

"What's that?"

"Maybe he was strangled and dumped in the water, but didn't actually *die* then."

"It's a thought," Gwen said. "Yes!"

"Maybe he tried to swim and keep afloat as long as he could. But he was losing blood from his neck, and not strong enough to get to shore, or get help. So he didn't die right away."

"You know what else? A large piece of canvas was still attached to one of his feet when he washed ashore," Gwen said.

"So he was wrapped up before he was dumped."

"It would take a huge effort to extract himself from that shroud."

They sat mulling this over for some time.

"It's all circumstantial evidence," Gwen said sadly.

"How else could—"

"Unless it was sharks."

"There weren't any bites taken out of him, Denise. It would have been in the report. Anyway, they don't come that close to shore—do they?"

"There might be fingerprints somewhere," Denise said.

Gwen shook her head. "We asked about that. If there were any, they were all washed off by being in the water so long."

Suddenly Gwen slammed her fork down on the table. "Oh, hell," she said. "That theory about his not dying for days is full of holes!"

"How so?"

"The coroner's report said there wasn't any water in his lungs. That means he didn't drown."

"Why didn't you say so?"

"I forgot. He was killed somewhere else, and then dumped off the cliff."

They finished eating in silence. Gwen thought, *such a good dinner, and I barely tasted it.*

Finally, Denise asked, "What about your mother's death? Any leads on that?"

Gwen breathed a long sigh. "No. I've been focused on Alex's murder, I'm afraid."

Denise nodded.

"You know, I'm still trying to find a connection between the two deaths, but maybe I'm barking up the wrong tree."

"How much do you know about Louis?"

"Louis. Why?"

"He knew your mother, right?"

"Turns out he did."

"How well?"
"I'm not sure, Denise."

~

Gwen talked to the coroner. "Is there any way Alex could have been alive for days before he died in the water?"

The coroner explained that even if he weren't dead when put in the water, no one could survive the temperature of the ocean for more than an hour.

"So much for that theory," she sighed.

~

Eric called, and asked could they meet. Gwen hadn't seen him since the sailing accident. She still felt uncomfortable around him. There were so many unanswered questions, and he hadn't come forth at all.

"Mm, I don't know. I'm really busy." She could feel her heart thumping in her chest.

"Please, Gwen. It's really important."

"For a few minutes. I'll meet you at Elephant Park." She sure wasn't going to rendezvous with him anywhere private.

He was waiting for her when she got there.

"Mind if we walk?"

"Fine."

He was quiet as they walked the first two blocks along Bridgeway. Gwen waited patiently.

"He shoved his hands in his pockets and looked skyward.

She waited.

Then he blurted it out. "I can't swim."

He seemed to be waiting for her to take this in.

"My dad threw me off the pier when I was about three. I still remember it. I thought I was going to drown. I took lessons later, but I never trusted the water."

"Yet you love to sail."

"Yeah. People don't know I can't swim. And they'd think I was stupid to sail not knowing, but well, I'm a good sailor and it was never a problem before."

Gwen joined the group that thought it was stupid to sail if you couldn't swim. But she didn't say so.

"We should have been wearing life jackets that day."

"Yes," she agreed.

"I knew that if I ever capsized I had to stay with the boat. That's rule number one. I kind of dog paddled back to it, when you got away. I'm glad you did—get away."

"So am I."

"I was too embarrassed to tell you. And I guess I half drowned you trying to save myself."

"Yeah, you did. I thought maybe you were doing it on purpose."

"Oh, God, no! Did you really think that?"

"I didn't know, Eric. And then, well, we didn't see each other."

"I was too ashamed to admit it."

"My other fear was that you really couldn't swim, and you would drown."

"Yeah."

They were quiet for a few moments.

Then Eric said, "It's been on my mind, and I knew I had to tell you."

She nodded.

"And apologize to you. Do me a favor, Gwen?"

"What?"

"Don't tell anyone else."

She smiled up at him. "Do *me* a favor? Learn to swim."

"I hope we're still friends."

"We are."

They walked in silence for awhile and Gwen breathed more freely knowing Eric was still her old faithful friend.

They continued over a block to Caledonia, and sat on a bench in front of an old antique shop. Her thoughts wandered to Louis.

"Eric, what do you know about Louis?"

"Do you two have a thing for each other?"

"Yeah, I guess you could say that."

"Do you sleep with him?"

"Eric!"

He shrugged. "Just trying to get the picture."

"Well, now you have it," she said. "So what do you know?"

"Not a lot. I saw him with your mother a couple of times."

"When was this?"

"Years ago. Once in a bar— Another time they were arguing, and he couldn't seem to stand it that she didn't agree with him."

"What was the argument about?"

"From what I gathered, they were arguing about age difference. She thought he was too young for her."

"Yeah, he told me it was puppy love. I'm almost sorry I asked him about that."

"Why?"

"It's just that our friendship wasn't tainted with suspicion and doubt. It seemed rather clean and *virginal*—well, maybe that was the wrong term."

Eric choked, then guffawed. "That's rich."

Gwen blushed. "Well, you know what I mean—it was devoid of suspicion."

"And now it isn't?"

"I suspect everyone who knew her. Didn't you know?"

"OK," he said, but he was still smiling. "He seemed like a nice guy. A little old for you, though, isn't he?"

"He's about thirty. I'm twenty-one."

Gee, if I'd known you were open to older men, I might have given it a shot."

She smiled at him. "You are— what? Forty-five?"

"Forty-something." He smiled back.

"Twice my age."

"Well, yeah."

Chapter 35

Sally Stanford was initiating a bill to provide public facilities for downtown shoppers. The shop owners were all in favor of it, believing it would increase trade.

Gwen said, "I think it's a great idea. They should have done it a long time ago."

"Yup."

There was a huge mailing to get out, and Gwen offered to help Sally with it after work.

About sixteen people were assisting Sally that evening.

"Can you stay when they leave?" Sally asked quietly.

Gwen turned, puzzled. "What's up?"

Sally shook her head. "We'll talk later."

At nine o'clock Sally sent the others home. "A fine evening's work," she said. "Thank you all for coming. A couple more nights and we'll have this job done."

When everyone else was gone, Sally said, "Have you seen your father lately?"

"A couple weeks ago. Why?"

"I'm not sure I should say anything. But he's been acting kind of weird lately—at council meetings."

"In what way?"

"You know in the past he's been very vocal on every subject."

Gwen waited for her to go on.

"He seems far away a lot of the time now—not focused on council discussions."

"That's strange."

"I miss his antagonism." Her eyebrows raised, not in unison, but independently. "Seriously, I wondered if you'd noticed anything."

"Not like that."

"Do you think he's ill?"

"I haven't seen any sign of it."

"I'm not saying this just because I don't agree with his politics. Excuse me, Doll, but I think the man has a hairline crack in his psyche."

~

This remark came as a shock to Gwen. She contacted her father. They met for lunch on the next Sunday, and took a short walk.

Richard seemed perfectly normal to her.

She asked him if he thought Conan could have killed Alex.

"I don't know. I really don't know that family. Conan is Alex's uncle, right?"

"Right."

"What do you think?" he asked.

"Well, he seems the most likely candidate. But sometimes I think it might be someone else." She had no idea who that might be.

Richard closed his eyes and rubbed his temples.

"What's wrong? Are you feeling OK?"

Something flickered in his eyes—a spark of emotion that quickly died.

"Yeah. I've just had a lot of headaches lately."

"What's bothering you, Richard?"

"Nothing to worry your pretty head over." He smiled at her.

~

Gwen didn't want to pin the blame on Conan for Alex's death, but if Conan was the guilty party, she did want some closure.

She called the pathologist who'd performed the autopsy.

"Is it possible for you to give me a piece of the canvas that Alex was wrapped in?"

"What's this about?"

"I thought if we could make a match between the material he was wrapped in, and the canvas the suspect used in his art, we might move further with this case."

"Wait—what suspect?"

Gwen swallowed. "Certain facts point to a person who's already in custody for another crime. If I could just have a small piece of the canvas—"

"Out of the question," the pathologist interrupted.

"Why is that?"

"The possible evidence, exhibits can't be tampered with. Nothing found with the body can be released."

"Why is that?"

"Not even after the trial. There could be a re-trial, even years later."

Gwen scratched her head. "What if I were to bring in a sample of the canvas? Could you then see if it matched what you have?"

"Do you have such a sample?"

"Yes," Gwen lied.

There was silence on the other end. Finally, the pathologist said, "I'm not a policeman, and I'm not a forensic scientist."

"Please," Gwen begged.

His reply was curt. "Bring it over. I can't promise anything."

The line went dead. Elated, Gwen wondered how she'd be able to get the canvas, and turn her lie into truth.

She sneaked back to Conan's houseboat. It had not been cordoned off as a crime as Conan was not officially a suspect for the murder.

The piece of plastic Varda had given her before came into use now.

She looked around for some canvas. Of course, she realized, it would all be in the locked studio. For a moment she felt pretty stupid.

Then she noticed a small finished painting of his on the wall. She'd take the whole picture to the pathologist. Of course, the work wasn't new, and there was no way of knowing if he was still using the same kind of canvas now.

She took it to Reardon's Funeral Home, and asked for Dr. Travis. She had to wait half an hour, but it was worth it to meet him in person.

He was tall and thin with sparse grey hair that was straight and dry. With bags under his weary eyes, he looked as though he hadn't slept in a week. His skin was so colorless, Gwen thought if he were lying prone, he might be taken for one of his cadavers.

He looked at the picture skeptically. "What am I supposed to do with this?"

"Well, as you can see here on the back, where the edges are attached, they're clean— not painted."

"I'll turn it over to the lab," he said.

"I'd appreciate that."

She left with little hope, but she'd done what she could.

Both sailing canvas and artists' canvas was plentiful in Sausalito. The lab ought to be able to at least discern which was used to wrap the body in.

~

Gwen missed Louis. Surely he had nothing to do with either of the deaths—just because he'd known her mother and had eaten her ham and pear sandwiches at one time. And he didn't know Alex at all.

Denise was gone for the weekend. She called Louis and asked if they could get together.

She hadn't realized how much she missed being in his arms, his strong hands caressing her everywhere. He had a way of touching her in one place that sent electricity running through her entire body.

He was more than glad to accept her invitation. Within the hour he was at her side, and not long after that they were in the throes of making love.

Encouraged by her response, he took her farther into the art of love-making than she'd experienced before. After three orgasms they lay sweaty and exhausted. Apart on the bed, their fingers entwined.

They fell asleep, and when Gwen awoke, she saw Louis looking at her. He moved closer and kissed her on the forehead.

"I could care about you."

"Oh, don't do that," she laughed.

"Why not?"

"This is just for fun, remember? No ties, no lies."

"Hmm."

"Are you hungry? It must be—" She looked at the clock. "Oh, Jeez, it's ten o'clock! We never had supper."

"Did you miss it?"

She giggled. "No. But I'm hungry now. Aren't you?"

He nibbled her neck. "I could eat you."

She made them a spinach and mushroom omelet. Half-way through the meal, she couldn't resist tonguing a bit of egg from his lower lip.

He was watching her mouth.

"What? Do I have spinach on my teeth?"

"I wish you did. Then I could lick it off."

Ten minutes later, they were in bed again, continuing their grooming.

Chapter 36

Megan called Gwen on June second, and in between sobs told her that the police had informed her that her brother would be tried for the murder of her son.

Gwen felt awful for Megan, who had not only lost her son, but now whose brother was being accused of his nephew's demise.

On the other hand, she was as eager as Megan and Chad to find the killer. She wondered if the wire she'd brought in or the canvas painting would provide any evidence against him. Or what had the authorities come up with that made them point the finger at Conan?

The law enforcement agencies were doing more than Gwen had expected. They had filed a formal report, which the judge then accepted and an arraignment was set for the next day.

At the arraignment Conan was charged with the murder of Alex Denison. His rights were read to him, and he was asked how he pleaded.

It was no surprise to Gwen that he pleaded not guilty.

Next, a date for a preliminary was set.

Chad and Gwen went to visit Alex in the San Rafael jail. She'd never been in a jail before. The heavy clanging of doors, concrete and steel surroundings did nothing to put her at ease. Possessing no windows, the only light came from harsh overhead fluorescents.

The prisoner was only allowed one visitor at a time.

"You go first," Chad said.

She was led into a room with chairs that faced a thick glass wall. She waited ten minutes for someone to bring Conan into the room on the other side of the glass.

When he sat opposite her, both were provided with microphones.

Conan's eyes were red and rimmed with dark circles.

"How are you doing?" She bit her lip. What an inane thing to ask a suspect of murder, she thought. She could see he was very agitated.

"How can they pin this on me? Christ, I was in here when it happened."

She listened to him for a few minutes. He seemed genuinely amazed that he was being accused of this crime.

Gwen could only nod. "What you need now is an attorney. Do you have one?"

"No. I don't know anyone."

"Look, the court will appoint someone to defend you."

"Yeah, some guy who can't make it in his field has to take court jobs like this." After a brief pause he added, "How about your dad?"

"Richard? Are you serious? I don't know, Conan. I don't think that's a very good idea."

"Why not?"

She struggled to find the right words. "Conflict of interest."

"How so?"

"I'm trying to establish a long-lost father-daughter relationship. I don't want to muddy the waters."

Conan looked at her with soft, injured eyes.

Sympathy struck Gwen like a knife in the heart. She had to get out of here. She promised Conan she'd ask Richard if he'd recommend someone.

She rose to go.

"Thanks for coming," he said. There was a note of despair in his voice.

When she saw Richard that evening, she told him of her visit to see Conan.

"He's distraught, very troubled by the accusation. And he needs a lawyer. Is there anyone you could suggest?"

Richard cupped his hands and blew into them. "Let me think about that."

"Actually, he asked for you."

"Me? Why me?"

"He doesn't want a court-appointed attorney."

"What did you tell him?"

"I told him 'No'. Conflict of interest—my relationship to you."

Richard looked at Gwen thoughtfully, and nodded. "Better someone else."

"He doesn't know anyone to ask."

"I'll see if I can find someone."

"The hearing's Friday."

"I'll get on it."

"Thank you, Richard."

~

The next day Richard called to tell Gwen that a Chris Macomb had agreed to take Conan's case.

"Great. Who is he?"

"Actually, it's a *she*. Chris is young, very active in the community, and in the local lawyers' association."

"Oh."

"He'll like her."

Gwen wondered if her gender would prejudice Conan. Oh, well, it was out of her hands. Anyway, she was glad to see women break into the Old Boys Club.

"She's heading over to the jail today to meet him."

"That's great. Quick work, Richard."

Chad and Gwen drove downtown on Friday to the old courthouse on Fourth Street where the trial would be if they had one.

The hearing went quickly, as the prosecutor presented his reasons for a trial. Macomb tried to counter them, saying there was no proof.

The Judge spoke up. "The purpose of a hearing isn't to prove guilt. It is to determine if there is sufficient reason to bring the accused to trial."

"Were any fingerprints found on the body or the canvas wrapping?" Macomb asked the pathologist.

"No, they'd have been washed away."

"Any traces of blood?" she asked.

"No."

"The same reason?"

"Yes.

"Nevertheless, scanty as the evidence was, the judge decided that the case should go to trial. Conan Galbraith had the motive, the means and possibly the opportunity.

Conan demanded a jury. He was assured that he would get one.

~

Gwen was conflicted. She was trying to keep an open mind, but she couldn't help thinking that Conan must have killed Alex. He certainly had a reason to. She couldn't think of anyone else, especially now that Useless had discovered that Conan was Alex's supplier.

On the other hand it was hard to believe that her friend and brother of Megan could do such a thing to his nephew. And she liked Conan. What made things worse was that California still had capital punishment, and murder would almost certainly lead to that sentence.

As the trial date approached, Gwen found herself in a position of comforting Megan again.

As often happens, it took days to decide on a jury. Both the prosecutor and defendant's lawyer found something objectionable with four of the candidates. They either knew the defendant, had work excuses or were clearly biased.

The day the trial began, Gwen was surprised to see Richard enter the building. She was further surprised when he approached her and told her that he would be representing the defendant.

"What happened?" This was incredible.

"Ms. Macomb bowed out."

"Why?"

"She said her mother was very ill in Idaho. She'd have to go to her."

"When did this happen?"

"She called last evening. I couldn't very well dissuade her. I don't know how long the trial will last. Then I tried to find someone else, but it was too last minute." He threw up his hands. "So here I am."

"Have you settled this with the judge?"

"Yes, he's OK with it. Doesn't want to delay the trial."

Gwen took a long breath. She put her hand on Richard's arm. "Well, thanks for stepping in. Conan will be glad."

"I have to go talk to him now. Apprise him of the change."

With that he strode out.

It was already hot in the room, and only ten o'clock.

The two ceiling fans did little to dissipate the heat in the crowded room on this hot August day in San Rafael.

Too bad the new civic center designed by Frank Lloyd Wright wasn't completed, she thought. The post office was finished, and the administration building, but not the Hall of Justice. She liked riding by the part that was completed, and walking around inside. It was such a change from any kind of architecture she'd seen anywhere. With a low sculpted dome painted aqua, the rest of the exterior was a soft peach color.

On the inside, gold anodized trim festooned everything from the front gates to hallway doors. Much conflict had arisen from the board and the community hiring this maverick architect—so much so that at one point Wright threatened to quit the project. Although negative comments were still made, on the whole it was considered the county's pride. And finally, all the various departments of the county, including the library would be put under one roof.

As one cynic pointed out, a person could get married there, choose some books for the honeymoon in the library, and on the way out, pick up divorce forms to be filled out later—perhaps after the honeymoon. Great time-saver.

Gwen waited impatiently while the crowd grew larger in number and volume.

Twenty minutes later the defendant was brought in, and beside him his new defense attorney. Poor Conan looked ten years older than the tall dapper artist Gwen had met last year. Whispers rose in the crowded courtroom.

Judge Donovan entered and all were asked to rise. Even though he was wearing a gown, Gwen could see he had an enormous girth. Although no more than fifty, his jowls were lumpy. He probably led a decadent life.

Opening statements were given by both sides.

Prosecutor Byers circumference would soon catch up with that of the judge, Gwen thought cynically. He was only ten years behind.

When a break was taken for lunch, Richard asked Gwen to join him.

"Is it going as expected?" she asked

"I think so. Of course, we've barely begun."

In the afternoon Byers presented several exhibits. First was the wire, which he maintained had been the murder weapon.

"Pardon me," Richard said. "Anyone can buy wire like that."

Harry Byers then presented as 'exhibit two' the canvas the body had been wrapped in. "This canvas is not heavy enough to be used for making sails, as two local sail makers are ready to testify. Rather it is a well-known weight and weave used for artists' canvases. Who but an artist would have on hand a quantity such as was used to wrap the victim in?"

"There are many artists in this town," Richard said. "All circumstantial evidence."

When Conan's prior crime of art forgery was introduced, Richard stated that it was not relevant to this case, but the prosecutor insisted that it was. The judge allowed Byers to continue.

"Is it not probable that when the victim showed the forger photographs of the forged materials, his purpose was to demand money? And if this were the case, isn't it conceivable that the defendant lost his temper and killed Alex Denison in a fit of temper?"

Suddenly Conan burst out. "He was blackmailing me, but I never killed him!"

An audible gasp was heard in the courtroom.

"Conceivable isn't proof," Richard stated.

But it gave the jury something to think about.

"The timing is all wrong," Richard insisted. "The victim couldn't have been killed before my client was incarcerated for forgery."

"We don't know the date of death," Byers said.

Prosecutor Byers called the pathologist to the witness stand, and Ronald Travis was sworn in. The man looked even more pale than he had at the morgue.

"I understand, sir that in cases such as this it is difficult to judge the date of death. But could you give us a window in which the victim could have died?"

Travis cleared his throat, and then appeared to have a coughing fit. He was offered water, which he accepted. Finally, he was ready to speak.

"In such cases, where the body has been preserved in the very cold waters of the Pacific Ocean, the body could have been submerged for weeks before it was found."

A general rumble rose in the courtroom.

Donovan banged his gavel.

"You cannot be more specific than that?" Byers asked.

"No. I'm afraid not."

"Had the corpse have been attacked by sharks?"

"No. The victim appears to have been thrown off a cliff somewhere near the point. There's nothing to suggest he was farther out at sea."

"Were there any other marks or signs that the body was in the water a long time?

"There was scraping on the skin where the tide brought him in and out."

"And this was caused by?"

"Gravel and stones as the body repeatedly raked the shore. First the canvas was worn through. Then the body was exposed to this thrashing," the pathologist said.

"Doesn't this suggest that the corpse was in the water prior to April 20th, the date of Conan Galbraith's arrest?" The prosecutor was almost foaming at the mouth.

"That would depend on where, exactly, on which part of the shore the scraping took place. As the tide brought it in and out, the body wouldn't have stayed in one place."

"So he could have been in the water a long time," Byers said.

"Then again, he might have only submerged for just a few days before the tide belched him up on shore."

The pathologist was allowed to step down.

Byers was visibly disappointed that the man had said nothing to confirm his theory that the victim could have been killed before the accused was incarcerated for forgery.

The trial wore on through the week, and the next.

Megan could not bring herself to attend. She relied on her husband and Gwen to give her diluted summaries of the trial.

Chapter 37

That Saturday Gwen was restless. She asked Chad if she could borrow his car.

"Yes, of course,"

She drove out Panoramic Highway to the Pantoll Ranger Station. After much hesitation she decided to stop in and see if Carl was there. He was.

After a brief moment the ranger recognized her. "Well, hello, Miss——"

"Harris. Gwen Harris." She extended her hand.

"So you're still here. You're missing the games, you know." His eyes twinkled. "Basketball."

She smiled.

"What can I do for you?"

"I know this might sound bizarre to you, but, well, I'd like to see the site where my mother's remains were found."

Carl nodded seriously. She could see his Adam's apple bob up and down.

"So if you could direct me to the exact site, I could go down there and——"

"Excuse me—do you mean by yourself? Alone?"

"Yes."

"No, no. That would not be wise. I cannot be party to sending you down the cliffs and drop-offs, brush and vermin, by yourself."

"I am strong, sir, and used to hiking. I have a brown belt in karate." She colored, wondering what possible use the last would be, and why she'd said it.

"No, I cannot advise it."

"Then what can you suggest?"

Again his Adam's apple bobbed up and down.

"I don't know, unless…"

"Unless what?"

"If you're willing to wait until I'm off duty, I could go with you."

"That would be splendid."

"It won't be until five o'clock."

It was twenty after four. "I'll wait," she said.

The room contained a rack of literature. She studied maps of the area, trails through the mountain. There were brochures warning of mountain lions. Above all, one should not travel alone, but if one must, he should sing so as not to take the lions by surprise.

Well, you learn something new every day, she thought.

When they were in his jeep, she thanked him for accompanying her. "I guess it would have been foolish to go alone."

"Very," he said.

They drove in silence until he pulled over and stopped at the same spot he had before.

"Are you sure you're up for this hike?" He looked at her shoes. "You should be wearing hiking boots," he said.

She was wearing well-worn saddle shoes. "I'll do fine with these."

They descended in silence. Carl walked ahead slashing at high brush with what she thought was a scythe, to make the terrain easier for her. A couple of times he reached for her hand, and helped her over difficult places. It was a steeper drop than she'd imagined. Twice she fell over grass and vines her feet became entangled in, and once tripped on a hidden rock. Her skirt caught on a thorny bush.

"Are you sure you want to go on?" Carl asked.

"I'm fine," she smiled.

They took a slight turn to the left, and descended an even steeper decline.

Finally, Carl stopped. "This is the spot."

Gwen felt a quick intake of her breath. All around she could see where disturbed foliage was gradually reclaiming its territory.

Gwen wasn't sure why she'd wanted to come. Maybe she was hoping to find something.

She took in her surroundings. "What caused all this disturbance?" she said gesturing to the ground.

"When the remains were found, it became a crime scene, was cordoned off, and a search was made for relevant artifacts—like the shoe that was found," Carl said.

Gwen kicked at some weeds.

Perhaps Carl sensed she wanted to be alone. "I'll be waiting for you over here," he said, and strode off about forty feet, where he sat at the base of a California oak, and lit a cigarette.

What did she hope to find? Probably nothing. If anything had been there, it would have been picked up at the time by the careful search of the authorities.

She extended her search past the disturbed area by a few feet. She used her bare hands to dig around in the brush for something that may have missed the eyes of the investigators.

Her hands came across slight bumps in the soft terrain. She dug them up—nothing but stones.

She walked over to Carl. He was extinguishing his cigarette with great care.

"Ready?"

She nodded.

On the climb back to the road, she said nothing. It took all her breath just to keep up with Carl on this arduous ascent. Grasping at branches, she used them to help her gain altitude.

She wondered what the point was of this sojourn into her mother's past, and had to be satisfied with the knowledge that, like visiting a cemetery, she now had experienced her mother's resting place for the last ten years. Tears welled up in her eyes.

Then on the drive, because she didn't want to talk about her mother, she asked Carl about his work. "Do you like it?"

"I love it, most of the time. My dad wanted me to be a doctor like he was, but I was always attracted to the outdoors. I was in Scouts and all that when I was young. I can recognize the call of almost every bird around here," he said.

"Do you recognize the sounds of the wild animals?"

"Yup. And I can recognize their paw prints and their scat. Can even tell how recently they dropped that scat. Sometimes that's very useful information, if the scat was just dropped where you're standing. That means he's pretty close. Might be you don't want to be that close."

"What do you do then?"

"You move away."

Gwen covered her face to conceal her smile.

"This place feeds the soul," he said seriously.

Yes," she said. In her present state, she didn't share his feelings, but she could imagine that under different circumstances she would.

When they returned to the ranger station, she thanked Carl and took his hand in appreciation.

"I know you did this on your own time. I want you to know that I really appreciate it."

"Glad to be of help," he said.

"So long."

~

On Monday the trial resumed. Gwen thought that Judge Donovan looked somewhat hung over. His hair disheveled, tie crooked, he leaned on his hands through most of the morning. She wondered what his weekend had been like.

Before the morning was over, Richard had made mincemeat of the circumstantial exhibits the prosecutor kept trying to present as evidence. The prosecutor brought in new material, much of which the judge declared irrelevant, and cautioned the jury to disregard.

Gwen noticed many of the people in the courtroom were the same as on the first day, but others were new, and some had stopped coming. At a break she went outdoors for some fresh air, and was disappointed to discover it was even hotter there.

She was approached by an elderly gentleman, dressed neatly in suit and tie. She'd seen him there since the first day.

"Like to go to the trials?" he asked.

"Not particularly."

"Then what you doing here? You a witness?"

"Might be."

"Now me, I been attending trials for the past five years. Ever since I retired. Better than TV. It's real life!"

"That's a new one on me."

"What is?"

"Coming to trials for the sheer entertainment of it."

"Oh, yeah, lots of folks do." He removed a clean handkerchief from his pocket and wiped his brow. "You ever been on the jury?"

"No. Have you?"

He shook his head. "Always wanted to be."

She thought about all the people who groaned when they were summoned for jury duty.

"I mostly go to murder trials. They're the most interesting." He took out a comb and ran it through his thinning hair.

"There aren't that many murders around here, are there?"

"Oh, I don't mean just here in Marin County. I go up to Sacramento, and to San Francisco. I've even been to a good one in Los Angeles. Cost me a lot, though. I had to stay in a motel."

She wondered what made people want to come to a trial as a voyeur and watch as a gawker might at a roadside accident.

"Where do you live?"

"In Petaluma."

"So you're not staying in a motel now."

"No. That's right." He checked his watch. "Well, we'd better get back in."

~

That afternoon Gwen was called to the stand by the prosecutor. After taking an oath, she was asked, "What was your relationship to Conan Galbraith?"

"We became friends, I suppose, because I was staying with the woman who is his sister. He was at the house frequently."

"And her son is the victim. How well did you know Alex Denison?"

"Quite well. We lived in the same house for several months, with his parents."

"Would you tell the court what you and the victim were doing on the night of March 30th?"

Richard interrupted. "I don't see the relevancy of this question."

Donovan waived him off. "Let's see where this is going."

Gwen was aware that Richard knew exactly where it was going, as she had confided the break-in she and Alex had made for the forgeries.

After she relayed the truth of that evening spent with Alex in Conan's studio, Byers said, "How many copies were made of the photos taken that night?"

"Two."

"Why two?"

"I wanted a set to give to Mr. Varda, to prove the forgeries. Alex asked that I have a second set made for him."

"And why was that?"

"I don't know. But he didn't want me to show them to anyone for a few days."

"Don't you think it likely the victim used his set of photos to increase the blackmail demanded of Conan Galbraith? And tired of this coercion Galbraith strangled him on the spot?"

The judge interrupted. "You're leading the witness. Strike the question."

Gwen felt she'd allowed herself to be caught up in a web of truths, damaging to the people she cared about. Whatever she said it was going to hurt someone.

Conan was put on the stand.

"Is it not true," began the prosecutor, "that the victim had been blackmailing you for a long time?"

"Yes," mumbled Conan. Sweat was running down his face.

"Speak up," ordered the judge.

"Yes, sir." Conan coughed.

Byers continued. "Then your nephew came to you with the photos he and Miss Harris took of your forgeries when they broke into your study. Is this not true?"

"Yes, sir."

"And didn't he demand more money? And didn't you get very, very angry?"

A cacophony rose in the courtroom. Judge Donovan banged his gavel to quell the crowd. "If there are any more disruptions, I shall clear the court."

"I didn't kill him!" Conan shouted.

Shards of light seemed to emanate from his eyes, fragments of violent emotions turned loose.

~

When the day ended, Gwen wanted most of all to see Varda. She called and he told her he'd be waiting for her.

When she started telling him about the trial, he put his arm around her, consoling her. She realized suddenly that this was her source of parental comfort, not Richard. Perhaps because she'd known him longer?

He fixed her a hot tea with a different flavor than she was used to. Before long she became very drowsy, and fell asleep on his sofa.

When she awoke, there was a quilt covering her, and a pillow had been placed under her head. She sat up, startled for a moment. Then she saw Varda, sitting across from her, making sketches on a pad.

She had a sudden revelation. "It was you, wasn't it?"

He looked alarmed. "Me—what?"

"Sending money to me all those years. It had to be you!"

"So you figured that out."

Gwen was embarrassed. "It took me long enough, didn't it?" She squirmed. "I am so indebted to you. How can I ever—"

"Now, please. It was and is my pleasure." He sat up proudly. "Remember, I am your godfather."

Self-appointed.

Flustered and embarrassed she was nevertheless in awe of his generosity and full of gratitude. "How did you find out I'd changed banks?"

"Easy. I saw you enter Bank of the West. I took a chance—-the next day I went there and asked that a check be deposited in your account. No contest. You don't need account information to make a deposit."

"But what if I'd been there for a different reason?"

"Then they wouldn't have accepted the check."

She smiled and blew him a kiss.

It was supper time, and Gwen offered to make him a simple American meal.

"And what might that be?"

"Do you have any eggs?"

"Yes."

"I was thinking of scrambled eggs."

"I love scrambled eggs."

He hopped to his feet, and she followed him to the kitchen, or did he call it the galley? Varda produced a frying pan, some eggs and a bowl. Gwen did get to scramble the eggs, but that was all. He could not resist enhancing them.

"Let's add a little cumin," he said. Then he shaved some ginger, and added pesto and sliced kalamata olives.

"Let's see, what else do we have?"

"I think this will be enough," Gwen offered.

"I know," he said with sudden inspiration, snapping his fingers together. He produced a jar of pickled red peppers.

"Hot?" Gwen asked.

"No, not hot. For color. And water chestnuts—for texture."

She saw an eggplant on the counter and was afraid he'd throw that in too. But it didn't appear that he'd noticed the purple vegetable.

The last thing he threw in was a can of sardines. "For protein. And flavor."

They were the strangest scrambled eggs she'd ever had. If she hadn't known, she might never have guessed the final product contained eggs.

Chapter 38

Gwen had taken two weeks off work to attend Conan's trial. On Monday she would have to get back to work. Her entire vacation spent in a musty old courtroom. And so hot.

But at least the weekend lay before her.

Richard called her. "I want to see you."

"I'm really tired. It's been a grueling two weeks at the trial."

"I know. For me, too. That's what I want to see you about."

"No. I want to clear my mind of all that."

There was a long pause. Then, "Please, Gwen."

She sighed. "Not tomorrow. Maybe Sunday."

"Alright. Sunday then, in the evening, before sunset."

She didn't understand why the sunset was important, but she didn't argue. That would mean she'd have most of the weekend for herself.

She talked to Denise about the trial that night.

"Do you think Conan will get nailed for this?" Denise asked.

"I don't know. There's still no real proof that he did it, but it certainly appears that he did."

"Is Richard a good defense lawyer?"

"He's been very good, I think."

"What do you think he's so anxious to see you about?"

"I have no idea."

"Where does he want to meet you?"

"In the headlands."

"Why?"

"I don't know. Something about the sunset."

"That sounds weird."

Gwen shrugged.

"Be careful."

Gwen went to bed early, but couldn't sleep. She kept having bad dreams that would awaken her, but then she couldn't remember what they were about.

In the morning, when she was finally in a deep sleep, Denise came in her room to tell her that Sally Stanford was on the phone."

"What does she want?" Gwen mumbled."

"I didn't ask, but she said it was important."

Gwen dragged herself to the phone.

"Can I buy you a cup of coffee?" the older woman asked.

"What's up?"

"Just something I thought you should know."

"Where are you?"

"At the restaurant."

"OK. I'll be there in twenty minutes."

She brushed her teeth, ran a comb through her hair, and pulled on her jeans.

When she got to the Valhalla Sally was waiting for her.

"Hungry?"

"No, what's this about?"

Sally brought a pot of coffee to a table by the window.

The restaurant extended into the Bay. Outside, two seagulls were fighting over a fish."

When she sat down Sally said, "I told you before how Richard was acting at council meetings—distracted, not focused."

"Yes."

"On Wednesday evening he blew up—just had a fit about something trivial, threw his pencil down and walked out."

"My God."

"Can you think of any reason he'd behave like that?" Sally asked.

"He's taken over the defense of Conan Galbraith, and that's no doubt created stress. He hadn't intended to—the previous attorney dropped out."

"Do you think his work load could cause this much disruption in his behavior?"

Gwen paused. "No. I don't understand it. He's been perfectly calm and tuned in at the trial." She sighed. Then she told Sally about the plans she'd made with Richard to see him Sunday evening.

"For a sunset?" Sally asked in amazement. "He isn't getting romantic, is he?"

"No, of course not."

"At this point nothing would surprise me."

At Sally's orders, the waiter brought over two orders of French toast and bacon. By now Gwen was beginning to get hungry. Food was just what she needed.

Before she left Sally took her arm and looked at her with great concern.

"Be careful, Doll."

"I'll be fine."

"You don't have to go."

Gwen kissed her friend, and walked the short distance home.

~

They had been in the headlands before. Many people thought the views here were the best in the county. One could see everything beautiful about the Bay, even the ocean, outside the Gate. Gwen spotted Richard's car, and locked her bicycle to a post nearby.

Richard was waiting for her. He was dressed in jeans and an old tweed sports jacket with leather patches on the elbows. He smiled and they began walking across the space toward the barracks.

"I want to compliment you on your defense of Conan," Gwen said.

"It's not over."

"But you're doing a great job."

"Can't let the wrong man go down for it."

"How do you know he's the wrong man?"

Richard didn't answer. He lit a cigarette.

"I didn't know you smoked," Gwen said.

"Seldom, any more. Only on special occasions."

What was special about tonight?

The weather had changed. The heat spell was over. Evening temperatures always dropped, and with the chill in the air, tourists were leaving the site.

They walked across the promontory. The wind was picking up; Gwen tied her scarf tighter. But the sky was still blue with just enough cloud cover in the west for a promising sunset.

The old dilapidated building was in front of them.

"Listen," Richard said.

"What?"

The only sound she heard was the clamoring of an unsecured door on one of the abandoned rooms.

"You said you wanted to talk about the trial," she said.

"Indirectly."

He seemed to be interested in the creaking and slamming of the unlocked door. He strode ahead and opened it. Gwen stayed behind, but she could see that the hut had been used for various purposes after the military abandoned it. All unsavory, she thought.

"This is fascinating," Richard called from inside. "A lover's tryst. Come on in—you've got to see this."

"No, Richard. I don't want to. I can see enough from here. Let's keep moving. It's getting chilly."

"But not in here. No wind at all."

Gwen was looking around to see if there were other people in the vicinity. No one. Suddenly from behind, Richard grabbed her and pulled her into the enclosure. Light from above shone through at an eerie angle.

"You have to listen. It's time you knew some things." There was a steel glint in his eyes she hadn't seen before.

Gwen tried to extricate herself from his grasp. His grip was like a bear's.

Suddenly she noticed the mis-matched button on his tweed sport jacket.

She gasped. The other buttons matched the one the ranger described that had been found near her mother's remains.

Richard had a wild look in his eyes.

"Just a few *Hail Marys*. That's all the priest gives us. I need more."

"Let me go, Richard!"

"Look at this."

Hurriedly he removed his jacket, and then his shirt. Gwen wrenched away from him, reached for the door. He grabbed her arm and pushed her against the back wall. He blocked the exit with his body.

"Look, look at this!"

Across his back Gwen could see the marks of flagellation.

Horror-struck, she could only say, "Who did this to you?"

"I did. It was the only way I could live with it. Now it's not enough." He pulled things out of his pocket. "Do you think this helps?" He threw his rosary on the ground. "Or this?" he tossed his bottle of medication at her. Involuntarily, she caught it.

"All props. Props to get us through this play we're in."

"No, Richard."

"But they don't help. They laugh at us."

He grabbed her by the shoulders and shook her.

"You're the real genesis of my sins. If you hadn't been born—" Suddenly he stopped. Blocking her escape with his body, he put his shirt back on.

Quietly, he said, "We shall have to make amends now. It's the only way we'll ever find absolution."

He dragged her out of the barracks toward the water. The fog was coming in. She screamed. She couldn't see another human anywhere. He tied her scarf around her mouth and held both her hands, then grasped her in a tight embrace.

"Don't be afraid, my little daughter. I loved you so much. I wanted to keep you when your mother was dying of cancer. You were mine. Don't you see? But it's too late. We can't have each other anymore."

He pressed her head against his chest and stroked her hair.

She wriggled her mouth free from the scarf.

"You killed her, didn't you?"

"She cheated me. She told me she'd registered your birth, naming me as your father. She lied to me, Gwen. I checked. Yes, I checked and she had not registered your birth!"

"So you killed her."

"I had to! I didn't mean to—I didn't plan it. You understand, don't you? She was going to die, and she wouldn't let me have my child!"

"And you killed Alex, too, didn't you?"

He spoke in a rapid frenzy. "He knew I killed your mother. He came to me for money, but it would never have ended. It would have hung over my head like a guillotine—a living ghost. He came to me one night—I told him to come back the next night. I bought the canvas and wire... ." He looked down at his daughter. "Those details don't matter. Come." He started pulling her again toward the water. "They had no right, no right to keep you from me. Afterwards, no one would back my claim. They all acted like they didn't know me, and sent you away."

Suddenly he seemed calmer. "It's alright now. The pleasant outings, dramas, opera—even their heroines die, Gwen. It was a good play, ours was, while it lasted. And like all plays, it must end. Would you like to die? The waves are getting excited—they know we're coming. They're ready to welcome us to the Great Mother. The sun is setting, and so too, must we. Come Gwen. We'll hold hands and float down together. The ritual of death should be as beautiful as birth and marriage."

"No!"

He was pulling her toward the edge of the cliff with its ninety degree drop-off. Fog and wind were roiling like a tsunami over the coastal headlands.

She let out a scream, but the wind carried it out to sea. The sun had set, and gun-metal gray clouds covered the western sky. Seagulls screamed above, before the fog obliterated them.

She broke away from him, ran, but he chased and caught her. Only the sound of the surf crashing against rocks below could indicate the direction of the sea. He forced her closer to the edge of the cliff.

"No, Richard, I don't want to die and neither should you!"

"What do you think I have to live for, when I have so much to live *with?*

"You didn't mean to kill her, did you? You said it was an accident."

"But I did it!"

"What good will your death do?"

"It will *cleanse* us, Gweny. The water will cleanse everything that has been sullied by us. You come, too. We'll get off this conveyor belt—now." He was gripping both her arms.

"Richard, your faith—"

"I have no faith." His face was wet with tears. He embraced her, sobbing on her shoulder.

Quickly, before she could think about it, she did a karate maneuver that landed him on his back. He looked startled, and sat there stunned. Gwen bolted. She was about fifty feet from him when he called to her. He had picked three wild California poppies at his side, and held them up for her to see.

What made her stop? Did she still think she could save him? Her lungs were heaving. Another voice said, *Run, while you can. Run, girl, run!*

"See, Gweny—one for you, one for me and one for Patricia."

Paralyzed, unable to move, she watched as he sat there in the field with the flowers.

Then suddenly he stood and came toward her. She was no longer afraid of him. He'd lost his fearsomeness. Gently, he held her face in his hands and looked deeply into her eyes.

Softly he said, "You don't have to come. I love you anyway."

He dropped his arms and left her. She saw him disappear through the fog.

And then he was gone.

From below she heard a crash. Cautiously she crept through the fog to the precipice where he'd jumped. Far below, amidst the waves that bashed the shore and the swirls of fog, she could see glimpses of his body. She watched it ride the surf until it was swallowed into the darkness below.

~

She didn't remember leaving the headlands and riding her bike back to Denise's. She felt a wrenching so severe she didn't know if anything could restore her to normalcy. She could barely speak and she was shaking uncontrollably.

Denise could see she was traumatized. She didn't insist that Gwen tell her anything right away.

"Catch your breath." Denise said, "Come, let's get you in the tub."

Gwen didn't resist her ministrations. The bath relaxed her muscles and after awhile stopped her shaking. Denise brought in a drink of brandy.

Gwen sipped it slowly, remembering the first time she'd had

brandy—with Conan at Pelican Inn. So much had happened since then. Was it over now? Finding her father and discovering he and her mother's killer were one and the same. And another murder thrown in the mix. Could she ever put it all to rest and lead a normal life?

She felt numb, not yet ready to absorb the full impact of what had happened this evening and before. She could remember facts, but had little emotional response to them. Perhaps it was nature's way of keeping her sane, until she was ready to process the ghastly events.

She knew her first obligation was to report Richard's death and the location of his body. She didn't feel prepared to do that. It would lead to a host of other questions. But she had to.

The bath water cooled, she got out of the tub and dried herself.

In the living room Gwen relayed only the part of the story that involved Richard deciding to end his life.

Although shocked, Denise remained calm.

"I suppose I have to call the sheriff now," Gwen said.

"No. I think that can wait until tomorrow," Denise said. "As soon as they know, they'll be all over you with questions. You're not ready for that."

"But—"

"I'll take responsibility for the delay," Denise said.

Chapter 39

Somehow she got through the next few days, and Denise protected her as much as she could from the sheriff and the press. She also brought the Denisons up to date.

Chad went back to the barracks Gwen described and retrieved Richard's jacket and turned it over to the sheriff's office.

Gwen had questions of her own. So many that crowded and clouded her mind. Was she ready to ask them? Would Megan be willing to give honest responses?

Finally, she thought she was as prepared as she'd ever be.

Inviting herself for coffee one morning, she said, "I need some answers before I can begin to bring a finish to ... what happened."

She saw Megan and Chad exchange quick glances.

"Of course," Megan said.

Gwen took a deep breath. "First of all, where was I born?"

"Here. In this house," Megan said.

"Was there a doctor present, or a mid-wife?"

"No. Your mother didn't want there to be."

Her questions wanted to take another turn, but she'd follow this line through first.

"Who assisted in the birth?"

"I did," Megan said. "And Chad."

"Were there any complications?"

"No."

She thought she knew but she asked anyway. "Why did my mother want a home birth?"

Megan bit her lip.

Gwen continued. "Was it to avoid filing a birth certificate?"

"Yes. She made the one out that you have. But she never planned to file it."

"You could still do that," Chad offered.

Gwen looked at him in amazement.

"I mean, you do exist, but there's no public record of it. Someday it might be useful to have that information available." He tried to smile.

Gwen nodded. Dear, practical Chad.

"You knew who my father was, didn't you?"

Megan and Chad dropped their eyes.

"Yes, but Patricia made us promise not to tell you," Megan said.

Gwen felt anger climb right up her spine and get stuck in her throat. Such a tangled web of lies she'd been told. But she kept calm. There were more questions to ask.

"She went to all this trouble to make sure Richard couldn't claim me, right?"

"Right."

"But it wasn't because he was Catholic, was it?" Gwen asked.

"She didn't want you raised as a Catholic, but the real reason was that he frightened her with his bad temper. And with good reason, it turned out. She said she'd go to any lengths to keep you safe from him. She was afraid for *you*."

"Why did she continue seeing him?"

"I begged her not to. But apparently he was under control most of the time, and could be very charming, but there were times when he wasn't rational."

Gwen let that information churn for awhile. Then she said, "Where were you the day she was murdered, Megan?"

Megan pursed her lips. "I was scared for her. He came to get her, and he looked—how shall I say—wound up too tightly. I tried to follow her. She told me she was going to the beach with him. I started out to follow them, but that's not where they went."

For a few moments no one said anything. Then Gwen asked, "Why didn't you tell me any of this?"

"Your mother didn't want me to. She didn't think you needed to know any of that. And considering what he did to her…at least not until you were an adult and could take care of yourself."

She thought of the previous week. *Take care of myself?*

"We think he might have been bi-polar, or something."

"He was schizophrenic."

"How do you know?"

"He threw his bottle of meds at me. I looked at it later. The label said Chlorpromazine. I took it to the druggist to find out what it was prescribed for."

"And he said?" Chad asked.

"Schizophrenia."

Silence.

"I should tell you this, Gwen," Megan said. "The circle was formed to keep her secret and protect you."

"You all knew?"

"Not the new people you met. Just our family, including Conan and Eric."

"But you invited me into the circle."

"We intended to tell you. But you seemed to find some pleasure in being with him. We thought perhaps he'd gotten over—"

"You don't get over schizophrenia."

"—Or had controlled it with medication."

"Until he didn't."

Gwen stopped quizzing them, pausing to take in what they'd told her.

"It was only later we called it the Goddess Circle," Megan said.

"So all that goddess stuff was a sham?" Gwen could contain her fury no longer.

"No, please understand. It was the best thing that happened to us. We really did study the teachings, and try to put them into practice. We still do."

You think Alex and Conan lived by these principles?

Megan paused.

"And in keeping with that, we'd like you to participate in a ceremony for Richard."

"Oh, God, I can't!"

"I think you'll find forgiveness very healing. To forgive is to let go. It's more for you than the other party."

Chad, who'd spoken little said, "We know it will help us get closure and peace over Alex's death, and the man who ended his life."

Gwen shook her head. "I'm not ready."

Megan nodded slowly. "Perhaps, some day."

There was a long silence in the room. Finally, Gwen said, "One more question: how did Alex know Richard had killed Mom?"

Chad spoke. "I suppose that's our fault. After you opened the envelope and found out who your father was, it was discussed openly in our family. Megan and I expressed our belief that Richard had killed Patricia."

"But we didn't *know*, Gwen, or we'd have told you." Megan said. "I don't believe Alex knew anything for sure, but he made Richard believe he did."

"Oh, my God!" Gwen said.

Megan sighed. "I think he'd become addicted to blackmailing, or to drugs, I should say, which led to blackmailing. He died for it."

"Perhaps he went to Richard because his former supplier was no longer available," Chad added.

"Conan."

"Yes."

"It's all so sad," Gwen said.

"And— Richard, I believe when he killed Alex, he lost control of his life. He couldn't live with another murder," Chad said.

Megan added, "But he loved you, Gwen, in his own disturbed way."

~

There was so much to digest. It was difficult for Gwen to reconcile all the lies she'd been told with the friendship she had with the Denisons. Were lies just part of common life? Not like these, no. Created out of necessity, she thought. At least believed to be necessary by those telling them. She knew Megan and Chad meant well. They had done a lot for her.

Forgiveness? This is where she should start. Not easy—so much deceit. So many falsehoods.

Flawed. All her friends were flawed. The Denisons, Conan, Eric— Yes, Eric had lied, too. *The Secret Circle*. Her father had been deeply flawed. She thought even Varda probably had a few flaws. He was very boastful, for one. Everyone was flawed to some extent.

Me too, she had to admit. Maybe especially me.

You have to decide what flaws you're willing to put up with, and what balances them. The Denisons—yes, she could forgive them; she loved them.

She mourned Alex. In his mistaken way he'd tried to protect her. And Conan, who'd been her friend.

It had been a roller coaster year and a half. She was no longer the naïve girl from the Midwest. She had gotten quite an education in Marin County. Not of an academic kind, but nevertheless she hoped some of it had made her a wiser person, and hoped none of it had turned her into a cynic.

~

The days that followed blended one into the other. Gwen returned to her job at the bank, finding that her work as a teller didn't require a lot of creativity or initiative. She stayed focused and made the numbers work. It kept her mind off recent events, which was all she asked for.

Murder charges against Conan were dropped. Although he was still incarcerated for forgery, she knew he was glad to face only two years instead of a lifetime—or worse— for a murder he didn't commit.

Denise, stable and supporting, was a great comfort to her. Gwen learned to laugh again.

"You are good for the soul," she told her friend. "I think you're the only normal person I know."

"Oh, thanks. Does that translate *boring?*"

"Not at all. Not at all."

Chapter 40

Louis was eager to see her, and wanted to know all about the murder. Gwen was tired of talking about it.

"Can we change the subject, please?"

"OK. Will you marry me?"

"What!"

"You heard me."

"I don't really know you," she laughed.

"You know we have a great time together."

"It's been fun. That's not enough to base a marriage on."

"What do you want to know?"

"Uh, let me think. What exactly is it that you do, since you gave up the insurance business?"

"I'm a sail maker—an apprentice."

"Really? Why didn't you tell me?"

"I love it. It's so visceral. I think it's my calling."

"OK. What's your religion?"

"I'm Catholic."

She froze. "You're serious."

"Yes."

Then she burst out laughing. Louis looked hurt.

"I'm sorry," she said, but she kept laughing, until finally she had to explain.

~

Gwen knew the person she most enjoyed being with was Varda. Godfather—yes, she liked that. She visited him several times in the weeks that followed the event in the headlands. He was a good listener. Being with him was healing.

It was autumn. The two of them were taking a walk through a park on Ebbtide.

Where fallen leaves had been blown by the wind into piles, she found herself seeking them out, and kicking at them as she had as a child. If only she was young enough to lie down and roll in them.

"Too bad we can't build a big bonfire," she said. "And cook potatoes in it."

"A happy Michigan memory?"

"Yes," she confessed. "Then trying to find them without getting burned—all covered with ash."

"You miss Michigan, don't you?"

"I'm trying to decide whether to go back."

"And your thoughts on the matter?"

Gwen picked up some leaves and tossed them in the air. "Marin is beautiful. But I have such awful memories here. At least Michigan holds only happy and bland memories."

"It is your decision, of course. But don't decide too hastily. If you stay on, perhaps good memories will replace the bad ones. Or at least put them in shadow."

Gwen smiled. "I have you as a good memory."

"And I shall miss you greatly if you leave."

"And I you." She took time to think. "I have to think about school, too. I still want a career in journalism."

"Not in detective work?" He laughed. "Don't they call you *Sleuth*?"

"I think I've had enough of that, thank you." She squeezed his arm.

"You're pretty good, you know. You were right that both deaths were connected."

"Intuitive," she said smugly.

"If you really want journalism, there are lots of good universities in the Bay Area."

They walked back to the Vallejo. "I have something to show you," he said.

When they were aboard the Vallejo, Varda left the room. What he came back with wasn't tea. He was holding a framed work of art.

"For you, dear one."

Stunned, she looked at it. Clearly designed just for her, it was a collage of snowflakes, a University of Michigan banner, a sandy beach and spring flowers.

"Does it remind you of your Michigan?"

She was too overwhelmed with surprise and gratitude to speak.

"It's not a forgery," he grinned. "See the little mark?"

She kissed him, seeing her own tear on his cheek.

"Now, when you get lonesome for Michigan, you can always lose yourself in this."

CPSIA information can be obtained
at www.ICGtesting.com
Printed in the USA
FFOW02n0030300914
7684FF

9 780990 518501